<u>**Writing As: J. Risk**</u>

THE ALTEREALM SERIES
1 *The Huntress*
2 *The Seer*
3 *The Empath*
4 *The Witch*
5 *The Chronos*
6 *The Warrior*
7 *The Telepath*
8 *The Healer*
9 *The Kinetic*

Solstice Heat

Book 2
Magic Seasons Romance

By Jacqueline Paige

Sparks flew off it, and the door remained closed. "What the..."

Dade grinned. "Quite the little witch you have there, Larkin."

Steven whistled out a breath. "Just how much trouble can they get into with all your stuff in there?"

Chris still scowled at the door while he answered. "A lot." He tapped the door with his hand. "Kassandra, unlock the door."

A gentle breeze blew over all four of them.

"That would be a polite no," Dade said quietly.

"Like hell I'll be locked out of my own temple room," Chris hissed. Stepping back, he stared at the door. The handle shook. When he thought it was going to open, it started to pour rain on the four of them. He waved a hand to stop it and looked at the men beside him. Dade's long hair was soaked, and the expression on his face was similar to how he was feeling about the whole thing.

"And that would be a mind your own damn business," Owen said, sticking his hands in his pockets.

Chris looked at Steven. "You have any ideas?"

Steven shook his head trying to get the water to stop dripping in his face, then took a step away from the door. "Oh no. I'm plenty happy enough to wait until it opens on its own. You might like lightning striking you, but I'm not too open to trying that."

Chris shook his head. "Are you all afraid of them?"

Dade nodded. "I've seen what each one can do alone, especially your little innocent there, my friend. The four of them together scare the hell out of me."

Chris sighed and looked back at the door. "Kasey?"

"Yes, Christopher?" Her voice came through the door again.

"You're making me angry, and I don't want to do something I've promised you I wouldn't."

A gentle breeze ruffled his hair. "I know you won't, Chris. Now go away. I'm trying to concentrate here."

Also by Jacqueline

ANIMAL SENSES
1 *Heart*
2 *Scent*
3 *Passion*
4 *Courage*

MAGIC SEASONS ROMANCE
1 *Beltane Magic*
2 *Solstice Heat*
3 *Harvest Dreams*
4 *Autumn Dance*
5 *Winter Mist*

MYSTIC GIFTS TRILOGY
Mystic Perception

Dreams
Three steamy stories that started with a dream

Curses
Two tales of curses.

After the Silence
Volume 1 Bree

SINGLE TITLES
Solitary Witchling
Salvation
Café Serenity

Published by Exordium Books FRP
Copyright © 2017 Roxane Kerr
Edited by Gaele L. Hince
Cover art by: Off the Wall Creations

Previous editions released in 2009, 2012
Excerpts from *Harvest Dreams*, *Salvation*, and *After the Silence Vol. 1* by Jacqueline Paige copyright © 2015, 2016, 2017 by Roxane Kerr

ISBN: digital 978-1-990763-00-7
ISBN- print 978-1-990763-01-4

DEDICATION

For my parents, Jim and Nancy for keeping up with the ever changing me over the years. I think we're almost there.

This was the original dedication I had for Solstice Heat when it was originally published. My mother has since passed, but I still couldn't have done half of what I did in my life, even after she was gone, without her. .

A note from the author

I have completely enjoyed going back into the Magic Seasons books and getting caught up with these characters again. (I even have a few thoughts to add a few more books to the series.)

The Magic Seasons was my first (serious) step into the world of writing and like everything else I do, I jumped in full speed ahead! The first book was written in 2006 (as a prank and 'last' word with a friend) and then we discovered it was good and that I could write.

I spent the next few years writing more, finally having Beltane and Solstice published in 2009. Then again in 2012. THIS edition is the final and best version.

A huge thank you to Gaele who persevered and helped me take my story back to the way it started and working with and around my little quirks. It would be a mess of repetition and blurry lines without you.

Many thanks to those that have read each edition of this series, you are amazing! To those that are reading it for the first time – you're seeing the best version first.

Jacqueline

❦ Chapter 1 ❧

Kasey had checked her bag four times now. What time were they supposed to be picking her up? She was tired from working a spell all night. Nervous about going to Solstice, where they expected a killer, she glanced at the clock and tried to exhale slowly. The thought of spending some quality time with Chris just added to her excitement.

Tired of waiting for him to make a move, she had no idea how to make any move, but the time was now.

You can do this, Kasey girl, she told herself for the umpteenth time. Maybe, just maybe, if she could manage to take a midnight stroll with him, she would come back looking as thoroughly kissed as Lee had at Beltane.

Her stomach lurched. The thought of kissing Chris, other than a quick one, tied her stomach into a complete macramé project of knots.

Owen's Jeep pulled up, and she was halfway out the door before it stopped. She smiled at Leena briefly, but her eyes quickly focused on the dark-haired man in the backseat as he pushed the door open for her. She stroked over the fairy pendant hanging at her waist, then looked back to Chris to give him an inviting smile.

Chris glanced at his watch as they entered the highway. Not bad, only half an hour behind.

Chris looked over at Kasey, his mind still stuck on how she looked running out of her house. Her hair wasn't helter-skelter for once. The short, choppy ends were soft and flitted about with each movement of her head. She'd done something with the color too, it was darker than normal. He wanted to run his fingers through her short locks to see if they felt as silky as he had imagined.

In the front, the newly engaged couple were talking softly and holding hands. This only made him turn back to look over at Kasey again. What was this, the tenth time he'd glanced at her since she got in the Jeep? She almost looked sleepy.

"You look tired, Kase."

She nodded. "I am. I ended up staying up most of the night trying to charm a talisman, took me forever to work everything out."

He touched her hand softly. "We're going to recharge the gris-gris bags…"

"Oh, no, it's not for me. I made it for Cassidy, only she's going to think it's a gift, which works out for the Solstice gift exchanges." She rubbed her eyes. "If I did it right, it will keep her safe." Her eyes were so sad when she looked back at him. "I don't want her to be the next victim, especially since we saw her in that vision…"

Squeezing her hand, he grinned at her. "I'm sure you did it right, Kase. Your gifts are getting stronger each day and soon you'll be able to take on anything you want."

"Thank you, Chris. Gosh, I am tired!"

He reached over and undid her seat belt. Without effort, he slid her over closer to him. "Lie against me and catch a nap." He kissed the top of her head. "I'll keep you from slipping off the seat."

"Thanks." She slipped down to rest her head in his lap. Shifting around until she curled her small body into a comfortable position in the backseat next him, she closed her eyes.

Resting his hand on the bare skin of her exposed waist, Chris grinned down at her. She was already drifting off.

"So…" Owen said, drawing his attention forward. "What is this about gift exchanges at Solstice?" He glanced in the mirror at Chris, and then turned to look over at Leena.

Chris nodded., "It's an old tradition, exchange a magical gift or tool at Summer Solstice with friends."

"Oh." Owen's eyebrows moved down before he looked towards the road again. "I didn't get gifts."

"Yes, you did," Leena whispered quietly beside him.

"I did?"

"Uh-huh."

"Thank you, baby." He lifted her hand and kissed it.

"You're welcome."

Owen turned back to watch the road. a puzzled look on his face. He was trying to figure out where to get something for Leena.

Chris studied the woman sleeping on him. She looked like a cherub when she slept and he stared intently at her face for several moments. Her small hand rested on his bare thigh by her head and he noticed, she had perfect hands.

Lightly, he ran his hand over her hair and almost groaned out loud. It was like silk.

An ugly, aggressive feeling came over him when he'd thought of Kasey being at risk at this gathering. Were they all crazy to be going if the killer from Beltane would be there? They did have advantages that few were aware of; hopefully the killer wasn't in the know. He pictured Leena and how she looked when she and Owen returned from finding the bodies. He'd die before he ever let Kasey go through that.

His eyes caressed her bare waist, imagining his hands doing the same thing. His long fingers lay across her belly button. He could feel the fairy he'd given her dangling there, keeping his fingers still was taking all of his self-control.

He had to curb the urge drop to his knees and kiss it, when she came out dressed in a tight belly top and short skirt. As she walked to the jeep, he'd seen her hand caress the fairy, making eye contact, ensuring he would notice wore his gift.

He had no fear she wouldn't like the Solstice gift he'd spent days deciding on, it was meant for her.

While allowing his eyes to wander leisurely over her bare legs, he noticed she'd kicked off her shoes. Her toes were painted at least four, no five, he counted, different colors.

By the time they pulled into the gates at the gathering, Chris wanted to jump out and stretch. He'd barely moved a muscle the whole trip, not wanting to disturb Kasey's sleep. Running a hand up and down her arm, he spoke softly. "Kasey, we're here."

She opened her eyes and turned to look up at him. His heart hammered in his chest when he caught her sexy, sleepy expression.

"Thanks," she whispered with a raspy voice.

He touched her cheek with the back of his hand, brushing his knuckles lightly over the soft, glowing skin. "Anytime, sweetheart."

Kasey smiled as she pushed herself up. "I feel so much better." She brushed her lips against his cheek, lingering for a short moment. "You are quite a comfy pillow, Chris."

"You can use me anytime you need, little Kasey," he said in a low voice, almost drowning in her pale green eyes.

"Are you getting out sometime today?" Dade looked in the window at them.

Steven winked at Kasey as she got out. "Kase, you look good enough to eat today." He walked over and hugged her, ignoring the glare from Chris.

Chris was almost certain Doc was doing that, just to annoy him.

"Oh! I love the belly ring, Kase! Where did you get it?" Rachel squeaked as she was bending down to look closer.

Kasey smiled up at Chris. "It was a gift."

Chris grinned down at her, liking the way she kept it between the two of them.

Cora walked over and looked too. "Oh my, those have to be real diamonds. Fake ones wouldn't sparkle like that." She reached out a finger to touch it and got a small zap. "Oh!" She put her finger in her mouth and laughed. "This dry weather is so awful for static charges."

Chris stuffed his hands into his pockets when he noticed Owen raise an eyebrow at Doc, and they both turned to stare at him. He glanced down at the ground, pretending he didn't understand their knowing looks.

Kasey chuckled. "I'll have to call her the electric fairy." As everyone started moving towards the registration, she pulled him and whispered. "The stones are not fake, are they, Chris?" He just shook his head. "Great!" She puffed out her cheeks. "I need an insurance policy on my belly button!" He threw his head back and laughed as she headed to join the others.

Chris followed along behind, still close enough to hear Owen as he leaned close to Steven. "Can he do that?"

Steven nodded. "Yes, and I'd say he definitely did."

Owen laughed.

"Who did what?" Dade asked, pushing between them.

Steven glanced towards the women and then whispered to Dade.

"No way! Really?" Dade chuckled. "Sneaky bastard," he muttered and then immediately walked ahead of them when Cora turned and gave him *that* look.

Leena stood by the registration, noticing that this site was more beautiful than the pictures on the website had shown. There were herbs and grasses growing wild around the whole camp. She couldn't wait to wander through the trees and along the creek to discover what was there. Harvesting herbs for her magic was very important whenever she had the chance.

She started a list of the herbs she most wanted to find. Wild catnip, of course, was always better than cultivated. Would there be motherwort here? Oh, and ground ivy would be at the perfect point to harvest. Grinning, she sighed and leaned back against Owen. Now seemed as good a time as any to get him playing in the weeds. She was just turning to tell him of her plans when Gwen, in her vintage, flowing, hippy skirts, came flying out of the little building. She ran over to Leena and hugged her tight.

"Cora just told me. Congratulations!" She picked up Leena's hand and looked at the ring. She then kissed Owen. "This is so lovely!" She smiled at them both. "It makes my heart so much lighter to know something this wonderful came out of the Beltane gathering." She kissed both of them again. "Oh! You'll be dancing your first coupled union tomorrow night. Oh, this is wonderful!" She sniffled as she walked back into the building.

Owen looked down at Leena. "Coupled union?"

Leena laughed and started towards the building. "I'll explain later." Justin was walking towards the group and she could see the strain of the past few months in his eyes.

"Justin, how nice to see you." She hugged him briefly.

The older man grinned back at her. "Gwen just told me the news, congratulations you two." He shook Owen's hand and grinned. "You're a lucky man, but you know that." He turned to nod to the others. "It's great to see all of you here. Thanks for coming back." He rubbed his jaw and glanced around. "You'll need to meet Mr. Blaine, the detective. I'm not sure where he is at the moment, but stop by at dinner, and I'll point him out." With that he offered a small grin. "It's certainly drier this time." He turned and went back into the building.

"Poor guy," Cora mused as she followed him into the registration building.

When Chris walked out to where the others waited, he noticed a few tense stares.

"Chris," Kasey said in her sweet tone. "Did you happen to pay for all of our registrations and the cabin?"

He grinned down at her. "What could be more magical then the eight of us together at a gathering? My Solstice gift to you all." He looked at them with a slightly smug expression, they couldn't refuse this gift.

Owen stepped forward until Leena put a hand on his arm and shook her head. "You can't refuse a Solstice gift, or you'll bring bad luck to the season." Unhappy blue eyes looked at Chris, and then Owen looked back at Leena and sighed in defeat.

Chris walked past them. "Shall we go check out our lodgings?"

Cora caught up to him and kissed his cheek. "Thank you."

Rachel did the same.

Kasey just looked up and frowned.

The outside of the cabin didn't look like a typical cabin. A simple square building with dark siding and white trim with a deck, or the white boards that could be referred to as a deck, were large enough for two or three people to stand, but not sit.

Once inside the cabin, they all stood in the small sitting area and looked around. There was a woodstove in the corner, with a well-polished wood floor that had seen many feet over the years. Two large armchairs, one of faded blue and one in red and a large brown wicker chair, with a green couch loveseat meant that gathering comfortably would be a challenge.

"Well, at least we *all* won't have to sit on the floor," Dade muttered as he walked over to open a door. "And people, we have a bathroom. Okay, a tiny sink and a toilet." He turned to grin at Owen. "You, big guy, might have to go in and out sideways, but at least it's not a sixty-foot hike outside."

Leena stood there and looked at the four closed doors. Sighing, she went and opened the first. "Double bed and a tiny TV-table-sized table. The wall is a foot from each side of the bed," she reported.

Opening the next, "Single, possibly a twin-sized cot in this room. Nothing other than that, including space." She lifted her brows at the others as they peeked in the rooms after her. The next door revealed two cots and a tiny window the size of a vent.

Chris looked in the last door over her shoulder. It had three narrow cots and almost a half-sized closet. "Well." Leena grinned at him. "We have four rooms, double bed, a single bed, two singles, and three singles, in addition to a closet sized space."

Owen grinned. "I'm calling the double bed that I'll be sharing with my fiancée." Everyone smirked, not arguing because it did make sense.

"I'll take the single then," Chris added as he stuck his head in and looked at the tiny space and realized Leena hadn't been exaggerating. He leaned against the wall beside the door.

Dade walked over and looked into the other rooms. "Guess Doc and I'll take the two beds in there, unless you ladies want to mix it up?" He lifted an eyebrow at the three women.

They laughed and walked into the room with the three single beds.

Leena dropped her purse on the chair. "Guess we'd better go haul everything in."

Dade shook his head. "I'll just drive the van over and park it beside the cabin. There's enough space."

It only took half an hour to get everything sorted out. Cora set the last package on the shelf they'd discovered behind a curtain they thought was a window. She looked over at Owen. "Were you expecting us to feed the whole camp?"

Owen shrugged and then grinned at Chris. "Just didn't want anyone to go hungry. You never know when those middle-of-the-night munchies will get you." Cora laughed.

Rachel was already putting some of the food back in bags. "If no one objects, I'm going to take this to the children's area. Munchies always come in handy there."

Steven nodded. "I'll go over with you and see if any of my fest kids are here."

Straightening from setting up the little travel table, Leena glanced at the women. "Before anyone goes anywhere ladies, shall we cleanse and protect?" The women nodded and went into their room. Leena looked around at the men. "A little tradition, although we could use this to recharge the gris-gris too."

Cora nodded as she walked back out. "Yes, good idea." She stepped forward and placed a wooden carved mask on the table. "To watch over all," she said and stood to the side.

Rachel stepped up and placed her large blue and black candles down. Holding her hand over them, they smoldered and then caught fire. "To protect and repel negative." She took her place beside Cora.

Kasey stepped up to set a large piece of raw jasper down. "To bring courage and tranquility to us all." She stepped over next to Cora.

Leena stepped up and opened her hand over a small dish. Herbs floated from her palm, then settled in the dish, immediately smoldering. She waited for the smoke to rise and then lifted her hands. "To cleanse and protect us all."

Chris watched as the smoke swirled around the small table, then around each of them before circling the room and coming back to the dish.

Cora motioned them to form a circle.

The four women joined hands with the men and as soon as the circle was complete a warm tingle shot through their hands before everyone let go.

"That should also strengthen the gris-gris bags," Cora said as she went to sit down.

Chris raised his eyebrows at Kasey. "Tranquility?"

She nodded. "I didn't know if everyone else was as uneasy as I was after Beltane, so I thought it wouldn't hurt." She looked down at her clasped hands.

"A perfect choice, Kasey, thank you."

Dade sat on the edge of the little couch and sent Chris a determined look. "To test your stone out, Kase, now would be as good a time as any to discuss what Justin asked the men to do, before we all head in different directions." All eyes were on him at once.

Dade glanced once at Cora. "Justin says this undercover cop asked if the four of us would help by making rounds, off and on throughout the next few nights." The other three men nodded, but none were jumping in to help Dade explain.

"Alone?" Cora asked. Dade nodded and started to speak when she stepped in front of him and looked down at him, hands on hips. "I don't think so."

"Coralee, the killer isn't after men, obviously from that vision..."

"No," was all she said and then sat down, crossing her arms in front of her.

Chris looked around at the women. He had been sure this wasn't going to go over smoothly. "I have a suggestion." Everyone looked at him. "We could take turns going out as couples and wandering around. It would look less suspicious." He grinned over at Kasey. "I don't know about you, but I'd feel safer knowing Kasey was with me. If we saw anything, she could work a confine spell while I ran for help." Kasey laughed and put her hand over her mouth.

Owen chuckled. "He's right, well, for the most part. I'd feel better with Leena beside me than worrying about her."

Dade laughed. "You just want to sneak off and have sex in the bushes with her, bro. Tell the truth."

Owen grinned back at him. "Hadn't thought of that, but not a bad idea, thanks." Leena lifted a cushion from the couch with a brush of air and tossed it towards him.

Ducking, Owen laughed and walked towards her. "Behave, woman." He grinned.

Steven stood up. "Other than the sex thing, which does have some merit, I agree with the idea." He looked over at Rachel and smiled. "Well, warrior woman, you want to protect me from the dark shadows?"

Rachel laughed and then shrugged.

Cora stretched. "I don't know about the rest of you, but I'm going to go try to grab a nap. It's going to be a long night, and getting up at dawn to light the Solstice fire will be even more difficult if we've all been in and out all night."

Dade nodded. "I'll head over and let Justin know our plans. I also want to see what this undercover cop looks like, so we don't attack him thinking he's the killer."

Leena sighed. "See if you can get the list of registrants too, Dade. We could check them with the Beltane list before dinner."

Dade saluted her and walked out the door grinning.

Rachel grabbed the bag of munchies and headed to the door. "You know where to find me."

Steven followed her. "Me too."

Leena grinned at Owen suggestively.

Owen held up a hand. "I know that grin, it says, 'Come get me,' but the eyes are saying, 'Owen, honey, I need a hand with something.'"

She laughed. "I do need your hand, to hold mine while we walk through the woods and meadows, foraging."

He shrugged. "I can do that." He took the bag she held out and opened the door.

⁗ **Chapter 2** ⁗

The list didn't provide any big clues. Twenty names were the same, not counting themselves and the organizers. Twenty names of the people who had all been at events for years.

The revel fire was more of a social gathering than ritual, as everyone knew the early morning and long day that would follow. The eight wandered through the attendants looking for something out of place or disturbing, but hadn't picked up on anything. Finally, everyone agreed to go back to the cabin and try to rest before their watch shifts began.

Leena and Owen took the first watch, and no one complained, knowing they were still so newly engaged they should be able to lounge in bed longer than the others.

Steven and Rachel took the midnight shift while the others tried to get a bit of rest before their turn.

Kasey wandered out to the sitting area to find Chris there. "Are they still out?" she whispered, not wanting to wake the others. He nodded. "Do we go out right after them, or is it Justin's turn? I keep forgetting."

Chris patted the cushion beside him, waving the puff of dust away that flew out. "We're out after them. Then at two it's Justin. It's either Charlie or Kevin at three. I'm not sure which order they're in. Dade and Cora will be out until we light the fires."

She nodded and then sighed. "I couldn't sleep. Maybe the nap was a bad idea."

Chris picked up her hand. "It's going to be okay, Kasey." His voice was soft and reassuring. "We're doing all we can do."

She nodded again and went to speak when Doc and Rachel stepped in quietly, grinning.

"It's all yours," Rachel whispered with a grin on her face.

Steven smiled at them too. "You might want to avoid the little ring of trees behind the dining hall. Another couple is busy there right now."

Kasey blushed but noticed that Chris grinned.

"We'll check there last." He turned to her. "Ready?" She nodded and grabbed her sweater.

They walked in silence. Kasey was happy to hold his hand, she felt less nervous about what they were watching and listening for. The only sounds they heard were the crickets, and their own footsteps.

She glanced up at him. At nearly a foot taller, he always made her feel smaller and more feminine. He looked so sexy in the almost-full moonlight. It cast a light that made him look stronger, almost invincible, she thought with a girlish grin. "Leena said there was a creek down that way. Do we look there too?" She kept her voice hushed.

Chris smiled down at her. "Sure. And I'd like to say, despite the reason we're out here, I'm enjoying walking with you in the moonlight. Kase. You look like a fairy in this light."

Kasey felt more relaxed. "It is beautiful out here tonight, isn't it?"

Lifting their entwined hands to his mouth, he kissed hers. "I think the woman beside me outshines the moon every night."

She felt her cheeks flush. "You say the nicest things, Chris."

"I mean them, or I wouldn't say them."

They both looked over as they heard the water trickling. Spotting a large rock, he headed over to lean against it, turning her to stand in front of him. They were face-to-face now. "I still feel guilt over how I behaved a few weeks ago, Kasey."

She was silent for a minute. "It's okay. You were right, in a way. I should work harder so I can stay focused during a ritual. I've been practicing ever since."

His hand moved up to caress her face. It was big enough to cover the whole side of it. "I could have told you in a friendlier way. I have no excuse for my behavior that night. It was just a bit of a shock, to be honest." His thumb moved slowly over her cheekbone.

"I'd like to explain what happened, Chris."

"There's no need..."

Kasey put her hand up to stop his caress. "There is, I need to."

He nodded silently and dropped both hands to her waist, resting them there. Could he sit here and listen to her explain about the lover he had seen with her in the vision? He wasn't sure he could, but he owed it to her to at least try, after being so rude to her over it.

"During the ritual, when we were all touching the edge of the dish, the currents flowing were very strong. The stones I used were doing their part really well, too. I guess you leaned up to look closer, I'm not sure. I was pretty deep in the vision at that point. I remember feeling your hand brush mine, an accident, of course." She paused and lowered her lashes, hiding her eyes from him.

Letting out a shaky breath, she looked back at his eyes. "When your hand brushed mine, it changed my focus to you, Chris. That was *you* I projected in the vision of... It was you."

She finished so quietly he almost didn't hear her. He stood there looking into her eyes. Her fantasy lover had been him? How had he missed that? As he thought of the dark-haired man's reflection in the bowl he felt ridiculous. How was he supposed to know what he looked like from behind? *Him.*

Chris searched her eyes for a moment, then looked at her mouth. She bit her bottom lip gently with her teeth waiting for him to say something. No words could be found to express how happy he was. Relief flooded through him. It hadn't been another man's mouth moving over her with frenzied passion. It had been his. A rush of heat went through him as he thought of the images.

"I've embarrassed you now," she said quietly.

"No, I'm not embarrassed to know that." He did wonder if everyone else had realized who the man had been. "Kasey..." He didn't know what words to use. His eyes moved over her face and he felt he had no choice but slowly lean closer, watching her eyes as he did. When his lips brushed against hers, she moved her hands to his shoulders.

Turning his head, he deepened the kiss and pulled her closer. Her mouth opened, allowing his tongue to brush against hers.

Struggling with whether he should pull her tight or release her, he groaned against her mouth and broke the kiss. "Kase," he whispered against her lips, "we'll have to continue this when we're not on duty."

"Oh!" She put her hands up to her cheeks and looked at him with wide eyes. "I forgot! You distracted me, and I forgot why we're out here."

He kissed her mouth gently. "That makes me feel better than you could ever know, sweetheart." Straightening up, he took her hand. "Let's head to check the other end of the camp."

Chris fought his impulses for most of the way touring the camp. He wanted to pick her up to lay her gently in the long grass, to play out the visions of the fantasy now running rapidly through his mind with new vigor. If he didn't let her know how he felt, soon, he was going to lose his sanity.

After they finished their hour, they saw Justin and Gwen step out of their cabin. Nodding wordlessly to the other couple, they turned and headed back to the own.

As Kasey reached for the door, Chris pulled her away from the door, to the side of the small deck. "We'll go in shortly." He picked her up quickly, seating her on the rail before she could react. "We're not on duty now," he whispered against her ear. "I want the rest of that kiss, sweetheart." Kasey ran her hands through his hair, pulling his head down.

Kasey held her hands in his hair as she pulled his mouth to hers. She didn't know if she'd get another chance to kiss him like this, when he'd asked, so she threw herself into the kiss and swallowed any hesitance.

With her tongue, she explored the inside of his mouth and stroked along his. He gripped her waist and stepped closer so his body was up against hers. She felt his hips push between her thighs, and gasped against his mouth.

Dropping her hands, she ran them down over his chest, loving the feel of his hard muscles.

When she touched him, he pulled his mouth away to run his lips across her throat. His hand cupped the back of her head as she leaned back to give him access to her entire neck.

Lifting her with one hand, he pulled her tightly against his hard chest and devoured her throat. She moaned softly, and he felt need jolt through him like a bolt of lightning. "Come inside with me, little Kasey." He groaned against her throat, and then felt her tense in his arms.

"I can't...the others...I'd..." She bit her bottom lip.

"It's okay," he said, pulling her to rest against his chest as he tried to regain his own breathing.

"It's not that I don't want to. I do. I just...if they found out..." Kasey stopped.

Chris leaned back and looked down at her flushed face. Her eyes were glazed with passion, and he wanted to carry her inside all over again. "I understand, sweetheart. It's okay, really."

He brushed his thumb over her swollen lips, almost dropped to his knees to beg when her mouth opened and her eyes drifted shut at his touch. She was the sexiest thing he had ever laid eyes on.

Dropping his hand, he pulled her into his arms again and held her. "Just let me hold you for a second while I settle down." Her little arms wound around his waist, and she nuzzled right into him.

Taking a deep breath, he straightened and picked her up from the rail and lowered her slowly to the deck. "Go get some rest, Kasey. I'll be in shortly." She looked up at him for a moment, then nodded and opened the door.

He watched her close the door, and then let out a long breath. This was going to be a very long, restless weekend.

As he turned to follow her someone stepped out of the trees on the other side of their cabin. His whole body tensed as he watched the man walk towards him.

He was a tall man, with short, dark hair with a bit of gray showing, and several years older than himself, he thought. Maybe it was that rough "seen it all" attitude.

"Mr. Larkin, isn't it?" the man asked with a slight Irish brogue.

Chris nodded, sizing up the other man.

When he put his hand out to shake his, he winked at Chris. "I'm Patrick Blaine, a special friend of Justin's."

Chris relaxed and shook his hand. Well, at least he didn't look like a cop, far from it, actually. To describe him, Chris would have used the word "dangerous."

"Just wanted to stop by and introduce myself. Saw the group of you at dinner last night and decided with all your men I'd better make sure you knew me." He winked again. "Appreciate the help you're all lending." He looked around the area for a moment, then pulled a dark stone of his pocket.

Chris grinned at the man as the stone hovered a few inches above his palm. Snapping his fingers, the stone fell into Patrick's hand. "Good thing you did at that, Mr. Blaine."

Patrick leaned against the rail for a moment and grinned. "It was thought I'd be best to handle this situation. I've been keeping an eye on the woman you all saw. She's been tucked in all night." He straightened up. "I need to talk to the lot of you before the fire-lighting about a few ideas I have, well, *now* that Justin has explained a bit about some gifts you all have"

Chris nodded.

"I'm off for a nap before everyone's all aflutter over the fire-lighting. I'll see you later on."

"Absolutely," Chris said as he watched the man walk away. *Well, well, they had a magical cop. Things were definitely looking up.*

As they stood in a circle with dawn only a few moments away, the silence prevailed. No one spoke or moved. Chris noticed Patrick looking silently at each face.

Justin asked Cora to give each person in the gathering a small token. With her moving slowly and Owen one step behind her, carrying a basket holding the tiny wrapped bundles, they moved around the circle handing them out.

They reasoned it would allow them to see if Cora, or even Owen, picked up on any vibe to point them in the right direction. Her hands would be close enough to the one accepting the gift to get a reading, of sorts, and with Owen being close, they hoped he would sense something also, or even amp up her abilities.

Chris glanced at Dade, who was very unimpressed with this plan. He stood rigid and waiting. At the slightest sign Cora needed him, he'd be there, Chris knew. Of course, it surprised him when the plan was being discussed that Dade hadn't just slung Cora up in his arms to march away with her. He smirked. Someday she would put him in his place once and for all, and that day wasn't far off.

He glanced down at Kasey. She was looking around the circle at each person when he felt his hair ruffle in the breezeless air. He glanced at her again, and she smirked. Looking at the ground, he concentrated and sent a brush of fingers against her neck without ever moving a hand. She smiled up at him.

When he lifted his head again, he saw Cora turn her head and glare at them both. Then she quickly handed Charlie and Kevin their gift bundles before taking her place back between Justin and Dade.

Patrick turned toward them as well and raised an eyebrow at Chris. So, using magic when so many witches were seeking hadn't been the best idea, he realized. Just what was it about the sexy little witch beside him that turned his usual logical, analytical mind to useless mush?

Shaking his head, Chris moved over to take his place with the drummers as the single women moved to the center of the circle. The sun finally crested the horizon, and as the first beat played, the women lit their torches and circled the fire pit slowly.

Dade had clipped on the waist strap of his drum and stood up without ever missing a beat. He moved slowly through the other drummers and out into the circle. Each woman walked past him as he went to stand in front of the wood that was to be lit.

As the last one passed by him, they began to throw their torches into the pit and walk slowly around the fire.

To someone without the knowledge of real magic, Chris mused, it would appear that Dade was drumming in the day as the lead drummer, with the others as a background. To many at this gathering who knew magic was a very real thing, they knew he was calling the sun spirits to keep this fire ablaze through the long day. They would feel the magic and know.

Cora passed Dade and ran her hand lightly from one shoulder across his back to the other. She would feel the spirits as they arrived and would feel the pull of the magic echoing from his drum on this bright early morning.

The women continued to circle the four-foot blaze, always moving more slowly by Dade, making sure they didn't step between him and the flames.

When he finally slowed the beat and finished, he was slick with sweat and out of breath. Chris watched Dade turn to Cora and give her a knowing glance. He stood for several moments by the fire letting the energy flow around him.

No one made a sound as they watched the Solstice fire burn as brightly as the newly risen sun.

Chris looked over to see Owen sitting with the other drummers and watching everything. One of the women walked to Cora and handed her a towel. Cora took it, smiling her thanks, and walked over to Dade to wipe the sweat from his face and chest, then slowly moving around to wipe his back. She whispered something to him, and he nodded. Then they both turned, and he walked out of the circle with the women following.

The Solstice morning had arrived.

Steven leaned over to Owen and spoke quietly. "The single men, that wouldn't be you, take turns keeping this fire going all day. At noon, we'll meet back here as a group and give offerings or thanks. We place them in the fire. Many will bring their Yule wreath to burn. Then we're back again tonight." He grinned at him. "The women will want to do the gift exchanges now, so you best cuddle up to your lady and see what she has for you to give out." Chuckling, he got up and walked over to Dade.

Chris watched Kasey go to Cassidy and speak for a few moments. With a smile, she handed Cassidy a small bundle. The other woman hugged her, and then Kasey turned to walk back to them.

Beside him Dade was guzzling a bottle of water. He stopped and smiled. "It was nice to see Cora giving someone else *the look* for a change." He grinned and walked towards the cabin, following after the others.

He dried the sweat from his body and reached into his bag to
touch the box.

He didn't take it out yet. It was too early for that.

Tonight he thought they would reveal themselves to him.

Tonight he would cleanse their souls from all their sins.

He lay back and closed his eyes.

He needed to rest to prevent the pain from coming again.

He had to be well enough to do as was expected of him.

He couldn't fail.

Chapter 3

Hugging her coffee cup like a cherished prize, Kasey sat in a chair with her feet pulled up under her. "Will we have time for a nap before ritual?" She yawned, "I couldn't get back to sleep after our watch last night."

Chris smiled at her knowing exactly why, as he'd had the same problem. He sat down on the arm of the chair and ran his hand over her silky hair. "We could probably fit a few hours in if you women don't take forever giving out the gifts this year."

She smacked him and grinned. "It takes a long time to do this sort of thing, silly. Each gift needs to be explained, especially if it's a spell or something charmed. Try using a wrongly charged oil or candle sometime."

He laughed and held his hands up in defeat. Looking around, he saw everyone was wandering in and out of the rooms or chatting quietly. Squatting down, he spoke quietly with his head close to hers. "I know I said paying for this trip was my gift to everyone, but I also got you something extra. I had to. It called to me."

"That's not really fair, Chris."

"Just take a look. If it's not something you want, I'll keep it for another time." Before he would open his hand, he grinned. "I put a little charm on it. It will only last as long as Solstice or not much longer, but I think you'll like it. You have to be happy or dancing for it to work."

Kasey gave him a curious look and wrinkled her nose in a childlike way. "Okay, I'll look."

He opened his hand. In it was a twisted silver chain with three little fairies hanging from it. They almost matched the one in her belly-button.

"Oh!" She touched it lightly, and when her fingers brushed over the chain, the wings on the fairies moved and appeared to be flying. "Oh my gosh! Look at that!" she whispered. "Oh, Chris, it's beautiful." She pointed a finger at him, "Later you're going to have to tell me how you managed to get them to move..." She touched them again to see the little wings flutter.

"Will you accept it, little Kasey?" he asked quietly, wishing they were alone.

Kasey studied him for a moment, her eyes excited. "You *so* cheated, Christopher Larkin," she hissed at him while smiling. "You knew I would take one look at those little wings and fall in love." She touched his cheek tenderly.

Chris sat back on his heels and pulled one of her feet into his lap. With hands not as steady as he'd like, he fastened it around her ankle and watched her grin as the little wings fluttered. She was clearly happy with his gift.

He grinned up at her for a moment. "They won't fly every second when you're happy, just the first few moments. They work with a change of emotion, but when you dance, they will dance with you the whole time." His hand lingered on her leg as they both watched the fairies.

Leaning forward, she kissed him quickly and then jumped up and danced around the room. "Look!" she said to Cora, walking out of the bedroom. "Look at the dancing fairies Chris gave me." She danced around as everyone turned to watch.

"That's amazing," Steven said, then looked over at Chris with his tongue stuck in his cheek. "You scare me sometimes, Larkin, the way you can charm things most could never do."

Chris shrugged and sat in the chair. "It's a small talent of mine."

"Small?" Owen croaked. "No, mine would be the small talent. Yours is like Mount Everest in comparison."

Everyone laughed.

Kasey stopped dancing around and looked at everyone. "I'm going to get my gifts!"

Owen looked around when she raced from the room.

Dade shrugged at him. "Kase loves giving gifts. She starts the day after Yule trying to figure out what to give for Solstice."

Owen shook his head and sat down quickly beside Leena. He leaned close to her and whispered in her ear. She smirked and nodded at him. Chris guessed it was about having gifts for Owen to give.

Kasey flew back into the room and stood in the center for a moment as she reached into the cloth bag she held. "It took me a few months to come up with some of them this year." She reached in, pulled out a tiny bundle, and walked to Dade while holding out her hand. "It's a spirit stone. Tanzanite, to be exact, it can connect you to any spiritual realm. You, of course, would work it better than most."

She watched him open it. "I had it put on the chain so you could wear it if you needed a little extra when calling, if you want, that is." She stood there and watched him examine the stone carefully.

Dade looked up at her and smiled, looking genuinely pleased. "It's wonderful, Kase. Thank you. It will come in handy when I'm having trouble focusing."

Smiling, she reached into the bag again.

Pulling out another small bundle, she walked over to Owen. "It's a protection stone, malachite. I got the idea when you were burned that very first time you used your gifts. It's on a chain too so you can wear it, and as long as you do, you won't be marked again when drawing negative energies from others." She watched him open it, then look up at her.

"This is wonderful, Kasey. I've been a little worried about burns, or worse, since the first time. Thank you."

She grinned, reaching into the bag again, and pulled out another gift. She walked over to Steven. "It's pretty much the same thing I gave you last year, and will probably give you every year until you slow down. An energizing stone, only this time I put it on a cord, and I charged it four times to make sure it would last you a few months, at least."

Doc grinned at her. "I think it's your stones that keep me going throughout the year."

Smiling, Kasey hopped around in her energetic way while she pulled the next bundle out. Grinning at Rachel, she held her hand out to her. "This one I worked really hard on, Rach. It's really rare and hard to get a hold of too, or so I found out. It's an amplifier. Moldavite, to be exact. You can use it when you really need to use a little extra for a spell or candle."

Rachel grinned widely. "Awesome! Will be trying this out soon. Thanks!"

Kasey turned to Leena and reached into the bag. "I didn't get you a stone charm, and I'm glad because you seem to have all that you need now." Smirking at Owen, she pulled out a marble mortar and pestle. "Although marble is made from magnesite, so I guess it's a stone after all, and it would be perfect for blending calming herbs."

Kasey quickly turned to Cora as she reached in again. "For you I had the strongest divination stone placed on a chain. It's electric blue obsidian."

Cora looked surprised. "Where did you get it? I have been bugging this one stoneworker for months to find me one. Thank you so much, Kassandra. I love it!"

Kasey danced around looking excited by everyone's praise.

"Kassandra?" Chris inquired softly.

Cora's head jerked up. "Oh, Kase, I'm sorry."

Kasey shrugged, "It's okay, Cora. They would have heard it at some point someday." She turned and looked at him. "Yes, my full name is Kassandra, not Kasey."

"It's beautiful. It suits you," he said calmly.

She grinned at him, then reached into the bag. "Thanks. Now, you were the hardest one to find a gift for. What do you get for a man that can get himself three of anything?"

Walking over, she held out her hand. "I guess you kind of get two things, as I had your stones made into cuff links. The stone is blue point celestite, it kind of looks like diamonds. They reveal the truth." She watched him open the bundle. "I know it would be cheating, but for those cases where you really need something...extra."

"These are quite amazing, actually." Chris beamed at her. "And occasionally I would be happy to have something extra, to prevent dangerous people from slipping through on small technicalities." He looked back down at them and gave a quick glance to her ankle. The wings moved. "Thank you."

Dade glanced at his watch. "There's not going to be a nap anytime soon, is there?"

Everyone glared at him.

He had been right, Chris thought. There was only an hour before the noon ritual by the time all the gifts were handed out.

Rachel had, of course, gave everyone charged candles, and Leena gave specific blended oils.

Cora gave them all a voodoo charm doll, with the exception of Dade, to whom she gave her grandfather's drum. He'd never seen Dade look quite the way he had when she'd handed over the drum. For a quiet moment, everyone almost expected to see a tear in his eye.

He, of course, made Cora cry by giving her his mother's favorite scrying dish.

Cora came through and saved the newly engaged Owen by bringing a gift for him to give his fiancée. It was a new boline to harvest her summer herbs. That took more than a few moments, as she all but made love to him right there in front of everyone. No one, of course, really wanted to interrupt that to speed up the gift giving.

Everyone gave him the usual magical aids of stones or rods, although the mirror was something new. He never had the heart to mention that he required no aids or tools. He'd use them for show sometimes, but his abilities were well honed and practiced. However, his temple room at home was quite the showplace for trinkets. He imagined Kasey would love seeing it sometime.

All in all, he mused, it had been much like Yule, and everyone was more than happy with what they gave or received.

❧ Chapter 4 ☙

Chris heard Owen objecting loudly and laughed, knowing the sarong discussion was underway. Getting up, he sighed and went to get changed.

He was just tying his own sarong around his waist, a new black one he'd found with white, he wasn't sure what, patterned all over it, when Kasey knocked on the open door.

His mouth dried up when he looked at her. She was wearing a short white sarong with a tiny white halter. His eyes lingered over the fairy sparkling against her stomach. She looked like one of the little fairies he'd fastened around her ankle earlier.

She leaned against the door and gave him a shy look. "I just wanted to say thank you again for the anklet. I love it, Chris."

Leaning against the wall beside her, he looked down at her for a moment. "I'm glad you like it, sweet Kassandra," he said softly. "I'd wear what you gave me, but I don't seem to have cuffs on right now." He watched her eyes move over his bare chest and waist.

"Cuffless looks good on you." Kasey blushed.

"And you look lovelier than I've ever seen you look, all soft and innocently seductive." He reached down and ran his hand lightly over the delicate fairy dangling from her belly button. "Every time I see this, it gives me several erotic thoughts." He rested his hand against her bare waist and pulled her gently away from the doorway. She looked nervously over her shoulder.

Chris lowered his head to her ear and spoke softly. "Everyone is getting changed. I'm not going to seduce you, sweet Kassandra, just kiss you." He feathered little kisses over her neck and across her jaw. "You taste so tempting," he whispered against her mouth before he closed his lips over hers.

He kissed her tenderly, almost hesitantly, knowing he couldn't kiss her as he wanted to. Not with everyone wandering around, and the door open. Her mouth responded to his, and he almost forgot what he'd just thought.

Shuddering when her hands brushed up his chest, he lifted his head and looked down at her. "Go, before I'm blind with wanting you." He kissed her lightly and released her.

She stood there a second with a dazed look before walking out. He glanced at her ankle to see the fairies in full flight. Shaking his head, he adjusted his sarong and dug in his pack for his noon offering.

As people walked past the group to reach the fire and place their offering into it, Dade gave Cora a look. She shook her head each time. Chris kept a bit of distance between Kasey and himself this time, not wanting to interfere with anything Cora might pick up.

Patrick moved to stand beside him. "Had a bit of a fright earlier. Two young girls didn't return after the fire lighting. They were found, ah, exploring the other side of their sexuality, we'll say, so if you can let Miss Cora know, it might explain some of the tense vibes flowing right now." He sighed. "Young people...jealous as hell," he muttered, then walked on by to Justin.

Kasey gave Chris a puzzled look when he stepped over to Cora and spoke into her ear. Cora smirked, quickly putting her hand over her mouth before nodding solemnly as he walked back to Kasey.

Chris winked down at Kasey. "I can't explain it now. I might laugh out loud."

Chris chuckled when he heard Owen thank Leena for making him wear the sarong. He understood completely. Standing in the noon sun in front of a blazing fire was too hot, no matter how you looked at it.

After a light lunch and several bottles of water later, they agreed to rest for an hour.

So why was he alone in the little rustic sitting area while everyone else was in their rooms sleeping? He doubted Leena and Owen would waste time to for sleep, however. Ah, he thought, he was sitting alone because he couldn't close his eyes without wanting Kasey, and he couldn't go in to her while Cora and Rachel were with her. So here he sat, wanting and alone. Sighing, he rubbed his hand over his face.

He just decided to go lie down, when Kasey stepped out of the cabin, closing the door quietly behind her. "Is everything all right, Kase?" he asked in a whisper.

Kasey shrugged and chewed on her bottom lip. "I'm just tense. Worried about what might happen tonight."

His heart ached for her. He placed his hands on her shoulders and ran them down her arms slowly. "Come stretch out on the bed with me, sweetheart." She gave him a surprised look. "To rest, we'll leave the door open. No one will care especially if you tell them how you're feeling."

She looked up at him for a moment, then nodded in agreement.

He took her hand and led her into his little room and stretched out, pulling her down with him. She cuddled tight against him and rested her small hand on his chest.

Turning her head, she looked at him. "Thank you."

Smiling, he wrapped his arm tight around her. "I told you anytime, didn't I?"

She smirked.

He kissed her softly, because he couldn't seem not to.

Kasey kissed him back just as tenderly. Then she suddenly propped herself up on her elbow and looked at him. "Chris, I really should tell you something." She bit her bottom lip and looked down at her hand on his chest.

"What is it?" His heart beat loudly as he studied her.

"I really like you. Well, that's more than obvious, I guess." She looked at his eyes as he searched hers. "I really, *really* like you. And when you kiss me, I..." She bit her lip again. "I don't know how to say this."

"Just say it, Kasey. It's usually best that way," he said, watching and wondering what she could possibly have to say that was so difficult to tell him.

"Okay. I really like you, and I'd really like to *be* with you, really be with you, but I can't. Not here, not with everyone else here." She looked at him for a moment. "I've never...I haven't ever... Well, you would be my first, Chris, if we, I mean, I'm assuming you want to with the way you kiss me. No one has ever kissed me like that before, and you do it so well. I know you probably like women that know what they're doing but I..."

Chris placed a hand over her mouth and looked at her for a moment. "Slow down a little, and let me catch up." He looked at the hesitance in her eyes for a moment and tried to steady his heartbeat. "You've never been with a man?"

She shook her head, no.

He moved his hand to rest against her cheek. Now would be the time to say something to reassure her, he ordered himself. So many things suddenly fell into place for him it was overwhelming. "Sweetheart, I can't even begin to say how that makes me feel. That you'd want me to be your first." *And only,* he thought to himself. "I would treasure that gift." He brushed his thumb over her bottom lip. "Yes, I want to. You have to know that. I have for a long time." Chris kissed her as tenderly as he could manage. "I understand you don't want it to be here in a cabin full of people, and I won't try to persuade you otherwise. Okay, that's a bit of a lie." He grinned at her sheepishly. "When I kiss you, I tend to forget how to think, but you've only to remind me, okay?"

She nodded and smiled, color rising in her cheeks. "I didn't know how to tell you. I tried last night, but you started kissing me, and when you kiss me, I don't want to talk. I don't want to do anything but kiss you." She leaned over and kissed him sweetly. "I'm kind of nervous, really. I don't know what to do. Well, I know sort of, but not from experience kind of know..."

"Nothing will happen until you tell me you're ready for it to, Kasey. That's a promise."

She smiled and let out a breath. "Okay. I was afraid you'd change your mind when I told you."

"Highly doubt that." He pulled her tight against him and kissed her roughly, stabbing his tongue inside her mouth and tasting the innocent taste that was Kasey. She wiggled tighter against him and pulled his mouth harder against her own.

He was hard as quickly as he took the next breath, wanting her more than he ever had before. Pulling back, he bit her bottom lip and sucked on it briefly. "This is not a good idea right now," he growled against her mouth.

When he pulled his head away, he looked into her big green eyes filled with passion and groaned. "And if you don't understand what I mean..." Grasping her hips, he pulled her tight against him so she could feel his desire. "That is how much I want you. Now stop wiggling against me and close your eyes or I'll forget all my good intentions, you sexy little witch." He grinned at her even though his voice was rough.

Kasey smiled that irresistible little smile of hers then kissed him quickly before lying down and nuzzling against his chest.

Letting his breath out, he closed his eyes. He wanted to jump up and yell in triumph. His little Kasey would only ever be his. Kassandra, lovely Kassandra, his.

There was no way he'd sleep with her tight against him, but he certainly wasn't going to let her go and get up.

Wrapping his arm possessively around her, he closed his eyes and rested his head against hers. His.

Kasey grinned up at Chris as they walked to the dining hall for dinner. "Thanks for waking me early," she whispered. He just smiled and tucked her under his shoulder.

When they stopped to talk to Patrick outside the building, a few celebrants stumbled out. All of them had over-celebrated at one time or another, so they laughed at the revelers.

Kasey stepped close to Rachel to let them pass when one of the younger drunk males put his arm around Kasey. "Hey, beautiful...come have a drink with us."

Kasey smiled sweetly at him. "Maybe some other time. I was just going to have my dinner."

He pulled her a few feet with him. "Aw, come on."

Kasey pulled out of his arm and shook her head again. He went to grab her and pull her again when he bent over double and gasped. "I think your friend has drunk a little too much," Kasey said sweetly to the bent-over man's friends. "Perhaps you should go take him to lie down." With that, she turned to join the others.

She glanced over to see Dade restraining Chris with a firm grip. She smiled up at him. "I'm starving." She walked by him and went inside with Leena.

Patrick looked at her, then at the men standing there. "Did she...just do that to that man?"

"Yeah," Dade grinned.

Patrick smiled. "I think I'm in love."

Chris straightened and looked at him. "Mine," he said quietly.

Patrick chuckled and looked at Dade. "Are all your women like that?"

Dade wiggled his eyebrows at him. "Yep, they keep us on our toes."

Walking along behind them, Patrick laughed. "Bunch of

lucky bastards ya all are." Laughing, Steven patted him on the back and nodded.

Chris walked along silently listening to Owen's questions.

"I just want to know what we're expected to do," Owen mumbled as they walked to the circle beginning to gather.

Leena smiled up at him. "It's nothing bad. We'll drum and dance, pretty much as we did earlier. Then when the fire has burned down, near to midnight, the couples jump over it. That's why it's a long, narrow fire pit instead of a round one." She reached up and kissed him. "We are, after all, a couple, right?" He grinned and hugged her to him. "Then it will bring health and happiness to our relationship."

Owen smiled again. "Baby, I get much happier, and I'll explode."

She brushed a hand against his cheek and kissed him.

"You two are going to make me swoon." Rachel grinned as she went by them.

Steven chuckled beside her. "I'm going to swoon just from looking at you four ladies. Those outfits look as hot as the flames." He glanced from one woman to the next.

Chris looked at the women again. Each outfit was a shimmering white that just barely covered what should be covered. "If I had a hat on, Leena, I'd take it off to you."

"I'm ready to drop and kiss her feet," Dade added.

Chris looked down at Kasey. She looked every inch a virginal temptation right now. "Let me just say it's a good thing I'm sitting with a drum in front of me most of the night." He winked at Kasey, and she blushed.

Cora stopped and kissed Dade. "Go give us something to dance to, Dade."

Dade grinned. "I'm all over that." He quickly walked away towards the drummers.

Chris's arms were heavy from drumming, but his heart wasn't. Every time he watched Kasey dance past him, the fairy in her belly button calling him, the ones on her ankles fluttering in time with every step, he almost lost the beat. He had to remind himself to not openly stare to let everyone know exactly where his thoughts were.

When someone signaled the last break before the drumming until midnight, he was more than happy to stop. It would give him a chance to spend a few moments with Kasey.

He guzzled his second bottle of water and then stood. Steven immediately jumped up beside him and nudged him, looking around. "What?" Dade looked to where Steven pointed.

Some man who had been sitting and resting grabbed Kasey by the waist as they'd walked past. She was pushing against his shoulders, and Rachel was trying to pull his hands from her.

Dade grabbed Chris's arm when the stranger bent forward with clear intentions of kissing her belly button. Dade kept a hold on Chris despite the jolt to his hand.

Owen stepped up, half blocking Chris. but keeping a close watch on the women at the same time.

"Let her go!" they heard Rachel demand.

Kasey pushed against his shoulders again. When he bent down and kissed the little fairy dangling against her belly, he jumped back so hard he tipped out of his chair.

"What the hell!" He rubbed his mouth. "Son of a bitch! Why would you wear something like that? That's sick!"

Turning quickly from the cursing male, Kasey looked at Rachel and then down at the belly ring. Touching it gently, she lifted her head and looked over to the drummers, to where Dade was holding Chris. Dade looked at Chris. He looked very angry.

He wasn't sure if he should release Chris as the women moved closer, or continue to hold him. Kasey glanced at him and then to Chris.

Cora touched Kasey's arm. "Kase, did your belly ring just

zap that man?" Kasey nodded, still watching Chris.

"Oh my," Cora let out a breath and looked towards him and Chris. "I think someone has definitely staked his claim on you."

Kasey huffed out a breath. "Someone better have a really good explanation for this. That man, jerk or not, could have been seriously hurt!" She stomped towards Chris.

Steven stepped away from Chris. "If you're smart, you'll drop to your knees right this second and bow at her feet."

Dade released his arm and rubbed his palm as he whispered. "You've got some serious explaining to do. Very clearly she had no idea your little gift would electrify trespassers." He glanced up at Chris. "I love fireworks, but not at close range, and you have one seriously pissed-off witch heading your way." Dade backed up a few feet away from him.

Chris went to step toward Kasey and was met with a blast force. He rubbed his hand over his chest and looked down at the woman who stopped a few feet from him, anger radiating from her. "Kase..." He felt an invisible hand slap over his mouth to silence him. His anger faded quickly.

Justin stepped up beside Kasey and said quietly enough so only the three of them would hear, "Take it out of the circle, where no one else will see." He glanced at the two of them and walked the other way.

Leena came up to put a hand on Kasey's shoulder. "Go for a short walk, and Kasey, let the man breathe." She gave Chris a sympathetic look and walked over to stand with Owen.

Kasey dropped her head down, and he instantly felt the hand move. She looked back up at him for a moment and then walked away towards the dining hall.

Chris cursed and followed her quickly. When he caught up to her, she was sitting on the steps. He held up his hands. "Don't. Please, let me explain." She glared at him, but also looked like she was going to cry.

Slowly, he sat by her feet and turned to look at her. "I was jealous as hell, Kasey...with that little fantasy vision at my place." He held up his hand when she went to speak. "I didn't know it was me. I was blind with rage and jealousy at the thought of another man touching you, so yes, I charmed it to shock according to intention." He started to say something else, then closed his mouth, changing his mind.

Her green eyes searched his for a moment. "He could have been seriously injured, Chris. You have to fix it." She stopped and looked at him. "Is my anklet going to do that too if some child tries to admire it, or worse they touch my belly..."

Chris hung his head down and sighed. "I wasn't thinking, obviously. I was just so jealous. I shook with rage." He looked back up, reaching to gently touched her cheek. "I'm sorry, Kasey."

Her eyes were so sad. "You need to get a handle on that temper of yours."

He smirked. "This from the witch that almost knocked me on my ass a few moments ago... And the hand on the mouth, impressive, but, who has to control their temper?"

"You deserved all of that."

Chris nodded. "I did." He leaned forward and kissed her mouth softly. He exhaled loudly. "Stand up, and let me see the fairy." She stood in front of him. He placed his hand over the fairy, and looked up into her eyes for a few moments. Brushing her tenderly, he stood up. "You won't shock anyone now."

She looked suspiciously.

"Honestly, go get someone to touch it."

Kasey looked at him a moment longer, then turned and walked back to the circle.

The first person she came to was Dade, so she walked over to him. "Dade, touch my belly ring."

Dade lowered the hand that had been lifting the bottle of water. "'Scuse me?" He glanced past her at Chris. "No thanks, honey, appreciate the offer, but I like my hands attached to my body."

She glared at him. "He's removed the charm." She looked at Chris.

Dade looked at him. Chris sighed and nodded, and then Dade slowly touched one finger against the fairy and grinned. "So he has." Then he sat back down behind his drum.

Kasey glanced at him. "Thank you." Then she grinned. "I'm still going to wear it, despite your little temper tantrum."

Chris reached out and brushed a hand over it. "Good, because it drives me crazy." He kissed her neck. "Go dance. Soon we get to see Owen and Leena jump across the fire."

Chapter 5

Almost four hours later, everyone was sprawled around the cabin.

"I'm exhausted," Leena groaned as she put her feet in Owen's lap.

"You asked for something to dance to," Dade reminded Cora, who was stretching quietly.

Cora stopped and grinned at him. "You could have taken a longer break from time to time, or at least played poorly, Dade Jones. You know I can't resist your drum when you want it."

Dade grinned teasingly. "Well, I wanted it tonight."

Everyone laughed, except Leena, who groaned and looked at Owen. "We have to go on our watch now." She looked over at Cora. "Anything tonight?"

Cora shrugged. "I felt little things off and on tonight. Nothing like before. I even wore the stone from Kasey, but didn't get anything strong enough to worry me."

Owen nodded slowly. "Good. Come on, baby. Let's go check out those bushes." He grinned as he got smacked.

Everyone else went to lie down, leaving Kasey sitting there in the quiet.

Chris stood in the door to his room and watched her rub

her finger over the fairy at her waist. "If you're trying to summon me, it worked." He grinned when she dropped her head back against the chair and laughed.

"I guess I was. I'm scared, and you always make me feel better."

His heart thudded at her confession. "Come here, Kase. I'll close the door so no one can see us, set my alarm so we're up before everyone else, and we'll try to get some rest before it's our turn." He held out his hand to her and smiled when she stood up and took it.

He didn't try to kiss her, even though he could think of nothing better. He just cuddled her into him and held her as they drifted off to sleep.

Chris suddenly woke up and wasn't sure why until he heard the tapping on the door.

"Chris," Dade whispered from the other side. "Chris, Cora just woke me. We can't find Kasey." He tapped again, and then the door opened a few inches.

Chris put his finger against his mouth to keep him quiet. "She was scared." Dade nodded, letting out a quick breath, and closed the door.

He had just put his head down when Kasey whispered, "Busted." Then she giggled. "Thanks for explaining." She snuggled back into him. "When is our shift?"

"Fifteen minutes." He didn't want to get up and wander around. He wanted to stay there and hold her for the rest of the night. Sighing, he kissed the top of her head. "We'd better get up. You are far too cuddly and warm and I'll end up going back to sleep."

She giggled again but moved away and sat up. Stretching, she stood up and turned. "Do you think I'll need a sweater tonight?" Her voice was soft and rasping, still full of sleep.

Propping himself up on his elbow, he found himself looking at the little fairy. "Oh please, don't cover her up." Chris leaned over and touched the pendant with his lips only. He gently ran his tongue around the little pendant once before giving it a light flick.

Kasey ran her fingers into his hair. "Oh. Hmm. I like that. Really like that." She smiled down at him. "I think we'll have to try that some more when we aren't on duty."

Chris groaned and dropped his face into the bed. "Don't say things like that to me when I have to watch you walk out of here, Kasey."

They walked around the campground. A few people still lingered here and there, mostly couples. They wandered slowly toward the creek, as they had the night before.

Chris frowned down at her for a moment. "You need to talk to me, sweetheart. I'm having one hell of a time trying to keep my tongue from playing with that little fairy again."

Kasey blushed but still smiled up at him. "Funny thing is, I've been thinking about that same thing."

"That doesn't help." He walked her over to the rock he'd sat on the night before and sat down. It didn't help that she'd done as he'd asked, and not covered her stomach up with a shirt. "Are you warm enough in that...bit of cloth?" His voice was strained.

She nodded, "I love the outfits Leena makes. Sometimes I wish I could wear them all the time."

"Feel free." He cleared his throat. "The one from her garden party tormented me all that night. I had to keep drumming to keep my hands off you."

She blushed again. "Why have you never told me this before?"

Chris closed his eyes for a moment. "The first time I saw you, I think you were twenty, I almost fell off the chair I was sitting on. I wanted you then." He grinned. "I was a bit of a, well, *bad boy* would be a good way to say it nicely. At that point, I felt dirty just looking at you."

She laughed. "I thought you were the sexiest man I'd ever seen. I still do."

He rested his forehead against hers. "Remember that talk about nothing happening until you say?"

She nodded, her mouth an inch from his.

"When you say things like that, or how much you like my mouth on you, it makes it very, very difficult to remember that talk."

"But I do like your mouth on me, and I do think you're the sexiest man I've ever seen. Am I supposed to lie?"

He let out a slow breath. "No. You're right, telling the truth is important, even if it makes me want to throw you over my shoulder and take you to my cave."

Kasey laughed. "I've seen your cave, Christopher. It wouldn't be a hardship. Trust me."

Chris growled. "I give up." He pulled her against him quickly and kissed her heatedly. He moved his mouth over hers, wanting to taste as much of her as he could. Her tongue met his, gasping when he felt her passion as she returned his kiss.

He slid forward on the rock and pulled her tightly between his legs while squeezing her perfect ass, holding her there. He tore his mouth from hers and nipped her neck roughly, then soothed it with his tongue.

Kasey groaned, grasped his hair, and pulled his mouth back up to hers. "I like your mouth," she gasped against his lips. He gripped the back of her head and pulled her back so he could taste her neck again.

Her breathing was ragged, and that was driving him closer to the edge. He was shaking with need as his mouth moved down between the patches of cloth covering her breasts.

She moaned softly, and he pulled her harder into him. He was throbbing painfully with wanting her.

She felt so hot and needy. She didn't want him to stop. "Chris, I need..." She moaned again as his mouth closed over her aching nipple, right through her top. Grasping his shoulder, she leaned back farther to let him move across to the other needy nipple. She rocked her hips against him, panting with a need she didn't understand.

Chris groaned as she pushed into him. Supporting her with firm hands, he bent her back farther and nipped her bare waist before running his tongue over her belly button. When she gasped again, he nipped the fairy with his teeth.

Kasey made a quiet whimpering sound, almost making him lose control. He opened his eyes to see her arched out before him, focusing as her breasts rose and fell with each rapid breath. He pulled her back to ravish her mouth as he kneaded her breasts with his hands.

Kasey suddenly tensed against him. He lifted his head and heard someone cough. Pulling her into him, he stood and looked around to see Patrick coming out of the trees.

Patrick lifted his hands and shook his head. "I'm so very sorry. I didn't see you until I was almost beside you." He cleared his throat and looked away from them. "It's pretty quiet around the camp now. I'll go check around up top and then let Justin know it's his watch."

Chris nodded to him, but still wasn't steady enough to speak. He sheltered Kasey in his arms until Patrick was well out of sight. Then he slowly pushed her back, and looked down at her. "Sweetheart, I'm so sorry. I should have heard him, shouldn't have gotten so carried away."

Kasey looked back at him with swollen lips, her neck red from his mouth. Her eyes were still glazed with passion and her breathing not yet normal. His heart thudded in his chest, and he lowered his head and kissed her gently. "I'm sorry."

She pulled back from him and shook her head. "Please don't say that. Don't regret it."

His eyes widened. "Don't misunderstand. I couldn't regret doing this with you. I'm sorry for the timing and letting it get out of hand. You need gentle and patient, and I all but took you standing right there." He brushed a hand over the back of her head. "You're dangerous, Kassandra. You took my control and shredded it into pieces."

Kasey smiled at him. "I like to think that I did that." He closed his eyes and let out a breath. "And I don't think I need gentle and patient always, Chris. I love your sweet kisses, but what you were just doing to me..." she blushed, "I really enjoyed that. I'm still so hot I feel itchy, and I'm so wet right now..."

Chris took his hands off her quickly and stepped a foot away from her. "For the love of the gods, Kasey!" he hissed. "You can't say that to me and expect me to kiss you sweetly then send you away." He rubbed his hand over the front of himself briefly. "I want you so much right now it hurts, and I'm trying, *really trying*, to give you time." He dropped his head down and took a few deep breaths.

She stood there quietly for a moment. She walked up and put a hand on his chest. "What do you mean you're in pain? I feel so hot and good right now..." She stopped. He looked down at her silently for a few moments. "Make me understand, Chris."

Chris let out a long breath. "I want you so much, Kasey. I'm so hard right now, from wanting you it actually hurts. Not an altogether bad pain, considering the cause..." He didn't know how to explain it to her. He grinned at her. "We really need to start heading back."

"Are you upset with me?" She looked up at him, worry clear in her eyes.

He shook his head. "No, I just need to settle down a bit."

"Okay, but walk slow. My legs are kind of Jell-O-ish right now."

Chris laughed. "What am I going to do with you?" He tucked her under his arm, and then they slowly walked back.

By the time they were almost at the cabin, he had himself under control again. All the way back his brain struggled with ways to explain, to help her understand, and he still had no idea.

"So, does this mean I don't get a goodnight kiss tonight?" She looked up at him.

"You get whatever you want tonight." He watched her

think about that for a moment.

"I'd like to understand better, but I don't think that's possible without causing you discomfort," she said quietly.

He pulled her to the shadowed side of the cabin. "Didn't you ever make out as a teenager, Kasey?" he asked.

She shook her head. "I was too shy to even talk to anyone new. It used to make me feel ill." She grinned at him. "It's taken me years to overcome that and talk to anyone outside my family, Chris. I don't expect you to understand, but it's the truth."

Chris felt his heart jerk in his chest from her confession. His little Kasey had never had a date, no petting in the dark, no necking, everything with him would be her first, and he wasn't at all sorry. He grinned down at her as he pushed her gently back against the wall of the cabin. "Then I'd say you have some catching up to do."

He lowered his mouth and began to kiss her slow, wanting to build her up to the excitement of earlier. "Let me show you, Kasey," he whispered against her neck. He ran his tongue over her ear. "I won't go too fast. I won't ask for more than you want." He nipped her neck tenderly with his teeth. "Let me show you what you needed earlier."

Kasey was already pressing into him, her hands traveling up his chest slowly. "I don't want you to be uncomfortable for me, though, Chris," she whispered as her mouth touched his chest lightly.

Reaching behind her, he and pulled her hips into his so she could feel how hard he was already just being near her. "I'm like this every time I look at you, sweetheart." He sucked on her bottom lip gently. "Let me show you, sweet Kassandra, what it means. I can wait." He kissed her deeply, drawing her tongue into his mouth, not wanting to give her time to think.

He wanted her squirming for him again, needed to hear her breath catch and tremble with need. He massaged her hip lightly, rocking her against him as his lips traveled to her throat. "Let me make you wet with wanting me again," he rasped against her skin.

Grasping her hips, he picked her up off the ground. "Wrap your legs around my waist." She did, and he shuddered at the feel of her legs against his skin.

He kissed her until she was panting against his mouth. Lowering his head, he nipped his way along her throat until his mouth rested over her breast. "Lift your top, sweetheart." She did with shaky hands, then grasped his hair when he licked over one hard nipple.

She was so beautiful, so soft. Biting the nipple gently in his teeth, he felt her jerk against him and moan softly. Taking it into his mouth, he sucked hard, then swirled his tongue around it until she shuddered.

Lifting her higher, he rested her back against the wall, and ran his mouth roughly over the soft skin from her ribs to her belly button. He gently licked around the fairy, pausing to nip at the soft fold of skin just below where the fairy hung with his teeth. She moaned. He felt the wet heat from between her thighs against him and shuddered with need.

Licking his way back up to her breast, he grasped one in his hand and sucked hard on the soft flesh, leaving a bright red mark behind. She whimpered softly and pulled at his hair. Biting the nipple between his teeth, he flicked his tongue over it at the same time. She gripped his head harder, almost pulling hair out as she did, and ground herself against him.

Lifting his head, he licked his way up to her throat. Her head was thrown back, and her bottom lip was caught between her teeth as she panted heavily. He groaned against her throat. "You are so beautiful right now I'm shaking." He kissed her throat roughly, and she rolled her head down towards his.

She pulled his hair until his mouth was against hers. "Chris..." She gasped against his mouth, then bit his bottom lip.

Chris jerked and felt his control slipping. Did she have to be so fucking sexy and wanton? He kissed her hard and fast as he reached to grasp her hips again. With a slow movement, he began to rub her up and down against the front of his sarong. Groaning in her mouth, he thrust against her as he moved her up and down him. She was gripping his shoulders, riding him.

His control was so close to snapping when she did that. They didn't have enough clothes on. not for him to restrain himself much longer. "Stand. I can't do it this way," he gasped against her throat. "Need you too much." She unwound her legs from him so he could slide her slowly down.

He devoured her neck as he reached a hand under the front of her skirt. She moaned when his hand came into contact with her wet flesh.

His knees were shaky when he felt how wet she was. He pushed aside the lace and slowly inserted one finger inside her. Her muscles squeezed around it as she gasped against his chest.

Cradling her head against his chest, he rubbed his hand over her again. She whimpered against his chest and clutched his arm. He cupped her again, and she ground herself against his hand, panting.

He groaned into her hair and began to rub her harder and faster until she bit his chest and groaned. He felt her convulse against his hand and held her tighter against him until the little squeaks stopped, and she stood gasping, her lips brushing over his too-sensitive skin with each breath.

His legs were shaking, and he didn't know at this point how he was going to let her go. "You okay?"

She nodded and looked up at him. The look in her eyes made him shake more. She lowered her head again and rubbed her still-bare breasts against his chest. When her wet mouth brushed over his nipple, he almost threw her to the ground.

"Tell me what to do, Chris. It's not fair," she whispered quietly.

He gripped her hair but then shook his head to clear the idea. He was not that far gone.

"No, sweetheart." She looked up at him with innocent eyes and rubbed her small hand over his throbbing erection, pausing to feel him under her hand. He gripped her shoulders and groaned. "Kase, I'm too close..."

"Good."

Despite his good intentions, he thrust against her hand and pulled her against him. He kissed her roughly, unable to stop.

"Harder," he groaned against her mouth. She rubbed him harder through the thin material, and he almost cried from the pleasure of finally feeling her touch him.

When her small hand grasped him tightly and continued, he shuddered and pushed into her hand, holding her tightly against him. "Yes," he growled against her lips. "Faster." When she did as he said, he tensed and came abruptly, almost into her hand through the material. Her small hand continued to move over him, sending him into aftershocks immediately.

He stopped her hand with his gently and lifted her chin to kiss her tenderly. "That was not part of the arrangement," he whispered.

"I know." Kasey smiled. "But you made me feel so good I wanted to do the same." He reached down and pulled her top back into place and hugged her.

"Now we just have to get back in the cabin unnoticed." Chris grinned when her eyes widened.

"I didn't think of that. Well, I couldn't think when you were touching me."

He took her hand and walked around to the small deck. Stopping, he looked down at himself. "You need to walk in front of me in case anyone is awake in there." She nodded and did that, still holding his hand.

They crept inside like two teenagers coming home late and sighed with relief when no one was up. "Sleep beside me, Kase," he whispered against the back of her neck. She didn't say a word, just led the way into his room.

He watched the couple sneak into the cabin.
He had waited and had watched.
Few were up and moving around.
He still had time.
He would wait and watch.
They would come to him.

ꙮ Chapter 6 ꙮ

"Owen!" Chris bolted up with Kasey still in his arms at the sound of Dade's booming voice. Scrambling off the bed he lunged towards the door and rushed to open it. Owen ran by it as he stepped out. Dade stood supporting a moaning Cora.

"She kept feeling off, so we walked around more. She wanted to try to get a direction..." He lowered her to the couch. "Fuck! I should have dragged her ass back here." Owen was already running his hands over her. "Then she just started crying out and shaking... I had to catch her when her legs gave out." Dade paced and watched Owen continue to run his hands across her shoulders.

Leena knelt down in front of her. "Cora, take deep breaths, and let Owen take some of it."

Steven reached down and grabbed her wrist. "Her pulse is really erratic."

Cora cried out and opened her eyes to look at Dade. Tears were running down her cheeks.

Dade was there on his knees in front of her immediately. "What is it, honey?"

"She's still alive... in pain, cold. She's alone."

He kissed her. "We'll find her, honey." He stood up and

turned.

Chris stepped back into the room and pulled the blankets off the small bed.

Cora stood on unsteady feet. "I'm coming."

When Dade turned back, he shook his head and looked at Leena. "Help her." Leena and Rachel stepped on either side of Cora as they all went to the door.

Kasey glanced around. "Did someone bring a phone?"

Steven nodded. "Yeah."

They stopped a few feet from the cabin and turned to look at Cora. She was still gripping her stomach. "Towards the creek. She can hear water."

Nodding, Chris turned. "We need to split up."

Patrick came running up from the direction of the circle.

Chris looked at him. "Get Justin and an ambulance and head towards the creek." Patrick didn't waste time with questions, just took off running in the other direction.

Kasey squeezed Chris's hand as they started jogging down the path they'd been on the night before.

Owen and Dade went down a different path while Steven stayed with the women helping Cora.

They were almost to the creek when they heard something in the longer grass close to the trees. Stopping, Chris let go of Kasey's hand and walked towards the sound. Kasey was right behind him. He saw something pale in the grass. Walking slowly closer, he squinted. It was a hand. Dropping to his knees, he began flattening the long grass.

There were two women lying in the grass. Their hands hand been pinned to the ground with wooden stakes. Kasey gasped as Chris knelt beside the one to check for a pulse.

There was a red cross painted on her naked chest. It looked like blood. Her face was streaked with cuts. Shaking his head, he pulled the blanket from Kasey's hand and covered the body and face. He turned to the other staked woman.

He saw her lips move slightly and touched her neck.

"Kasey," he said quickly, "get the Doc and Owen here, *now.*"

Kasey handed him the sheet before turning and stumbling back the way they'd come.

Owen burst through the trees first and dropped down beside Chris. His hands shook as he held them over the woman. "What do I do?"

Chris shook his head, trying to think, as Steven came running through the brush from the left.

Steven fell to his knees and checked her pulse and eyes. "She's in shock." He lifted the sheet and looked under it, then glanced at her hands. "Pull those stakes from the ground. Leave them in her hands, though, or she'll bleed out more." Steven looked at Dade. "We've got to lift her gently so I can see where all this blood is coming from."

Dade nodded and waited until Chris had pulled one stake free. Gently he lifted under the woman's shoulder and hip so Steven could see her back.

"Fuck!" Steven hissed. He turned when Owen set the other staked arm gently on the ground. "Owen, get your hands over this and see if you can't stop some of the bleeding. He's sliced her back up... I don't know how deep."

He checked the woman's pupils and pulse again. "Chris, she's going to crash." He gripped Chris's hands and placed them directly over her heart. "When I tell you to, I want you to give her a good jolt, understand?"

Chris nodded and looked down at his hands for a second before watching Steven again.

Patrick and Justin came running through the grass and stopped quickly. Patrick looked at Rachel as he spoke. "You stop anyone that doesn't have magic from coming in here until the ambulance arrives." She nodded with the tears running down her face and turned to walk back on the trail.

Patrick went over to the Doc and knelt down. "Can you save her?"

Steven looked up from where he had been tying a strip of his shirt around the woman's wrist and took a breath. "I don't know. How far out is the ambulance?"

Patrick glanced down at his watch. "They should be at the gates anytime now." The woman's lips moved, and Steven glanced to Owen. "Keep holding, Owen. She's coming around."

Owen was sweating now, and pale, but he nodded at Dade.

Dade went to kneel behind Owen to support him. He took the stone Kasey gave him and dropped it inside Owen's shirt to rest against his skin.

Steven cursed. "Pull him free, Dade, now!" He motioned. "Now, Chris!"

Dade pulled Owen's hands free just as the sparks burst from Chris's palms, barely touching the woman's skin.

Steven bent down and checked her eyes. He looked to Patrick when he heard sirens. "Take him over there, Dade." He motioned with his head. "I can't even attempt to explain any of this to the paramedics." He motioned to Chris. "Stay ready until they get here with the paddles."

Chris nodded and didn't dare lift his hands to wipe the sweat from his eyes.

Justin stepped in to help Dade lift Owen to his feet and move him to the edge of the area.

Leena stepped away from Cora, and she went over to help sit Owen down. She looked at Dade. "Will he be all right?" Dade didn't answer, just continued to slowly lower the large man to the ground.

Chris turned his head to see Cora walking hesitantly toward the covered body. She knelt down and placed her hand on the bare leg sticking out from under the blanket. She cried out suddenly.

"Stop her!" Dade yelled.

Kasey spun around and grabbed Cora's hands, pulling her away from the body.

"Cora?" Kasey pulled the trembling woman into her arms. "Cora!" Cora continued to shake. Close to tears, Kasey looked to Dade as he left Owen to come over.

He reached down and scooped Cora into his arms. "You

know better." He turned and carried her a little away from the others, then sat down with her in his lap.

Rachel ran up. "They're here."

Chris pulled his hands back from the body and stood up, quickly taking a step back. He got no farther than a few feet when Kasey launched herself into his arms and hugged him tightly.

Looking down at his hands, he saw the blood. Hugging her tightly to him, he made sure his hands didn't touch her body. He stepped back with her as the paramedics came into the group.

Patrick lifted the blanket and examined the body under it. Looking up, he met Chris's eyes and shook his head. Chris closed his eyes and lowered his head to rest his face against Kasey.

Everyone watched the paramedics and Steven work to further stabilize the woman before asking for assistance in getting her, with the stakes still in her hands, onto the stretcher.

The four women crowded around the listless Owen and kept back out of the way. Charlie came running through the grass looking bewildered. He stopped when he saw the covered body and then sat quickly, putting his head between his knees.

Kevin was right behind him. After looking around, he sat down quickly beside Charlie and spoke quietly to him. Chris waited until Steven left with the paramedics before turning to help Dade and Justin lift the body of the other woman onto the second stretcher.

Dade motioned to Leena. "Take Cora to the cabin. Chris and Justin will help Owen get there. I'll be there as soon as we're done." He nodded to Kevin on the other end of the stretcher.

Everyone watched in silence as they carried the second stretcher away.

Chris hugged Kasey again quickly and then walked to where Patrick stood. He reached into his pocket and pulled out a piece of paper and held it out to him. "I pocketed this before it got stepped all over or lost."

Patrick took the page and read it. "Shit!" he spat. He looked around at everyone as he put the paper into his pocket. "Get everyone to the cabin. I'll be there as soon as I look around here." He cursed quietly, "With the way we all trampled it, I'll be lucky to find anything."

When Steven and Dade walked into the cabin, Kasey wiped the tears from her cheeks and looked at them. "Is she still alive, Doc?"

Steven nodded and let out a long breath. "For now. They're going to let Patrick know what's going on."

She nodded but didn't know what to say.

Steven looked at Cora curled up in the chair. She looked back at him with clear eyes. He turned to Owen, who was propped up on the little couch. "How's he doing?"

Leena looked up from Owen. "Better. I'm using some herbal teas to replenish him." A tear slipped down her cheek. "I didn't know it could affect him like this."

Steven lifted Owen's arm and felt for his pulse. "Well, that was the worst-case scenario, Leena."

Dade stepped past him and knelt down to Cora. "Speaking of that..." He picked up Cora's hand and held it. "You know you can't touch death, Cora. You've seen what could happen. What were you thinking?"

A tear slipped down Cora's face. "I just wanted to see him. To stop him. She was in so much pain. I wasn't thinking. Oh, Dade..." She threw her arms around his neck and started crying against his neck.

Stroking his hand over her hair, Dade lifted her until she sat resting against him. "You saved her, honey. You saved one. If you hadn't, she would have been dead before we found her." He rested his face against her hair and rubbed his hand up and down her back.

Owen opened his eyes and looked to see a teary-eyed Leena leaning over him. "I'm okay, baby," he whispered and pulled her down to hold her close to him. "I'm just a little shaky now."

Unable to watch, Kasey turned and left the room quietly.

Chris came out of his room after changing and looked around for Kasey. Not seeing her, he walked to her room. She was curled up on her cot crying so hard it shook with each sob.

He walked over to her quickly and curled his large body around her. Pulling her tightly against his chest, he held her shaking body.

Kasey lifted her tear-drenched face to his and looked into his eyes. Her eyes were filled with so much pain and grief he couldn't breathe. "You're breaking my heart," he whispered to her. He kissed her teary eyes and took a hitched breath. "Tell me what to do, Kasey."

"H-Hold me. Just hold me. Don't let go."

He pulled her tightly against his chest and ran a gentle hand down her back, rubbing in small, little circles. "I won't," he said into her hair.

Chris didn't know how much time had passed, or how long they lay there. She finally stopped sobbing, and her breath was steady, but he had never been so unsure of what to do in his life.

Rachel came in and stood at the end of the cot. She looked at him. "Patrick, Justin, and Gwen are here."

He nodded and spoke softly, his voice still shaking. "We'll be out in a minute, Rach. Thanks." Chris waited until she left to look down at the swollen green eyes looking back up at him. "We need to go out and talk to Patrick, sweetheart. Are you going to be okay with that?" She nodded. He kissed her mouth softly and then moved away from her and stood up. Taking her hand, he pulled her to her feet and wrapped his arm around her.

When they walked in the room Patrick looked at her, and then to Chris. "She okay?"

Chris nodded. "As well as can be expected."

Patrick looked down at the notes he'd taken. "I think I have most of it for now, but I do have a question, off the record, if that's okay." He shrugged. "I have to know everything so I can figure out how much I have to tell my superiors and how much they don't need to know."

Chris sat and leaned against the wall feeling exhausted. He pulled Kasey down into his lap. He glanced around to see Owen was now sitting upright, Leena right beside him.

Cora was in the chair with Dade sitting protectively at her feet. Rachel was comforting Gwen, and Steven was writing something quickly on a notepad.

He cleared his throat. "What do you need to know?"

Patrick studied him for a moment. "I understand what Mr. Grey was doing, well, at least I do now. I'd like to know how exactly you were able to become a human defibrillator. Aside from restarting her heart and possibly saving her life, I've never encountered anything quite like that in all my travels or in dealing with magic."

Chris rubbed his jaw against Kasey's head for a moment before speaking. "It was a simple manipulation of energy."

"Simple?" Patrick grinned, "I don't think so."

Chris shrugged. "It takes a lot of practice."

Patrick was silent while Steven handed him the notebook. "Takes a lot of talent too." Patrick raised an eyebrow. "Okay, I want all of you to go try to eat, or at least bring food back here and try. After that I may know something I can tell you." He started to turn until Kasey spoke to him.

"He's going to do it again, isn't he? That's what the note said?" Her voice was hoarse with emotion.

Patrick stood looking down at the floor for a moment. "Yes, in forty-one days' time, which would be Lammas." He glanced over at Justin and then around the room. "We've told everyone it was a horrible accident, the reason for the ambulance, and I'm going to be advising my superiors they suggest you don't hold another gathering."

Gwen put her hand on his arm. "But then he could just

go to another festival somewhere else and do it there."

Patrick sighed. "Yes, he could."

Gwen looked up at him. "He could get away with it again and again, moving around the country to do so..." She looked up at Justin a moment. "We will be having another gathering, and you will be there to help find him, Mr. Blaine. We have always held them, even when many authorities tried to stop us. The seasons don't stop, the cycle doesn't pause, and the gods don't wait." She watched him a moment more, then turned and looked around the room. "Kathy and I will bring all of you some lunch. Go outside and rest in the sun." With that, she got up and left the cabin.

Patrick let out a long breath. "I'll talk to you all later, before everyone starts heading home tonight." He held the door open and looked back. "That woman, regardless of the outcome, owes all of you her life." He turned and walked out with Justin.

Leena stood slowly. "Let's go sit outside and let the sun relax us. Then we'll start packing up to go home."

One after the other, they silently followed her out the door.

୬୧ Chapter 7 ୨ର

The ride home was a quiet one. Owen insisted on driving, and Leena watched him the whole way carefully. Chris hadn't had to pull Kasey over closer to him. She had been as close to him as she could manage before he was completely in the Jeep. She hadn't spoken, and the longer she went without speaking, the more worried he became.

Chris didn't want to think of her alone tonight in her little house. He didn't want to let her go, not now that he'd finally gotten close to her. He wanted her in his house, where he could watch over her, care for her. He actually didn't know how he was going to get out of the Jeep and walk away when they got back.

Kasey leaned into him. As long as he was there, she felt safe. It was going to take her a long time to forget what those women looked like when they found them. She remembered the blood on all the men. Looking down, she glanced at Chris's hands. There was no blood on them now, but she would still see it there for a while.

Her stomach tightened, and she felt herself start shaking. "Owen, please stop for a minute." She couldn't stop shaking.

Chris turned to her and reached out to hold her

shoulders. "Just breathe, Kasey. Breathe through it."

She shook her head. She couldn't catch her breath.

Owen pulled over quickly.

Pushing away from Chris, she opened the door and scrambled out. She ran into the ditch and stood there bent over with her hands on her knees.

Chris was out and around the Jeep before Dade could pull up behind them. He slid down the slope into the ditch and ran to her in a few strides. He placed his hand on her back and talked softly to her. "Just take deep breaths, sweetheart." He knelt down and looked into her face. "Just breathe. It will pass."

He glanced up to see Owen looking distressed. Leena wouldn't let him come and help after what he'd gone through that morning. "You have to relax and let it go." He shook his head at Owen.

Kasey was gasping, trying to draw air in. He brought her chin up so she would look at him. "Kassandra," he said softly. "Look at me. Don't look away. Just keep looking at me. Listen to my voice, sweetheart. Let me bring you through this." Chris stood, slowly straightening her up. "That's it. You're doing fine. Just keep looking at me. Take a deep breath now, and let it go." He smiled as her breathing became quiet again. "That's it... Keep looking at my eyes, sweet Kasey. You're going to be fine."

It had been a long time since he'd used his gift in this way. He'd promised himself long ago to never use it this way on someone again. But this was Kasey, and it was for all the right reasons this time.

Chris lowered his lashes, looking down and breaking the connection. Then he quickly looked at her again. "Are you okay?" he asked her quietly.

She nodded. "It was awful. I looked at your hands and saw the blood and all of it again, and then I couldn't breathe, Chris." Kasey wrapped her arms around him and hugged him tightly.

He kissed the top of her head and held her close for a moment. "Kase, look at my hands, sweetheart. They're clean. It's gone." He held them out in front of her. She took each hand and turned it over slowly and looked at them. He held one of hers and brought it to his mouth. "Let's get you home."

Leena and Cora practically pulled her out of his arms when they climbed to the edge of the road again. He let them hug and comfort her as he stood there with his hands in his pockets, beside the other men.

Dade grinned at him. "You've been holding out on us, Larkin, big-time, huh?"

Chris looked at the others standing there and let out a breath. "There is a slight chance I know a few things I haven't shared." He looked seriously at Dade for a moment. "For very good reasons, my friend."

Steven looked down at the ground for a moment then back at him. "If the women caught a feel of that, you're going to have some serious explaining to do."

Chris grinned, "You forget my profession. I excel at finding loopholes."

"Be careful, or that loop will turn into a noose around your neck." Dade laughed.

Chris sighed, knowing he was right. He glanced at Owen. "I don't want her alone tonight."

Owen stuck his hands in his pockets. "I'll make a suggestion to Leena."

Chris nodded and walked over to try to get Kasey back into the Jeep.

He hadn't been lying. He didn't want her alone. But he also didn't trust himself with her alone right now either. She lifted her face for a kiss as he opened the door to the Jeep. He lowered his mouth to hers to feather a brief kiss against her lips. Brushing his fingers over her cheek, he smiled before he closed the door.

Chris had Owen drop him off first, leaving most of his

stuff in Dade's van. Kasey would be spending the night with Leena and Owen at their house. The worry of her being alone was gone. The worry of what he'd done wasn't, and he needed some time to sort that out.

He stepped into his large, quiet home. It felt empty after the weekend of being so close to the others. He dropped his pack by the door, only to pick it back up and carry it with him to his temple room. As the door opened, he flicked a hand and the lights came on.

He looked around, comforted by the familiar space. It always soothed him. The dark blue of the walls relaxed him. His bookshelves were lined with any book that had ever been written on magic and all varieties of the occult, dark or light. He'd read every one of them, too.

Beside them on the shelf was a large leather bound journal that contained his experiences with what did and didn't work.

The marble floor was polished to a brilliant sheen. Sighing, he walked to stand in the middle of the pentacle carved into the floor.

One wall, lined with cabinets that were filled with various magical ingredients and items. He didn't require them, but having them provided a sense of security.

Setting his pack down, he took out the Solstice gifts and placed them on a table. Holding the cuff links in his hand, he walked over and placed them inside a carved wooden box on the shelf.

Then he went and sat on the cushions in the far corner, away from the window. He waved a hand towards a shelf, and several candles moved to settle down on the stands throughout the room. With a snap of his fingers, the flames grew from the wick. Sighing, he flicked his hand, and the electric lights turned off, as the soothing candlelight caressed the room.

He studied a fairy sitting on a shelf next to a wolf and grinned. The irony of that didn't slip by him. What, he thought with a sigh, was he going to do about beautiful, sweet, innocent, little Kassandra Wright? Could he tell her everything about himself and his past, then watch her run the other way? He was sure he wouldn't survive that ending.

He could keep his mouth shut and continue as he had for the last several years, yearning, wanting. He groaned when he thought of how she'd felt against him in the dark.

Chris couldn't go back to the harmless banter and a chaste kiss here and there. Was he able to give her the time she needed? Running his hands through his hair in frustration, he swore under his breath. He stood up and paced to the door. With a snap, as he walked out the door, the candles snuffed out, and he closed the door to darkness.

He was almost to the kitchen when he realized he'd left his pack and phone in the temple room. Dropping his head, he took a deep breath and focused. Down the hall he heard a door shut and opened his eyes to see his pack floating towards him. Catching it in midair, he grinned.

Now he needed a drink and some time to get his brain together before he went to the office in the morning.

Dropping the pack on the kitchen counter, he fished his cell phone out of it and flipped it open. He stared at it for a few minutes, then sent Leena a message.

Everything ok there?

He glanced towards the fridge until a beer was in his hand. He had just taken off the cap when she replied.

Yes. Kase is soaking in the tub.

He grinned at the image that came to mind with that.

Good. Call if you need anything.

He set the phone down and took a long drink. What was it with beer? Why did man think it fixed all? He chuckled and was studying the bottle when Leena's message came back.

Will do. And Chris, you and I are going to have to talk.

He grinned at the phone. He had been expecting that.

Name the time and place and I'll be there. Tell Kasey good night for me.

Setting the phone down, he picked up his beer and leaned back, taking a slow drink. Leena would be the easiest of the four women to talk to, and he knew at some point he'd have to do a lot of explaining to all of them. The only one he feared telling was Kasey.

Grinning into the bottle, he remembered what she'd done to him over the belly ring being charmed. Oh, she was more powerful than she let on too, for the little thing she was. He sobered for a moment thinking of how strong she'd be when she was older, that was almost frightening. He finished the beer and grabbed his phone, deciding sleep was the best plan of action.

Chris had just flicked off the lights and dropped down onto the mattress when his cell phone rang. He flipped it open to see Kasey's number on the screen.

"Hi, sweetheart. How are you doing?" There was a pause.

"Better. You don't mind that I called, do you? If you're busy..."

"I just laid down in my bed. You can call me whenever you want, Kasey. You should know that." He pursed his lips wondering if she had his home and office number.

"Do you want me to let you go to sleep then?"

Her voice was so soft, so sweet, his muscles clenched just hearing it. "No, I'm not tired, really, just trying to relax. That was not the weekend I had planned."

He heard her sigh softly into the phone.

"Yes. That's one of the reasons I called, to thank you for being so good to me today."

"You don't have to thank me for that."

"I know, but I wanted to anyways. Will you let me know if you hear anything?"

"Of course."

"Good. The other reason I called was, well, I was relaxing in the bath, Leena's filed me with so much herbal tea I may never be tense again, but I was just lying there, relaxing with my eyes closed..."

His mind filled with that image, and he smiled to himself.

"And I started thinking about you and when we were alone those few times." He imagined her blushing right now.

"I never really got to talk to you about any of that, Chris."

He could be there with her in his arms in twenty minutes. "We can talk about it if you like, sweetheart." His voice was suddenly huskier.

She giggled. "Well, I guess I really don't want to discuss it like the weather or anything, but what I meant to tell you was I was thinking about you and how we were, and um... I wouldn't mind being with you like that again, if...if you want to."

He grinned into the phone. "Kassandra, just hearing your voice over the phone has me hard and wanting."

There was a pause "Oh, good, that makes me feel better...because the sound of your voice almost has me wanting too, just listening to it, Chris."

He groaned, "You're killing me, Kasey. I'm ready to drive there now and carry you out the back door."

She laughed. "Oh, see? You've distracted me completely from the other reason I called. Now I'm just all hot."

He hissed out a breath. "Now you're just being a mean and sexy little witch."

She giggled again. "I'm sorry. Really, I can't help it. Every time I see you standing there in the moonlight wearing just your black sarong... God, Chris, do you know all I could think about when I saw you was licking every inch of that muscled chest..."

His hand not holding the phone grasped the pillow and squeezed. "Kasey, please! Have some compassion for me here."

She gasped. "I'm sorry. See? You did it again."

He closed his eyes and tried not to think of the way she would look doing as she said. "What was the other reason you called? And I warn you, if it involves any part of your body or mouth or anything close to what you've got me thinking now, I will hang up and be on Leena's doorstep in twenty minutes or less." There was a pause.

"Oh. Hmm."

"Kasey!" The little witch had him so hard he was almost panting like an animal for her.

"I was thinking," she answered quickly.

"I know what you were thinking, you little witch." He took a deep breath. "And the other reason you called?"

"Okay, but it involves body parts, but not in that way. The parts like your eyes and what you did tonight on the way home when I had that attack."

He sat up. So she did know.

"I didn't completely realize it at the time. It hit me after we dropped you off. Chris, what did you do?"

He let out a slow breath. "It's similar to a hypnosis technique, but more of a spell. I wanted to help you, but talking you through it wasn't working."

"Is it like mind control?" Her voice was suddenly very quiet.

He pinched the bridge of his nose and thought. "Not completely, no." He waited.

"Would you ever use it against me, for any reason other than like today?"

She spoke so softly he could barely hear her. "No. Never. That wouldn't be fair to either of us." And he knew then he wouldn't, and it was the truth.

"Okay, good, then. I have one more question, Chris."

"Go ahead." What more could she know?

"Did you like what I did to you after...after you made me feel so good outside the cabin?"

She caught him completely off guard. He was shocked. He closed his eyes and remembered. "Kasey, say the word, and I'm in the car and coming to get you."

She laughed softly. "That's not an answer."

He growled into the phone. "Yes. Yes, I liked it. Are you enjoying teasing the hell out of me right now?"

"Oh, yes."

Her voice was low, and he groaned into the phone. "Go

get some sleep, you sexy little witch," he whispered.

"Same goes for you. Good night, Christopher."

"Good night, sweet Kassandra." He closed the phone and took a deep breath, holding it before letting it out slowly. Teaching that woman was going to be more than worth it..

✸ Chapter 8 ✸

Leena waved her off the floor the next day. Kasey checked the machine and then walked over, taking her safety glasses off. Grabbing her hand, Leena smiled. "She made it through the night. Steven just called. She's not out of intensive care yet, they had to operate again late last night, but she's holding on."

Kasey hugged her quickly and let out a breath. "Oh, I hope she holds on. That's good, though, that she has so far."

"I've got to get back and get this order sorted before Cora hurts someone. Tell Rachel when she goes flying by the next time."

Kasey nodded and walked back to the air knife that had spent most of the day jamming up.

Kasey couldn't wait to get home. When Leena dropped her off, she ran in the house. She had been thinking about some of the revisions Owen had suggested to use in her story, and a solution had hit her just after lunch.

Dropping her stuff at the door, she kicked it shut and ran into her bedroom. She grabbed her laptop off the dresser and opened it quickly. While it booted up, she sat there bouncing, trying to keep the idea clear in her mind. There was nothing worse than thinking of the perfect dialogue or scene and not having anywhere to write it down. Of course, then, by the time you did, half of it was lost and you never quite got it back.

Ha! She raced to find the part she was looking for and started typing quickly. Oh, this was it. It just all fit together now. Grinning to herself, she continued typing.

When she got uncomfortable where she was, she just pulled the computer onto her lap and continued.

It took her an hour to get it all out the way she wanted, but she was so happy she'd gotten it written before she forgot the details. Congratulating herself, she closed the lid and went out to get something to eat.

Now she was definitely starving. She had just stepped into the kitchen when someone knocked on the door. With a puzzled look, she walked over and opened it.

"Chris?"

He grinned. "I was going by, and that's not a line, by the way, and I thought I'd pop in and see if you had gotten the news from Steven today." Chris stood there, his eyes moving over her.

Kasey suddenly wished she'd changed when she'd come home. She was wearing stained work jeans. Her T-shirt was much the same. At some point it had been a dark blue, but it was now faded to a washed-out almost blue. She wore a baseball cap, backwards. "Oh, come in. I got distracted when I got home tonight and haven't even changed yet." She was mortified she looked like this and he saw.

Chris stood there in a dark gray suit, an expensive one if the fit was any indication. He'd undone his tie, and it rested loosely against the very white pressed shirt. Was it possible he was even sexier this way than half naked in a sarong, she wondered.

He smiled down at her. "Am I interrupting then?"

Kasey shook her head and then took off her hat, running her hands quickly through her hair to fluff it.

"No. I'm finished." She looked up at him for a moment.

"I was going to have a drink of wine while I decided on food. Would you like one?" She fidgeted with her hat as she spoke to him.

Stepping in farther, he took off his jacket and laid it on the chair. "I would love one. It's been one of those days. And I couldn't sleep last night." He sat on the arm of the couch as she went into her little kitchen area. "Steven reached everyone?"

Kasey stretched up on her toes to reach the wine glasses. "Yes, he called Lee at work, and she came out and told us." She poured one glass and then looked over at him. "Is she still the same?"

"As far as I know."

She walked over and handed him a glass, then sat in the chair. "Well, that's good, I guess. At least she's holding on." She ran her finger around the rim of the glass. "I didn't even ask anyone her name. I wanted her to remain nameless until we know if she'll be all right." He came over, in his expensive suit she noted to herself, and sat on the floor in front of her.

"I haven't asked yet either so don't think of yourself as a coward."

"You always say the right things. Did you know that?"

"That's good. It really helps with being a lawyer, that I can say the right things."

She laughed. "I think I'll heat up some stew Cora made. Would you like some?"

"I would." Chris started to get up so she could stand, but then he stopped in front of her on his knees. "Are you going to make me beg for a kiss?"

"I didn't want to get too close and get your nice clothes all dirty."

Chris laughed and pulled her forward in the chair by her legs. "They'll wash, or I could just take them off." Her eyes widened. "I was kidding. Come here and kiss me."

Kasey leaned forward, careful to keep her glass away from his shirt, and placed her hand against his cheek. Brushing her mouth slowly over his mouth, she tasted the wine on his lips. Leaning back, she whispered, "I'll go put the stew on.

He watched her as she stood and walked quickly to the fridge. Shaking his head at his own weakness, he stood up and walked quietly over to her. "If you want to go change, I'll start this."

Kasey turned. "Oh. Okay, thanks." She set the pot on the counter and smiled at him before walking to her room.

When she walked back out a few minutes later, he was placing dishes on the table. He grinned over at her. "It's nice that you asked me to stay. Most of my nights end with me eating at my desk over paperwork." He watched her walk over. She had put on a little black tank top and red shorts. He smiled at the fairy hanging at her waist. "You wore her to work?"

Kasey grinned and rested a hand against her belly. "I didn't want to take her off. Of course, if anything ever happens to her, I'll cry for a month..."

She stopped when he walked over to her. Her eyes widened when he dropped to his knees and placed a kiss on her belly button. Gripping her hips, he grinned up at her. "You've ruined me, you know. I'm standing in the courtroom today, in the middle of a hearing, and the image of you popped into my head, and all I could think of was kissing this fairy hanging on your soft, sexy body. I had to ask for a ten-minute break." He dipped his head and ran his tongue slowly around the pendant.

Kasey ran her hands through his hair and held him against her. "Well, that's only fair. Every time I touched my own waist today, and her, I'd be standing in the middle of a factory full of people and machines rubbing my tummy and blushing."

He laughed against her stomach. Standing up slowly, he pulled her into his body. "I told myself five minutes. Stop for five minutes, behave myself, and then go home. I'm not doing a very good job of listening."

Smiling, she ran her hands up his shirt. "You're doing a fine job, and you have enough time to kiss me again before the stew is ready."

He grinned and lowered his head, savoring the mouth he'd thought of all day. He ran his tongue along hers, taking the taste of her into his mouth. It was a struggle to keep his hands gentle and the kiss slow and lazy.

When he lifted his head, she smiled up at him with a dreamy smile. "Mmm. I like those as much as your hungry kisses."

He straightened his arms and moved her away. "Behave, or the stew gets turned off and you get thrown over my shoulder."

She bit her lip for a moment and then gave him a small smile. "Stew wins. I'm starving."

Laughing, he sat down while she went over to the stove.

They sat on the couch with a third glass of wine after dinner. Kasey giggled to something he said, and he grinned at her. "I forgot you shouldn't drink more than one glassful."

"I am not driving or operating machinery, so I think it's okay." She gave him a wide-eyed look. "Unless you'd like to take advantage of me, and then I'm afraid I've had just enough that I might let you."

Taking the glass out of her hand, Chris set it on the table. "You're cut off before you say something that really gets you into trouble."

She fidgeted with the collar on his shirt. "Like I want to sit here and make out with you?"

He studied her face. "If you mean that Kasey, prove to me you still have your wits about you and light us a few candles."

Kasey just looked at him silently, watching the surprised expression he gave her when a large candle came across the room and sat on the table. She looked at the candle a moment, and the wicks became flames. "Is this one enough? It has three wicks." She smiled sweetly.

He studied her a moment longer before motioning to the light above them. With a flick of his hand, it went off, leaving only the candle and a small light in the kitchen casting shadows over them. "Come here, you sexy witch." He reached and pulled her onto his lap.

Supporting her back in his arm, he kissed her once softly. "Don't let me take you further than you want, sweetheart," he whispered against her lips. "My mind isn't able to function when I have you in my arms."

She ran her tongue over his bottom lip. "Kiss me, Chris."

Lowering his mouth to hers again, he kissed her long and slow. He fought to keep it slow. Her tongue tasted of the wine, and she wiggled against him trying to get closer.

He deepened the kiss, sensing what she was looking for, and hissed out a breath against her mouth as she sucked gently on his tongue. Pulling his mouth from hers, he moved down and traveled over her throat softly. "That's advanced making out, sweetie, and could get you more than you're looking for."

Kasey undid a few of the buttons on his shirt and ran her hand inside. "I'm a pretty good student, and I have an excellent teacher." Before he could stop her, she leaned forward and kissed his throat tenderly.

His hand tightened on her hip as he pulled her closer. She slid her mouth to the side of his neck and pulled the shirt open to get to his skin. She nipped his neck tenderly before she ran her tongue over it as he'd done to her. He took a ragged breath and tilted his head, encouraging her to continue. She sucked gently on his neck, and a breath hissed out of him. Enjoying how she affected him, he let her continue, even when she ran her tongue around his ear and he growled.

Moving her mouth, she sucked harder on the side of his neck, then slowly ran her tongue over the part of his chest that was exposed.

He pulled her head back and leaned her back over his

arm. "Your turn," he gasped against her throat. He nipped along her skin as she had done to him and ran his tongue around to the side of her neck. Pushing her top aside so his mouth could continue to taste across her shoulder.

When he returned to her mouth, he held her head to kiss her deeply. His mind said slowly, but he ignored it as his mouth ravaged hers, stabbing his tongue in quickly. She moaned against his lips as he ran his hand over her waist and up under the edge of her top. His thumb brushing over the thin material she wore underneath made her gasp into his mouth.

Pulling his mouth from hers, he pushed her top up and looked down at her. The material covering her was sheer enough he could see the hard, pink nipples pushing out against it. He dipped his head down and pinched one between his lips. She whimpered and grabbed his head.

For one brief moment, he wanted to tear off her bra and taste her. But he leaned back, reasoning with himself. "Kassandra...sweetheart. We stop here or we don't stop at all." He kissed his way gently up her throat while pulling her shirt back into place. "I can't continue this right now. I want you so much, if we go further, I won't have enough control to stop. I don't want to hurt or scare you."

She looked up at him with eyes of lust, her body still draped over his arm, and his throat dried up. "Sweetheart, I want you more than I've ever wanted another, but if you don't stop looking at me like that, I'm going to start begging."

Kasey smiled at him and ran her fingers over his mouth. "You are the sweetest man."

He kissed her hand. "If you could read my thoughts, you wouldn't think that."

"I don't care what you say." She sat up until she was face-to-face with him again. "I know this isn't easy for you. I mean, how many men encounter a twenty-six-year-old virgin? Not many, I'm sure." She searched his eyes. "I know you're experienced, and not used to having to stop." He went to speak, but she shook her head. "But you do. You could have any woman you want, and here you are with me, patiently trying to give me the time I need."

He kissed her softly. "I don't want any other woman. I only want you." He kissed her cheek and down to her jaw, his lips lingering slowly over her skin. "I don't suppose you could give me a time-line on the completion of this future seduction, could you?" he asked against her throat with a grin.

She moved her head so he'd continue. "I just feel like I don't understand any of it. I like it all, but it's a little overwhelming." He nuzzled her throat softly. "Then sometimes I think, Oh, now!"

He stopped and lifted his head. "Get up." He lifted his hands and held them up.

"But I like sitting on your lap." She bit her lip. "I like feeling how much you want me."

He clasped his hands behind his head and looked at her. "Kasey," he said with exasperation, "please, have mercy on me. I am one step from being a bloody angel, and you tease me endlessly." He put his head back and closed his eyes letting out a slow breath. He jumped when he felt her warm lips move over his throat. He growled, "I have to go home. Get off me, you sexy little witch, before I give you what you keep asking for without even realizing it."

She laughed softly against his throat. "If that's what you want, I'll get up."

Chris scooped her up quickly and stood holding her. "It's not. But I do have to go. I'm tired, and my restraint is fading quickly."

He set her on her feet and picked up his jacket and tie. "Oh, the other reason I came by is that I've been invited to the birthday dinner of a rather influential judge. I'd like you to go with me."

Her eyes widened. "You do?"

"Yes. It will be pretty dressy, so you'll need a cocktail dress."

She stood there looking at him without saying anything.

"Kasey, will you go with me?"

She nodded.

"Don't get all nervous. You'll be with me." He kissed her softly. "At least if we get bored out of our minds we can zap people and sit back and laugh as they try to figure out what happened."

She grinned.

"I'll pick you up Saturday at six, and I'll see you at the Wednesday meeting. I think I'm going to have a Sunday brunch again this week too."

"Okay."

He pulled her close for a soft, lingering kiss. "Good night, Kassandra."

"Good night, Christopher." As he stepped through the door, she stopped him. "Were you really driving by?"

He grinned at her as he backed up a few steps. "If I drive around long enough, yes." With that, he walked to his car.

As soon as she closed the door, Kasey flew over to the phone and called Cora. Where did you buy a cocktail dress? Why did they call them that, she wondered as she dialed.

A few moments later, she hung up the phone and flopped down into the chair. Cora agreed to save her life and go shopping with her Friday night.

Had he chosen the wrong one?

She still lived. Her soul wasn't cleansed.

She had fought him, unlike the rest.

The evil flowing through her had been strong.

He had failed to save her.

Wiping his hand over the blade of the knife again, he closed his eyes against the pain in his head.

He wouldn't fail the next one.

ᴄ₢ Chapter 9 ᴖᴄ

They were sitting around Leena's living room when Kasey stormed into the house looking flustered. Chris's smile faded when he saw the look on her face.

"I've just had the worst day of my life, the past hour at least." She waved a piece of crinkled-up paper at them. "You'll never guess what this is!" She waved it some more, then looked down at it. "I'm so screwed!" she spat out, and then the page flew up to the ceiling and stuck as if it had been glued there. She threw her hands up in the air and stomped into the kitchen.

Everyone looked at the door she'd slammed, then stared up at the paper still on the ceiling. Dade got up and stood under it looking up at it. "Oh." He turned to Chris. "I believe this would be a legal matter, counselor."

Eyebrows drawn together, Chris got up and walked over. Holding out his hand, the page floated off the ceiling into it. He read it for a moment. "I believe you're right."

Leena stood there looking at Dade. "What is it?" she whispered.

Dade scowled. "I think it says Kasey's landlord has sold the property she lives in and the new owners are tearing it down, giving Kasey three weeks to move out."

Leena's mouth dropped open. "Oh no! Can they do that?"

Dade shrugged. "I guess that's for Chris to figure out."

All eyes turned to Chris. "Give us a moment." He walked into the kitchen.

Kasey turned when Chris walked in. She was boiling mad and wanted to beat something, but curbed the urge because this wasn't even her house.

"Kasey. Calm down." Chris stood looking at her all calm and relaxed, and that annoyed her right now.

She whirled around to face him completely. "Calm down? Easy for you to say, you're not going to be living in your car!" she spat at him. "I tried to call my landlord. Oh, I don't blame him. He's such a sweet old man, probably just wants to retire and travel. He apologized, said he had no idea they intended to tear it down." She put her hands in her face and groaned. "What am I going to do, Chris?" Kasey flipped a hand out, and the crinkled paper flew from his hand into hers. She looked down at it.

Chris walked over and pulled it from her hands gently. "You're going to let me have it. I'll make a few calls. If there's a way around it, I'll find it for you."

She went from mad to teary-eyed and looked up at him. "I can't afford to move, Chris. I can barely afford where I'm living now."

He leaned down and softly kissed her mouth before straightening and smiling at her. "Just let me handle it, all right?" She nodded. Tucking her under his arm, they went back out to the others.

Dade winked at her and glanced up at the ceiling. "That was pretty impressive stuff, Kase."

Kasey let out a deep breath. "Sorry about that. I was just so upset. I almost blew up my cup of tea when I read it."

Leena went over and hugged her and then looked at Chris. "Is there anything you can do?"

Chris shrugged. "I don't know at this point, but I'll see

what can be done tomorrow."

Owen grinned at Kasey. "I will never run out of ideas for books as long as I'm around you guys."

Kasey chuckled halfheartedly. "Yes, I'm sure you could write a whole book about short-tempered witches."

He laughed. "I haven't even begun *that* series yet."

Steven sent a cushion floating over at Owen's head. "Now that the show is over, would anyone like an update on the recovery of Rhonda?" All eyes went to him when he said her name.

Not one of them had known her name, Kasey realized. Suddenly she became something more than she had been to them. Rachel nodded and sat on the floor looking up at him.

"She's still in ICU and pretty incoherent. They're keeping her medicated and relaxed. She has a lot of stitches everywhere, so they want her comfortable through the worst part of recovery. But she's getting stronger each day. They're not certain how much use she'll have of her hands at this point."

He paused to watch a tear roll down Rachel's cheek. "But the damage to her back wasn't as bad as first thought, and she should be able to walk." Steven reached down and wiped the tear gently off Rachel's cheek and offered her a small smile. "She's still alive, and at this point, Rach, that's all that matters."

Straightening, Steven looked around the room. "I'm going to go see her on Friday afternoon when I'm off duty, so I'll have more to tell you after that." He gave Chris a serious look for a moment. "I spoke to Patrick. They weren't able to get any DNA to trace, or prints, or anything, really. His only thread of hope is that Rhonda may have seen something."

Chris stuck his hands in his pockets and looked down. "I talked to him last night too. He's placed a guard on her room just to be sure nothing else happens to her."

Leena leaned into Owen's arms. "Take her some flowers from us, Steven, and if you speak to her, tell her we're all pulling for her." Leena turned and looked at Kasey for a moment. "Maybe Kasey can charge a stone or two to leave with her."

Kasey nodded. "I'll do it tomorrow night and drop it off at the hospital for you."

Cora had sat there quietly through the whole conversation. She looked from Kasey and Leena to Steven. "Will they let us see her once she's out of recovery?" Dade leaned forward and watched Cora. "I'd like to see her when we can. It was such a strong connection..." She looked at Dade. "I think she sent out the call for help to me, which would mean she has real magic inside her."

Dade sat squatted in front of her and touched her hand. "You're sure?"

Cora nodded. "Yes. I wouldn't have been able to hear the creek she heard. or known as much as I did, if she wasn't able to send the information out to someone. To me." She looked up from his hand. "I'd like to find out. I still feel her inside my head sometimes, Dade."

He reached up and touched her cheek. "The Doc will let us know as soon as we can see her, and then I'll take you."

She nodded and looked back down at their hands. "Thank you."

Rachel studied Cora for a moment. "That must have been so awful for you, Cora, to feel what she did. I want to go with you when you do see her." She looked at Steven. "I've been working on a spell to bring peace, and I'd like to do that for her."

Steven nodded slowly for a minute. "I'll have to make sure she's stable before any of us try anything more to help her. It could possibly hurt her further."

Chris cleared his throat. "Just let us know, and we'll all go together. If she's as Cora suspects, she might feel better knowing we're still around."

Owen nodded. "I know I would." He looked over at the Doc. "Would I be able to help her recovery at all?"

Steven frowned. "It's possible. Of course, you all realize

any of us doing anything magical while inside the hospital is risky as hell. Too much energy flying around could set off alarms and wreak havoc with monitors."

Dade stood up and looked at him. "We'll be careful, Doc, no worries there."

Chris glanced at his watch. "On that note, I need to go. I think a Sunday brunch at my house is in order, and then Steven can update us, and hopefully we'll come up with a plan to help Rhonda."

Chris looked at Steven for a moment. "When I spoke to Patrick, we discussed what was going to happen if she does know who attacked her. No one outside of us and Justin and Gwen can hear of anything that takes place. He's told Justin no one gets told anything. If she remembers anything, she's going to need to disappear until the killer is caught."

Kasey looked up at him, knowing he would see the fear in her eyes, but she couldn't hide it right now. "What about her family?"

He rested his hand on her shoulder. "There's going to be a lot to figure out, Kasey, but one step at a time. First she has to get stronger." He kissed her quickly. "I'll call you when I find out about your situation."

Kasey smiled at him. "Thank you. You've quite possibly saved some corporate jerks from falling off a building."

Chris shook his head laughing. "You're really starting to scare me, woman." He saluted to the others and walked out.

Rachel waited until the door closed, then grinned at Kasey. "I want in on this shopping trip Friday."

Leena leaned forward and whispered, "Count me in too."

Cora grinned over at her around Dade's shoulder. "You're going to look so good he'll be speechless."

Dade lifted an eyebrow at Owen. "Have I missed something here?"

Owen nodded towards the kitchen. "Let's go have a beer."

Grinning, Steven got up. "I need beer too."

The door had barely closed behind them when Dade turned, lifting his hands. "What is going on? Who's going to be speechless? What shopping trip?"

Steven hopped onto the counter. "Yeah, fill us in here. You get the inside scoop now being coupled up with one of them."

Owen handed them a beer. "It seems Chris finally worked up the courage to ask Kasey to some big fancy dinner with a judge or something."

Dade took a long drink, then grinned. "Really? Does he know he's got all the women coaching little Kasey?"

Owen shook his head and looked over the bottle at him. "Nope."

Steven laughed. "I would kill to see how this date goes. Chris has been wanting to drag her off to bed for so long."

Owen sobered. "Well hopefully he doesn't actually drag her."

Dade paused in drinking. "What do you mean?"

Owen cursed softly and then looked at the door. "Lee will rip my heart out if I tell you and she finds out." *Please don't let her find out,* he thought.

Dade leaned over closer as Steven stepped to listen by the door. "That's why we won't let her find out. Give."

Owen hissed, "Chris had just better...well Kasey..." He cursed again. "Leena's gonna kill me." He searched for a moment on how to say this without saying it. "Let's just say there's a really good reason why little Kasey looks so innocent all the bloody time."

Steven straightened away from the door and looked at Owen blankly. Dade stood back and stared at him for a moment, and then his eyes widened. "You're serious?"

Owen nodded.

Steven's mouth dropped open. "Lucky bastard!"

Owen nodded again.

"Well fuck!" Dade said before taking a drink. "This just keeps getting more interesting." He grinned. "Don't suppose either of you have a talent for seeing?" They shook their heads. "Well that sucks."

"What sucks?" Cora asked, pushing through the door.

Dade took a drink quickly, and Owen turned and opened the fridge, trying to appear as if he was getting something out.

Steven shrugged. "They wanted a guy's night out Saturday, and I have to work."

She grinned. "It will keep all of you out of trouble then."

Dade nodded. "Yeah, probably just as well."

She looked at him for a moment. "I came in to say good night. We're all heading home."

Owen closed the fridge. "Oh, I'll go out and say good night to everyone then." Steven went out the door Owen held open.

Dade grinned at Cora. "Come to give me a kiss good-bye, honey?"

He watched her smile slowly. "No, I didn't." Then she walked back into the other room.

❧ Chapter 10 ❧

Kasey stood in front of the mirror, deep breathing. If he didn't get here soon, she was going to have a nervous breakdown and back out. Cora had slipped over and helped her with her hair, leaving quickly before Chris got there. She checked it again. It looked pretty good dark, but she still missed the blonde.

She almost jumped out of her skin when he knocked on the door. She opened it, and her jaw dropped. He looked sexier than she had ever seen him look. His dark suit was tailored to fit him perfectly. His usual dark, messy hairstyle was combed perfectly, bringing her attention to his dark green eyes, which she noted were appraising every inch of her at the moment.

Any words he had disappeared when she'd opened the door. She'd slicked her hair back, and tiny thin silver chains hung from her ears almost to her bare shoulders. She was wrapped in a deep emerald green, silk dress. The neckline plunged low enough that he could see the rise of her breasts. It hugged her waist perfectly, then fell gracefully to mid-calf length.

Inordinately pleased when he saw the anklet he'd given

her wrapped around one smooth, tanned ankle. Looking back up at her eyes, he smiled and held one hand over his heart. "There are no words I could use to adequately describe how gorgeous you look right now." Then remembering the flower in his hand, he held it out to her.

She smiled and took the single, de-thorned white rose from his hand. "It's beautiful, thank you." She stepped back to let him pass. "I just have to get my shoes and purse."

Chris watched her walk into her bedroom, having to take a shaky breath when she turned and he saw the dress dipped down to leave her entire back bare. Unbuttoning his jacket, he let out a slow breath. This was going to be one long evening.

When she walked back out in dangerously high heels, barely held in place by a thin strap, he swallowed. Images of things best not thought ran through his mind. She had fastened a fine silver chain to her neck as well, and just below her collarbone, which he wanted badly to taste, hung a perfect dark green stone. He reached out and feathered his fingers over it. "Bloodstone?"

She nodded. "I need a little help in the courage department tonight." Kasey looked down at her dress. "So, is this okay?"

He leaned down and kissed her cheek gently. "More than. I'm going to have to stand guard over you all night." Taking her hand, he opened the door. "Let's go before I change my mind and try to persuade you to let me take that temptation off you."

She blushed and followed him out the door, still holding the rose he'd given her.

When they walked into the hotel, Kasey knew she was out of her element. Every woman there seemed to have been born and bred with a sophistication she would never have.

Kasey stepped closer to Chris's side, and he put his arm gently behind her. Feeling his palm resting against the skin of her lower back made her feel secure. She looked up at him.

"I'm just going to sit and smile all night. If I speak or move, everyone will know I'm a fraud."

He smiled down at her. "The only person here that's genuine will be you, sweetheart. Relax."

When he guided her towards an older couple surrounded by several people, she reached and stroked a hand lightly over her the stone hanging around her neck, trying to stay calm. *You can do this, Kassandra Wright,* she told herself. *Just smile and be polite.* When she looked up again, she found herself standing right in front of the couple.

Chris stepped forward and shook the man's hand. "How is my favorite judge tonight?" He kept his hand on Kasey's back. "I'd ask how many years we're celebrating, but I think it best I just say many happy returns."

Chris picked up the woman's hand and kissed it softly while smiling at her. The older man threw his head back and laughed. Pulling Kasey closer, Chris smiled down at her. "Judge Wilson, Mrs. Wilson, I'd like to introduce Kassandra Wright. She took pity on me and agreed to be my date this evening."

Kasey shook the hands offered. "Pleased to meet you."

The man grinned at her. "Call me Greg, and this vision of loveliness is my wife, Violet. I see you let this rake charm you into his company." He grinned at Chris. "I'd say he's unworthy of the company of such a lovely woman, but I'd be lying."

Chris laughed and put his arm back around Kasey. "No, you probably would be quite accurate, Greg." When another couple walked up, Chris smiled politely. "We'll go find our seats and talk to you later."

Kasey allowed him to sweep her through the room. They stopped several times when people spoke to him, and he'd go through introductions again. She smiled and stood by him trying to follow along with questions being asked him or make sense of comments. *Way out of your league, Kasey girl,* she thought.

When they finally headed to a quiet table, she looked up

at him. "This," she motioned to the ten or more large round tables, "is just a dinner party?"

Chris grinned down at her as he pulled out a chair. "This is politics, sweetheart, and unfortunately something I have to put up with if I ever want to be in Greg's shoes." He winked at her. "I'll go get us something to drink. Something watered down." She blushed at him remembering the last time they'd had a couple glasses of wine together.

She watched him walk through the room. Everyone seemed to know him and stopped him to speak to him. He smiled and took the time for each person along the way. He was so good-looking tonight she almost sighed every time he glanced back in her direction. He wanted to be a judge? He'd make a good one, she imagined. Not that she really knew why she thought he would. *What are you doing with him?* She frowned down at her clasped hands.

"Well it looks like it's my lucky night, to be seated at the same table as you."

Kasey looked up, startled to see a young man, probably close to her own age, with sandy blond hair and a Boy Scout smile.

He held out his hand. "I'm Chase Taylor. I'm actually doing my internship with Mr. Larkin."

She almost let out a breath of relief, someone on her level. She took his hand and smiled sweetly.

"Kassandra Wright. I'm here with Chris tonight."

He sat down a few chairs from her. "Yes, I noticed, as did everyone in the room, I think." He glanced over at Chris still working his way back across the room. "Mr. Larkin always makes a good entrance, but with you beside him tonight..." He grinned "well, it was quite something to watch."

Kasey blushed, smiling shyly, not knowing how to reply to that, so she didn't.

Chris walked up with two drinks and winked at her. "Sweetheart, you keep smiling like that at Chase and he's going to fall head over heels for you."

Chris set the glasses on the table, then sat on the other side of her, putting his arm around the back of her chair. "How are you, Chase?"

The younger man just grinned. "Plotting on how I can get Miss Wright to leave with me."

Kasey blushed again and put her head down.

Chris laughed. "Try it, and you will find your time with me long and trying."

Chase grinned at him. "Yeah, I figured that." A tall dark-haired woman wrapped in a tight red dress was walking towards the table. "Uh-oh, here comes the Black Widow."

Kasey turned to look, and for some reason, Chase's description of the woman walking toward them seemed to fit the predatory insect he'd called her. With the way her blue eyes moved over Chris and then Chase, she was definitely a predator. The way she seemed to glide with a gracefully inviting sway and the smile on her overpainted mouth invited every male to her.

Chris leaned forward and spoke quietly to Chase. "She's not seated with us, is she?" Chase shook his head, still watching the woman move through the crowd towards them. "Small blessing," Chris muttered before he took a drink.

Kasey smiled up at her as the woman reached the table. The blue eyes gave her a distasteful glance before moving to see Chris's arm over her chair. "Christopher," she all but purred at him, "I wasn't sure if we'd see you here tonight." She flashed him an inviting smile.

"Vickie, it's always a pleasure." His voice seemed hard, and Kasey turned to look at him. His jaw had tightened, and his eyes were cold as he looked at her.

She reached out a hand to Kasey. "Victoria Wilson. I'm so pleased you could come to my father's party."

Kasey had to struggle to not let her jaw drop. *This* woman was related to that sweet couple? Kasey smiled sweetly and took her hand and shook it. "Kassandra Wright. We wouldn't miss your father's birthday." She took her hand back from the woman and placed it on Chris's thigh, noting the other woman's cold blue eyes followed the movement slowly.

Smiling coldly, the woman turned her inviting smile to Chase. "Chase."

He nodded, almost hesitant to speak to her.

"Come with me and get a drink."

Chase glanced at Chris and then nodded to her. "Be happy to." He winked at Kasey. "Save my plate if I don't get back on time."

They watched the couple move away before Chris leaned down and whispered close to her ear. "Little Kasey has claws too, how interesting."

Kasey blushed when she looked at him. "Well, it was either that or make the string barely holding that dress in place pop off her."

Chris chuckled. "I like the claws." Kissing her hand, he looked up to see another couple walking towards them. "That man is a close associate of mine. I took the liberty of making sure they were sitting with us." He grinned at her. "His wife won't take a bite out of either of us."

Kasey just grinned, feeling more than a little lost.

The next hour was a whirlwind of chatter and talk she didn't quite follow. The dinner confused her even more. She wouldn't move a hand towards anything until she waited to see which fork or spoon to touch.

The courses seemed endless, and she didn't dare ask anyone what half of them were. A few almost made her make an *eww* face, but she'd put her head down and eaten it in silence.

As the main course, at least she hoped it was that, arrived; Chase leaned over closer to her. "If you know what that was we just ate, please don't tell me. I don't want to know."

She put her head down to cover her mouth as she tried not to laugh.

Chris leaned over on the other side of her. "Put samples

in your purse to get Cora to identify it."

She dropped her head and laughed harder. "Stop it. You're going to have me crying in my plate." She looked up at the plate the server set in front of her and had to drop her head down again to breathe through the laughter she felt.

Chase groaned quietly. "Oh no, more."

Turning her head, she glanced at Chris. His eyes searched hers and looked quite pleased. He smiled at her and then winked as he picked up his fork.

Kasey looked around the table at the other five people sitting with them and noticed they were all smirking, having heard the conversation, and obviously no one at the table knew what they were eating.

The man Chris had introduced as his closest associate, Lester or Lorne or something, she couldn't remember the name, leaned toward the middle of the table and whispered, "The only person I know that would think of all this as a meal would be the Black Widow. She probably spent all her father's money to put this horrid menu together."

Chris coughed loudly at the chuckles that broke out. She grinned and put her head back down trying to bring herself to taste the items in front of her.

With dinner out of the way, finally, Kasey waited until most of the others were mingling around the room again before she leaned over to Chris. "Please point me towards the bathroom. There are at least thirty doors in this room."

He grinned and nodded towards one. "It's out there."

She smiled and leaned in to kiss his cheek softly. "I'll be back."

Chris watched her walk through the room, noticing with every step she took the way the material swayed suggestively across her backside. The way she smiled politely whenever someone looked at her made him proud that she was here with him.

He watched her place a hand on Greg's shoulder as she walked by the table, leaning down to speak briefly to him. He noticed that Greg smiled a real smile and patted her hand.

Lorne cleared his throat until Chris turned to look at him. "Quite the lady you have there, Chris."

Chris grinned at him. "You have no idea." He glanced to see she had reached the door finally. "Just have to convince her she needs to be with me."

Lorne laughed. "Has that ever been a problem for you?"

Chris sobered. "Not until now."

Lorne laughed again. "It's about time."

His wife nudged him, and they turned to her. "I think I'll visit the ladies' room also. The man-eater you have to put up with just went out the door, right behind your friend."

Chris smiled at her. "Appreciate that, Justine." He turned to watch the door and wait for Kasey to return.

Kasey stepped to the mirror to check her make-up and saw Victoria step beside her.

"How long have you known Chris?" There was no purring in her voice now. It was hard and cold.

Kasey didn't give her the satisfaction of seeing her falter. "Oh, wow, must be six or seven years now."

Victoria looked at her in the mirror. "Really, that long? That's surprising. I didn't think Chris kept female acquaintances that long." She grinned at her with spite. "Sorry, that was mean of me." She pouted. "I'm just a wee bit jealous." She rolled her eyes. "He's quite the man. That's one flame I would love to rekindle." With that, she smiled and walked out of the room.

Kasey glanced up at her reflection to see Justine standing there. She smiled a shaky smile at her.

Justine walked over and opened her purse. "Don't give that piranha the satisfaction of knowing she has upset you." She applied some lipstick and then grinned at Kasey. "She's just mad as hell because every man out there is looking at you, and not her for a change."

Kasey blushed, then sighed. "I *so* don't belong here."

Justine laughed. "That's the exact thing I said about ten

years ago, when Lorne all but dragged me to one of these." She closed her purse and smiled at her. "Just keep smiling and looking as good as you do, and you'll have everyone falling at your feet, Kassandra."

Kasey grinned at her. "It's Kasey, and thank you."

Justine smiled again. "I'm Tina. You're welcome."

Chris watched as Vickie came through the door with that smug evil look on her face. He stood up. He should have strangled her years ago when he'd been close enough to. He had only taken two steps when he saw Kasey and Justine come through the door. They were laughing. Kasey looked so beautiful when she laughed.

Lorne patted him on the back as he passed him. "I'd go grab her before the dancing starts, or you're not going to get near her."

Chris grinned. "I'd like to grab her and get the hell out of here."

Lorne chuckled. "That would be so rude, not to mention completely unfair to every man here dying to dance with her."

Chris glared at him. "The things I do for this bloody job."

Kasey saw him walking to her and smiled. Forgetting everyone else around them, she walked towards him slowly. When he was right in front of her, she rested her hand on his chest and stretched up to kiss him softly. "Miss me?"

He put his hand over hers. "I was ready to come and find you." He glanced over towards Vickie briefly. "Did she play nice?"

Kasey pursed her lips and looked at him for a moment. She still wasn't happy to find out that he had slept with that nasty woman. She grinned at him sweetly. "No. Didn't anyone ever tell you to put all your toys away when you were done playing with them, Christopher?"

The look in his eyes sobered, and he threw a cold glare towards where Victoria was standing, then looked down at her again and put his hand gently under her chin to bring her eyes to his. "I cleaned out my toy box the day I met you, sweet Kasey." He kissed her lips gently. "The dancing is going to start, and I want to hold you in my arms and make every man here cry in their drink."

Her heart started pounding in her chest.

Justine, now on her husband's arm beside them, leaned over. "If you two don't stop, I'm going to be a puddle of mush on the floor."

Kasey laughed and looked at her. She would have been lost without her a few moments earlier. She was about to say something when she heard the music and felt Chris take her hand, gently pulling her towards the floor.

When he wrapped his arms around her and began to gracefully lead her around the room, she smiled. "How long do we have to stay?"

He smiled at her with his boyish grin. "You're not having fun with all the fake people?"

She lowered her head. "I'm not really in my element here. Give me a wrench and a hat, and I'll be much happier."

Chris grinned and kissed the top of her head. "I will get us out of here as soon as the cake has been sliced."

Kasey glanced past him to see Victoria walking towards them with a predatory grin on her face. She was going to cut in and take this first dance from them. Maybe the only dance she ever got with him. She looked up at Chris for a moment and noticed him studying her silently with his sexy eyes. She smiled and looked back towards the other woman.

Turning her head slightly, she watched as someone stood and splashed some of their drink on the front of the tight red dress. Not watching the remainder of it, she rested her head against Chris.

He chuckled softly into her hair. "I don't want to know what you just did, but I felt the surge of your magic, my dear, and Ms. Wilson seems to be having a tizzy fit now."

Kasey smiled up at him sweetly. "I made sure it was white wine and wouldn't stain that trashy red dress."

He laughed. "Oh, I love those claws."

Kasey slumped back in the seat of Chris's car. "My feet are going to fall off!" She took off the heels and rubbed one aching arch. "What torture specialist invented heels?"

Chris watched her rub her foot for a moment. "Well, no one said you had to dance with every male in the room, Kasey."

She looked over at him. "No, but excuses didn't seem to work. Every time I got close to sitting down, some other man was in front of me. You could have rescued me."

Chris looked at her hands again. "Every time I tried to go to you, someone else cut me off. They were conspiring against me tonight," he growled.

She looked over at him and laughed. "You're jealous?"

He snarled at her, not quite joking. "Damn right I am! I've never had to spend the night watching my date whirling around with every male but me. I almost grabbed you and ran when the birthday cake was rolled out." He let out a long breath. Then he turned to start the car. "I'd like to take you back to my place, Kasey, but I know it's too soon." He started the car and looked at her. "So, I'll take you home."

Kasey sat there quietly for a few minutes. "Chris, didn't tonight show you how much in common we *don't* have?"

He glanced over at her briefly. "What do you mean?"

She shrugged. "I didn't understand anything anyone was talking about. I spent the night avoiding questions about my profession. Slopping about in mushy paper with greasy machines isn't exactly a profession, I'm sure." She picked up the rose he'd given her and studied it. "I didn't belong there, Chris," she said quietly.

"You didn't want to be there with me?"

She looked up quickly. "I didn't mean that. Yes, I wanted to be there with you. I just didn't belong *there*."

He looked at her for a moment, then turned back to the road. "I don't see the problem, Kasey."

She pursed her lips and looked down at the rose again,

running her fingertip over a soft petal. "Look at you, Chris. You're at home in your suit that probably costs more than a month of my salary. I live in a three-room house. My entire house could fit in your sitting room."

She paused as he pulled the car over and turned it off before turning to look at her. "I work in a factory, recycling paper. When I come home from work, I look like I did on Monday night. Look at how you look when you're done for the day." She looked at his eyes trying to gauge what he was thinking. He had his lawyer face on, and she couldn't read what he was thinking now.

"I love being with you. When we're together as a group or at an event, it's great, really great." She motioned towards his suit. "But this is the real you the rest of the time." She looked down at her dress. "This is not the real me." She tried to grin to lighten the atmosphere. "I'm sure you didn't have to spend a week's pay to buy your suit. I did, Chris. What does that tell you?" She needed to know what he was thinking.

"I see. I had no idea this is what you thought, Kasey." He searched her eyes and tried to find the words to tell her none of it mattered, and it didn't to him, but clearly it meant everything to her. "I don't know what to say." She looked over at him, her hand holding the rose stem tightly. "Kasey, none of that matters to me at all. None of it. I don't care if I live in a castle and you a mud shack. It doesn't matter."

Her eyelids dropped, hiding her thoughts so he couldn't see them. "The man sitting here in his dinner attire is still the same man that held you wearing nothing but a sarong. I am that man, Kasey." He touched her cheek softly wishing she'd look back at him. "Both of those men want to be with you. I have to go to things, like tonight, because it's my career. It's what I do, but it's not who I am." He didn't know what else to say.

He was the man of words for reasoning, yet he couldn't find the ones he needed. She leaned into his palm for a moment and closed her eyes. When she opened them and looked at him, his heart stumbled in his chest. He was going to have to watch her walk away.

"Chris, I can't be someone I'm not. Not even for you. It matters to me that we're from two very different, far apart lifestyles." She looked at his eyes, searching. "I need to be on equal ground, and I'm not." Her voice was soft with emotion as if she was going to cry.

He straightened away from her and put a hand on the steering wheel. "I see." His jaw clenched for a moment. "I'll take you home now."

"Chris..." She let out a breath and then turned towards the window.

Kasey sat silently looking out the window watching the scenery go by. The buildings all seemed gray to her, or perhaps that was her heart right now, she wasn't sure. The lights on the taller buildings usually caught her eye, but tonight she kept her eyes level and focused on not allowing herself to cry.

Who had she been kidding, thinking she could have something with Chris? As much as she'd always remember him taking her out tonight, her, not someone else, she would also remember how much she didn't belong there and how much he did.

When he pulled up to her house, he turned off the car and sat back looking at her. "Nothing I say is going to matter, is it?" he asked her quietly after a few minutes.

She shook her head without commenting.

Chris looked at the steering wheel. "This is a first for me. I've never before met a woman that didn't want me because of my money and status."

Kasey spoke so softly he almost didn't hear her. "Then I'd say you'd been keeping company with the wrong women." She picked up her purse and held it to her. "Chris..." She stopped for a few seconds. "I didn't mean I don't want you. I just wouldn't like myself very much if I lied and told myself it didn't matter."

He ran his hand through his hair and looked at her. "That's not much help. You want me, but want nothing to do with me." He bit out the last part, and then took a ragged breath and looked out the windshield. "You had better go in the house now, Kassandra."

"Thank you for tonight, Chris. I felt like Cinderella going to the ball." She touched his hand gently before opening the door. "I'll see you at brunch in the morning."

Without looking back, she walked quickly to the door and unlocked it. She went in, closing it quickly behind her.

Chris sat there looking at the closed door to her house. She had just walked away from him. *Sorry, buddy, your lifestyle makes me uncomfortable. I'm out of here.* He gripped the steering wheel and started the car. What did he do now? The woman he'd thought of constantly for six years, the woman he'd gotten to hold a few brief times, the woman he wanted heart and soul, had just thrown him a curveball, and he'd caught it right in the face!

Pulling away from her house, he headed in the direction of his house and drove without really seeing anything around him.

<h1 style="text-align:center;">✤ Chapter 11 ✤</h1>

Kasey chatted quietly with Rachel at Chris's the next morning. He was on the phone and hadn't done more than stuck his head out of his office when they'd arrived saying he'd be there in a moment.

Rachel grinned at her. "How was last night?"

Kasey rolled her eyes. "Way, way out of my comfort zone."

Steven came into the dining room and dropped into a chair grinning at them. "Am I interrupting girl talk? I hope so."

They both grinned back at him.

Kasey watched Cora and Leena come in and sit down. "No, not girl talk, I just wanted to know how Kasey found the party Chris took her to last night."

Leena leaned over and grinned. "I'll bet you looked fabulous, though. That dress looked so good on you."

Kasey smiled.

"I had to watch every man in the room drool on her feet all night," Chris said as he stepped into the room. Kasey watched as he walked around the table. He hadn't even looked at her.

Dade winked at her. "I can see that." Then he turned to

Chris. "Change of pace for you, counselor, you're used to the ladies drooling on you."

Chris gave him a brief smile and sat down.

Cora picked up the juice and poured some. "How was the food?" Everyone looked at her. "What? I need to ask. It's an obsessive thing." She laughed.

Kasey crinkled up her nose. "It was never ending courses of unidentifiable and not altogether tasty blobs of stuff."

Cora's mouth dropped. "Really? You don't know what any of it was?"

Kasey shrugged and went to speak when Chris answered for her again. "It was imported delicacies, mostly the type that people with *money*," he looked right at her with a cold look, "indulge themselves with from time to time." His eyes brushed over Kasey's face with harshness. "I'm afraid Kasey didn't find them enjoyable, or familiar." With that he turned to Steven. "You went to see Rhonda?"

Kasey dropped her head down and played with some food on her plate, not wanting to meet anyone's eyes. When she looked back up, Steven was looking at her.

Steven studied her for a moment, then turned a curious look to Chris before starting slowly to answer. "Yes." He looked around the table at everyone. "She's been conscious several times now, but as I explained before, she's very medicated. All of her vitals are really good, though, so her doctors are thinking of moving her out of ICU."

Steven paused and picked up his cup and then looked at Kasey for a second. "Kase, can you pass the coffee this way?"

Kasey picked up the coffee urn and stood up. "Allow me to serve you, Dr. O'Reily." She gave him a sweet smile. All shocked eyes were on her as she walked to the other end of the table and poured the coffee into his cup.

Jaws dropped when she turned to Chris and asked sweetly, "Could I pour your coffee for you, Mr. Larkin, sir?" She bit out each word slowly.

Chris met her eyes with as much determination as hers

held. "Please do." He gritted his teeth and watched her unsteady hand pour his coffee. She set the urn gently down beside his cup and went back to her seat.

He picked up the cup and took a sip, watching her with an angry stare the whole time. Nonchalantly he looked back to Steven, who looked shell-shocked. "You were saying?"

Dade sat up closer to the table and studied Kasey.

Steven took a few drinks. "Her hands are a mess, but she has been moving them in her sleep, so that's a good sign that there isn't too much nerve damage."

Kasey glared at Chris, and he glared right back at her.

Shaking his head, Steven continued. "Her back will always be scarred. No surgery will ever remove those completely. The cuts on her face weren't as bad as they looked. It's as if he started cutting her there and then got angrier as he went." He took a bite of a croissant. "Uh...oh, Patrick still has the room under guard, and it will stay that way. They're going to start..."

Kasey jumped up to take the bowl of fruit around to Dade when he'd been leaning over to reach it.

Steven paused and watched until she was sitting again. "They're... going... to start lowering her meds and try to bring her back slowly so she doesn't just jump up and try to move too much. By the end of next week, if all has gone well, she should be completely conscious and able to move around a bit." He shrugged. "She's not going to be able to get up and walk without therapy, though. There was far too much area involving too many muscles and nerves. It's going to be months before she's functioning at a close-to-normal level."

Kasey broke her stare from him and looked at Steven. "Do you think we'll be able to help her?"

Her voice was vibrating with an emotion Chris had never heard from shy Kasey before.

Steven smiled at her. "Well, I don't think anything we do would hinder her in any way, Kase. I left the stone you charged hanging by her window, but once she's conscious, something stronger would definitely be of help." He winked at her. "I have had more than enough energy since you gave me that one at Solstice."

Kasey's eyes were cloudy as she looked up at Steven, but she still smiled briefly. "I'll find the right one for her before next week then." She sat back again and played with the glass of juice in front of her.

Steven sat back when Kasey got up and walked to the end of the table again and refilled Chris's coffee cup. Without a word, she went and sat back down. Chris picked it up without hesitating and drank.

"So, are we going to be able to see her next weekend then?" Cora asked Steven.

Steven had to turn his head slowly away from Kasey before speaking. "As long as there aren't any setbacks, yes, I don't see why not. Patrick is actually anxious for us to go see her, feeling we may be able to help more."

Chris sat back and flicked his eyes over Kasey before speaking. "We'll plan a visit next Saturday?"

Everyone nodded. No one spoke.

Leena cleared her throat. "Chris, were you able to find out more about Kasey's house? Does she have to move?"

Chris realized at that moment he'd forgotten to tell Kasey the night before what he'd been able to do. "I actually hadn't even gotten around to discussing it with Kasey yet, Leena. But unfortunately, the new owners are within their rights and have done everything without any loopholes." He paused to see Kasey watching him quietly, her chin held high. "I was able to get her another week's time to find a new residence, and a bit of compensation for the inconvenience they've caused her." He picked up his cup and took a sip.

Kasey watched him silently. She had to move. She had few weeks and then was homeless. It made everything she'd said last night seem even more of a reality to her. Here he sat in this house, sipping coffee, looking not one bit disturbed by the fact that he'd gotten someone to pay her off quietly so she would go away and find somewhere else to live.

Kasey sat back and looked over at him again. "Make sure you bill me accordingly for your time." She would not fall apart in front of him. She let out a hushed breath.

His angry eyes met hers. "I didn't do... it... for... the... money," he said, pausing on each word.

Kasey lifted her chin higher. "That's fine, but I'm sure it took time away from more *important* things you had to do." She crossed her arms and sat back, wishing she could melt into the chair.

Dade hissed out a loud breath and sat back. "Well, I don't know about the rest of you, but I've about had all the light brunch conversation I can stand."

Several heads nodded in agreement.

Kasey stood up. "Why don't all of you go relax on the terrace, and I'll clear this up." She began picking up dishes and stacking them.

"Enough!" Chris bellowed as his closed fist slammed on the table hard enough that the dishes rattled.

Kasey turned and glared at him, her hands on her hips. "Oh, I don't think so!" she spat.

Chris shoved his chair back and stood.

She flashed a hand out at him, and an unseen force sent him flying back into his chair and sent it sliding back three feet. "Don't!" she practically growled.

Chris flicked a hand, and all the dishes from his end of the table went crashing onto the floor.

Everyone scrambled back from the table as he slowly stood again. "Do. Not. Slap. Me. Back. Again," he growled quietly.

Dade ran around the side of the table and stood beside him, his hands out to his sides. Chris didn't even turn to look at him. "Stay out of it."

Dade lifted his hands and backed up a few feet.

Kasey's chest was heaving with ragged breaths. "At least I slap at you with something tangible instead of taking cheap shots with words, Christopher Larkin!" Her fists were clenched at her sides. She opened them, and the table shook with a force she'd never used before. The dishes lifted up, and then they dropped down hard enough, several shattered. Kasey watched the glass and china scatter everywhere and then looked back at Chris. "Take that out of the payoff money you've swindled for me!" With that she ran out of the room.

Chris stood there feeling every bit as angry as she had looked. He wanted everyone to go away and leave them alone. He started to step towards her and then stopped and clenched his hands at his sides. His knuckles were white.

Leena went to go after Kasey and smacked up against an invisible wall. She felt her hand over it for a second, then turned and looked at everyone in the room.

"Someone tell me what the fuck just happened!" Dade bellowed.

All eyes turned to look at Chris as he stood there trying to gain some control over his temper. He looked around the room.

Rachel puffed out her cheeks and then exhaled noisily. "I didn't even get to give her the present we got her. Gee, you don't think she's all pissed because she thinks we forgot her birthday, are you?"

Not intimidated in the least with how dangerous Chris looked, Leena walked over to him with her hands on her hips. "If you're not going to explain, then you damn well better find a way to remove that wall and go find Kasey and make sure she's all right." She glared at him.

Chris watched Owen suddenly stand to his full height, seeming ready to protect his woman if Chris didn't tread carefully. He looked down at Leena and then dropped his head down trying to breathe his anger away. His mind searched for Kasey. "She's sitting outside on the steps." He looked around the room at the worried, lost looks on everyone's face, and the mess of broken dishes and food all over, and sighed.

He put his hands in his pockets and stood there. He'd

forgotten her birthday. What a present he'd given her. He had belittled and hurt her. "I am an asshole. Kasey hurt my pride last night, and I took it out on her this morning." Sighing, he walked towards the door she'd gone through. "I apologize." He flicked his hand at the unseen wall and walked out.

Chris stepped out the door and studied Kasey from behind. She was shaking and no doubt crying with her face hidden against her knees. All he wanted to do was sit down and pull her into his arms and hold her. A part of him knew that wasn't the solution. The other part of him was almost afraid she'd throw him on the roof if he tried. She had scared him with the force she'd shown inside. Yet a small part of him fell deeper in love with her for putting him in his place in such a manner.

Kasey turned her head and glanced behind her. "Please leave me alone, Chris," she whispered with a wavering voice.

He put his hands in his pockets and leaned against the wall. "That's part of the problem, Kasey. I can't." His voice shook with emotions he couldn't control.

She clasped her hands around her knees and looked out across his large lawn. "I'm sorry about the dishes. I'll replace them."

Chris bunched his hands in his pockets. "I don't give a fuck about dishes, Kasey," he said quietly.

She turned and gave him a startled look. "Is everyone mad at me for all of that?"

He sat beside her, careful not to get too close. "No, I'd say you scared everyone half to death more than upset them. They're worried." He looked down at the ground. "Leena tore a strip off me for my behavior." She still didn't speak. "And you had every right to put me in my place."

Kasey sighed. "I may have overdone it a tad."

"You think?" He wanted to hug her, but knew it was too soon. "When my temper has finally cooled and my nerves are a bit steadier, you're going to have to explain to me how you managed that slap, as strong as it was, not to mention the wall

Leena ran into."

She threw her hands over her face. "Oh no! Is she all right? She's not hurt, is she?"

He shook his head. "She's fine, a little shocked. Everyone is fine." He looked at her tearstained face. "Kasey, I'm sorry. You hurt me last night with your honesty, and I lashed out. It was childish, and I should know better."

Kasey studied his face for a moment. "I'm sorry too, Chris. The last week has been a bit overwhelming for me, and I'm not coping very well. I mean, I find out the man I've been having fantasies about for several years, that would be *you*, so there is no misunderstanding this time." He smirked at that. "I find out he actually likes me and shows me a few things I... well, I could never have fantasized accurately. Then those women..." She took a deep breath. "Then I'm evicted and being whisked off to a fancy party. I still don't comprehend any of that last night, and I'm not sure I want to." She let out a shaky breath. "To top it all off, I'm having this breakdown on my own birthday! It's all been very overwhelming, and I'm a little lost right now."

Her honesty staggered him. The truth of what she said floored him completely. He hadn't stopped to think what the last week's events would do to her. He just kept rushing full speed ahead, forgetting that sweet little Kasey, his sweet little Kasey, was used to a much slower, much more uneventful life.

Chris let out a breath. "I'm sorry, sweetheart, I didn't even stop to consider how everything one right after the other would affect you. I should have." He looked out across the lawn. "And you'll never know how sorry I am. I was so caught up in things I forgot your birthday." He hesitated in taking her hand, but felt the strain ease when her little hand closed around his.

"I don't know what I'm going to do, Chris. I have three weeks to find a new home." She leaned against his shoulder.

Three weeks, he thought, and she'd spent a week's pay to play dress up for him.

He stood up and pulled her to her feet. "That's what you have friends for. Those people in there worrying about you, and I, are here to help. That's how it works for all of us, sweetheart."

She stopped in the door and looked up at him. "Thank you, for understanding, Chris."

He leaned down and kissed the top of her head. He wanted to crush her in his arms and vow to protect her always, but her words still filled his mind, so he led her back inside to the others.

The present of a jeweler's heat pen that they had all chipped in to buy, was accepted with shrieking and bouncing. She could finally make her own necklaces for people by mounting the stones to the metal clasp herself.

❧ **Chapter 12** ☙

Kasey ran back into her bedroom. Several pairs of eyes watched her come out again. "I don't know." She stood with a stone on a silver chain in one hand and a crystal on a gold chain in the other. "I have two, and now I'm not sure which one to take."

Chris, who had been leaning against the wall, sighed and walked over to her. "Let's see what you've got." She opened her left hand and held it out to him. He studied the stone but didn't touch it. "Where do you find some of these, Kase? That is spinel, isn't it?" She nodded, looking down at the almost white crystal in her hand. "What did you focus on with it?"

"Rejuvenation, kind of overall, inside and out, mentally as well. I did it first, but then I got to thinking that maybe she might need courage more."

He opened the fingers on her right hand and looked down at the bloodstone that she had worn to the night he took her out. He studied it for a moment, remembering how it looked against her skin. "I'd go with your first intuition and go with the spinel. It will help her mind, as well as her body, heal." He took the bloodstone from her hand and placed the chain over her head.

She smiled up at him and took a deep breath. "This is hard. Is anyone else finding this hard?" She looked around the room.

Cora nodded. "I had to run back in the house four times. I thought Dade was going to give up and leave without me."

Dade grinned. "I'd never leave you behind, Coralee."

Owen sat up on the couch. "Maybe we should do one of those healing circle things before we go?"

Leena smacked him and laughed. "Ignore him."

Everyone knew what had happened at the last circle started laughing, except Rachel and Steven, who still didn't know.

Chris turned and looked around. "Are we ready to go now?"

Steven came into the waiting room with Patrick beside him. "Okay, I've finally convinced them to let us all in. We have fifteen minutes. I couldn't get any more than that." He looked at Patrick. "As I've just been explaining to Officer Blaine, Rhonda doesn't have use of her voice completely yet. Between the trauma and being intubated for so long. Don't expect her to speak. And, the men are going to have to stay back as much as possible. She is very nervous around men." He looked at Owen. "We'll see what happens and see if she'll let you help."

Chris took Kasey's hand as they went into the room. He'd never seen her quite this nervous. She looked up at him in silent thanks.

When they stepped into the room, everyone stood just inside the door as Patrick walked over beside the woman in the bed.

She looked very frail and listless. Her eyes were wide with fear. Across her face there were two long scars running from her forehead down to her jaw and one lower from her jaw to chin. They were very raw and angry-looking marks. She was covered with a blanket to her neck, but her two bare arms rested against it with bandages covering from her wrists to her fingers.

Patrick leaned over her and spoke softly. "Miss Caruthers, these are the people that found you. The ones I explained to you about."

Her eyes flicked up to his face and then back to everyone standing near the end of her bed. With nervous eyes, she searched over them, stopping on Cora. She swallowed, squinting as she did, before lifting one bandaged hand off the bed a few inches towards Cora.

Stepping away from Dade's arm that she'd been hanging on to, Cora walked over to the side of the bed. Patrick backed up and let her get close. Cora smiled down at her. "You did call to me." Rhonda nodded slowly at Cora. Cora smiled. "I'm Coralee. May I call you Rhonda?" She nodded slowly again. Her eyes continuously searched Cora's as she spoke softly to her. "Rhonda, we'd like to help you again, speed up your recovery a little if you'll let us." Her eyes flicked back to the group and over them again.

Cora smiled and hesitantly placed a hand on Rhonda's arm. "I'll explain as we go, and you just give me a look if you're uncomfortable with any of it." Another nod. "Okay, first I'd like you to meet the couple that found you. I'm afraid I was all but debilitated feeling your pain, and couldn't get there fast enough."

Cora motioned to Chris and Kasey. He slowly stepped to the side of the bed with Kasey clinging to his arm. "This is Chris and Kasey." Her brown eyes teared as she looked at them. Hesitantly she looked down at Chris's hands. Cora nodded. "Yes, he used a little energy to bring you back to us. Kasey is very gifted with charging stones."

Rhonda's eyes flicked to the stone in the window. "Yes, she did that one too. She's brought you something today as well. Can you wear the chain, or would it hurt you?"

Rhonda looked to Kasey and nodded, attempting to lift her head.

Kasey rushed over and supported her head gently. "It's

to rejuvenate, your body as well as your mind." There was a tear rolling down her scarred cheek as Kasey placed the chain gently around her neck. Leaning down closer, she dropped a kiss on the woman's cheek. "Get well," she whispered, then stepped back beside Chris. He squeezed her hand as she placed it in his.

Cora then turned to Rachel. "This is Rachel. She wants to help you feel some peace if you'll let her." Rhonda looked at Rachel as she stepped up beside the bed.

Rachel leaned over and spoke softly. "I'm going to need Dr. O'Reily to help me. Do you mind?" She slowly turned her head, indicating she didn't.

Steven stepped up beside Rachel and smiled down at Rhonda. "Just close your eyes and relax a moment. I'm going to put my hand lightly on your forehead. If you're uncomfortable with this, just open your eyes and we'll stop, okay?"

She closed her eyes.

Standing behind Rachel, he held his fingertips over Rhonda's forehead and leaned close to Rachel as she placed her hand over his and they chanted quietly in a whisper that Chris couldn't hear clearly.

When they lifted their hands, Rhonda opened her eyes, and a tear slid down her cheek as she looked at them. Steven placed his arm around Rachel as they stepped back to the end of the bed.

Cora leaned over her again. "This next couple would also like to help you, Rhonda. Leena has a talent with herbs, and she brought some dishes of healing herbs she's going to place around the room. She also brought you some tea. We'll leave them here with you."

Chris watched Leena place a few open packets around the room, then looked back at the woman lying so still in the bed.

Cora spoke softly again. "Leena's fiancé, Owen, helped you a great deal when you were found." Her eyes flicked to Cora, then back to Owen again, and looked down at his hands. "Yes, he stopped the bleeding on your back. He'd like to help you today if you'll let him."

She looked nervously back at Cora.

Cora kept her voice steady and soothing. "I was thinking if you'd just let Owen hold your hands for a few minutes each, maybe he can help with those."

Without taking her eyes off Owen, she nodded slowly.

Everyone watched big, gentle Owen walk around to the side where Cora stood. He smiled down at her. "You gave us quite the scare that morning, Rhonda." He picked up her hand as he spoke and lifted it up closer to where the stone hung around his neck. "When you're back on your feet again, you need to come sample Coralee's fine cooking. I think she feeds all of us more than we do ourselves. We'll have a party at Leena's for you. How would that be?"

She nodded slowly.

He set her hand down and walked slowly around to the other side of the bed. As he picked up her other hand and placed it against his chest, he saw her eyes move in Dade's direction. Owen grinned. "That would be Dade. You would have danced to his drum when they lit the fire." She looked at Owen for a second, and then back to Dade, while Owen continued to talk. "Other than drumming, his basic function is looking good." She looked at Owen again, and her lips formed a weak smile. He gently placed her hand back on the sheet.

Dade spoke quietly without moving from where he stood. "When you're well enough, I'd be happy to drum for you again, Rhonda." He smiled at her.

Cora leaned over and whispered, "He's a walking flirt too, Rhonda." Rhonda turned her eyes back to Cora. He thought he saw something in her eyes that was close to humor, a far cry from the frightened look she had when they walked in.

Steven motioned to the clock. "We have to go now, Rhonda. They want you to get your rest."

Everyone moved a little closer to the bed and smiled at

her. Rhonda reached out and touched Cora's hand as she started to move away. Cora turned back and looked down at her.

Rhonda licked her dry lips with a swollen tongue "Th-Thank you a-all," she barely whispered.

No one spoke.

Chris looked at her a moment, studying her eyes. She looked silently at him. "We'll come back and see you soon."

She closed her eyes and drifted to sleep.

Patrick stood outside the room with the group. "You've all done well today." He shook hands and smiled at the women. "I'll keep in touch."

When he went to step away, Cora stopped him. "She sent me an image, Mr. Blaine." He stopped and looked at her with everyone else. "The left shoulder of the man that did that to her has a thick, ugly scar on it." Cora lifted a hand to Dade's big arms and pushed up his sleeve. "It went like this." She ran a finger over Dade's shoulder in the place the scar was on the killer.

Patrick pulled out his notebook and looked at Dade's shoulder, then wrote something down. He nodded. "It's more than we had. Thank you, Coralee."

Patrick watched her pull Dade's sleeve down, and she held the man's hand. "I'll be in touch. You look after each other, all of you," he said roughly, then walked down the hall.

Kasey looked around at everyone for a moment, knowing they all felt the peace they brought being able the do some good. "Let's have mead at my house when we get back." She walked down the hallway, leaving everyone to follow her.

Chris was the last person through the door. He shut it, then turned with envelopes in his hand. "Your mailbox was full."

Kasey nodded. "I know. I didn't want any more nasty letters, so I've been ignoring the mail." He smirked as he handed them to her. "I've got a letter from a publisher?"

Chris looked at Owen, who stood beside Kasey with his arms around Leena. He glanced at the envelope Kasey held. "Oh shit." he whispered, and pulled Leena over and into his lap as he sat. He motioned with his head for Dade to sit. Chris wasn't sure what was going on.

Dade gave Owen a weird look, walked over, and sat down.

Kasey was walking to the kitchen, opening the first envelope as she went. She squealed from the kitchen and came flying back into the room, the other letters flying all over the floor.

"Oh my gosh!"

She launched herself into Chris's arms, wrapping her legs around his waist. He stumbled back three steps before he got his balance holding the shrieking woman.

"Oh my gosh! Do you know what this says?" She was hugging his head and waving the paper around in the air. She kissed his face all over, then shrieked again.

Chris had no idea what was going on, and at that point in time, he didn't really care.

Kasey leaned back and looked at him. "My story! Book! They're going to publish my book!" She bounced again and hugged him.

Chris was speechless. He didn't even know she'd written a book, although at the moment the reason that had landed her in his arms didn't seem important.

She squeezed his neck again, kissing him hard on the mouth, and then dropped to the floor. Turning, she pointed to Owen. "Did you know?"

He nodded.

"Oh my gosh! I'm going to faint." She jumped up and down, and tiny little fireworks exploded above her head in bright red and yellow hues. She bounced a few more times. "I'm going to be a published author." She spun and looked at Chris as she waved the paper around. "They're publishing it!" She wrapped her arms around his waist, and as hard as he tried, he couldn't hold on to her.

She let go and whirled again in a circle before going towards her kitchen. Stopping, she spun around and grinned at him. "Come grab glasses. We need to toast!" She was bouncing so much as she poured the mead, he was surprised any of it landed in the glasses. When she turned, everyone was standing smiling. She started towards Dade with the glass in her hand.

He reached over carefully and took it from her.

She spun quickly and grabbed another. "Let's make a toast! Here is to helping Rhonda. To Owen for having the patience to show me how to write a better story. And to my book!" She took a sip, then quickly set the glass down and raised her hands to the ceiling. As she pulled them back down beside her, a trail of tiny fireworks flew over everyone's head.

If Chris didn't already love her as deeply as he did, he would have fallen in love with her all over again. Her temper, when triggered, was volcanic and fierce, but as he just witnessed, so was her happiness. He'd sort out his not knowing she wanted to be a writer later. He'd seen her for years scribbling in notebooks but never stopped to wonder what she wrote.

He wanted to pick her up and carry her to her room and hold her away from prying eyes. Then he remembered all that had happened to her in the past few weeks and knew she was already teetering the very fine line of emotional overload. Sighing, he leaned back against the counter watching her hug everyone in the room before they had a chance to sit down again. As she bounced around, her short shirt pulled up, and he saw the fairy still nestled against her skin. Knowing she still wore it gave him some hope, and a good case of lust as well.

Kasey turned in the middle of the room, then looked over at him and smiled. He had no choice but to smile back. "I'd like to try brunch again at my place tomorrow." He held up a hand before anyone spoke. "I promise to behave this time."

Kasey looked down and clasped her hands in front of her. "Me too," she said solemnly.

When they decided to call it a night, Chris spoke softly from behind her. "I'd like to speak with you for a moment, Kasey."

Dade turned as he was going out the door, and looked at Chris. "Don't piss her off this time. I don't think we could handle another brunch like last week."

Chris held up his hands. "I won't." But he grinned as Dade shook his head and followed the others out.

Kasey turned back to him when she closed the door. "This has been quite the day." She flopped down in the chair and grinned up at him.

He smiled at her, perching on the table. "I'm happy your book is being published, even if I didn't know you were writing one."

She shrugged. "No one really did. Leena told Owen, and he humored her by asking to see some of it." She smiled. "He really helped me zero in on the weak parts and fix them. I had no idea he sent some of it to his editor until after he did. Then they wanted more. It's kind of crazy the way it happened." She stopped and looked at him. "What?"

Chris shook his head. "You, little miss fireworks, are amazing."

She blushed. "Not really. I'm sure you can do much flashier things, Mr. Larkin. But thank you anyways."

He shrugged. "Maybe, but with you its pure emotion, and it's amazing." He cleared his throat. "I didn't want to bring this up in front of everyone, but have you had any luck finding a place?"

She let out an exasperated breath. "No. They're all too expensive." She fidgeted with her hands.

"I have a suggestion, and now that you're going to be a published author, it makes even more sense." He paused and thought for a moment. "Will you stay at the factory?"

Kasey was silent for a moment before nodding. "Yeah.

I'm not going to give up a steady income."

He nodded. "You could stay with me until you find a place, Kasey..." He held up a hand when she raised her eyebrows. "In your own room, your own bed. My house has four bedrooms. I use one and very little of the rest of the house except my library and the kitchen. Stay until you find somewhere suitable. Maybe once the book is published, it won't be as tight financially."

She smirked at him. "I'm sure one book isn't going to make me rich." She pursed her lips together and sat there for a few minutes. When she stood up and paced to the other end of the room, she moved with slow steps. "Won't that be hard?" She stopped and looked at him. "It is a solution. I was afraid the others would take pity on me and make an offer they'd regret. I know Owen has a house, but I didn't want them to rush into any decisions. They spend some nights and weekends there, and Cora was on the verge of offering a few times, of course I'd have to sleep on her couch, but I changed the subject."

Kasey stood in front of him. "Won't that be hard to deal with?" She motioned between them. "With all of these other feelings between us?"

Chris took her hand and studied it for a moment. Then he looked up at her. "I honestly don't know, Kasey. The house is big enough we won't be in each other's way. Most nights I'm in my library with motions or going over cases. I just want you to have the time to find a decent place and to be happy." *To be where I can be close to you,* he thought. "I'm not using this to get you into my bed. I've told you that won't happen until you tell me, and I still mean it." He let out a slow breath. "I have so much, and I've worked hard to get it, but at times it feels empty and meaningless because I have no one to share it with. I'd like to share it with you as long as you need or like."

Kasey stood there looking at him, her eyes searching his. "I accept, and thank you." She grinned. "And if you don't want me to jump on you again, you need to take cover. That is so totally the nicest thing anyone has ever done for me...said to me." She was bouncing again.

Chris grinned and opened his arms. She almost knocked him off the table when she went into his arms. Holding his head against her chest, she squeezed. He held her tight and closed his eyes. Later, he would ask himself if it was going to drive him closer to insanity having her that close to him.

He pulled back. "I brought a set of keys, and tomorrow, before brunch, you can pick which room you'd like. I don't see any reason to wait and move everything all on the last day." Chris paused and looked around. "There's an empty room at the back of the garage you could store your furniture in for now as well." He stood and pulled three keys on a ring from his pocket and held them out to her.

Kasey reached over slowly and took them from his hand. The smile on her face made his heart stutter. He started to say how happy he was to help, but she launched herself into his arms again. This time he caught her against him and held on to the bouncing woman as she kissed his face.

Kasey giggled. "I'm so happy. This has been such a good day. First we helped Rhonda, and then the publisher's letter. Now I don't have to live in my car." She grabbed his face and kissed him hard.

He was only a male, he thought as he supported her bottom with one arm and reached to hold the back of her head so he could kiss her properly. Angling his head, he took her quick kisses and turned it into a long, smoldering one. He almost whimpered. He had missed those lips on his. She'd stopped bouncing and started moving against him in a completely enjoyable manner as he kissed her. His body screamed yes. His mind reminded him that if he continued this, there was a very good chance she wouldn't move in and she'd walk away, again.

Burying his face in her throat, he held her for a moment. She was as breathless as he was, and that didn't help his internal argument.

When he could think clearly again, he lowered her slowly

to the floor he rested his forehead against hers. "This is me behaving and going home." She looked at him with those sexy eyes for a moment. "I don't want to, sweet Kassandra, I really don't want to, but you have a lot on your mind, and me taking you to bed isn't going to help anything right now." He grinned mischievously. "Okay. It would help some things, but not altogether in the end." He kissed her softly again.

"You are the sweetest man, Chris." She sighed against his lips.

He shook his head. "No, I'm not, Kasey. Remember that." He turned and quickly went out the door before he changed his mind.

❧ Chapter 13 ❧

Chris was the last one into his own dining room again. "Sorry for being late again. I can only catch up to one judge on Sunday mornings." He bent down as he walked past Kasey and dropped a kiss on the top of her head.

She smiled up at him. "Good morning, roomie."

Dade choked on his coffee and shook his head. "'Scuse me?"

Everyone turned to Kasey as Chris went and sat down.

Kasey grinned. "Chris is going to rent me one of his rooms until I find someplace suitable."

Chris leaned back in his chair. "I don't recall rent being mentioned in the discussion last night."

Kasey leaned back in her chair and looked at him. "Well, I won't stay here for free."

He watched everyone sit back slowly in their chairs, waiting. "We'll work out the details later, when the dishes are out of harm's way."

She laughed. "Okay."

Dade picked up his cup again. "I've done some renovations for Chris. Which room did you scoop?"

She sighed. "I don't know yet. I haven't been upstairs." She looked down at Chris for a moment.

He grinned and motioned to the door. "Go." She was out of the chair so fast, literally running for the stairs. He shook his head, then turned back to everyone. They were all looking at him, all with smirks on their faces. He held up his hands and grinned. "She'll have her own room and her own bed."

Leena smiled. "You're just a big softy, Chris Larkin."

He scowled at her, then grinned. "There was a time, not long ago, no one would have ever thought that about me."

They heard a shriek of delight from upstairs, and all turned to the doorway before looking back to Chris. He grinned. "I really have to go see what it's about now. I'll be back."

He only had to follow the muttering and laughing to locate her. She was in the main bathroom at the end of the hallway. She was standing in his Jacuzzi tub.

Kasey looked up as he leaned on the door. "Look at the size of this thing! I could use it as a pool." She laughed when he held out a hand to help her out of it. "Sorry. You probably thought I'd seen something scary. I'm kind of a screamer." She blushed. "I don't mean that way, well, maybe I am. I've never had the chance..." He cut her off with a withering glare. She grinned and raised her hand. "Right, that would be one of those discussions you don't want to have."

Chris smiled and walked down the hallway and opened a door. "You can have any room up here but this one. It's mine."

Kasey let go of his hand and stepped a foot inside the door. "Wow, are you Dracula and you've just never told us?"

Chris threw his head back and laughed as she slowly looked around the room. Rubbing the bridge of his nose for a moment, he thought. "No, I'm just a man that likes dark colors."

She looked from him around the room. He had nothing but dark wood furniture in the room. The walls were almost black. The drapes were actually black, and when her eyes landed on the bed, he understood why she'd called him

Dracula. He had a black satin coverlet with deep blood-red pillows. Hmm.

"Wow," she whispered again when she stepped out. She looked at the room across the hall, and he nodded.

She opened the door, almost bouncing, and then she stopped and looked around. "This would be the day version of the night on the other side of the hall."

The room was completely white, the walls, the furniture, the bedding.

"The bed is huge." She ran over and flopped out on it. "Is everything in this house giant-sized?" She fell back spread-eagle on the bed. "I'd have to change directions every night to use up the whole mattress." She looked over at him leaning against the door grinning. Sitting up, she smiled. "Sorry."

He shook his head. "Don't ever apologize for being yourself, Kasey." He motioned down the hall. "Would you like to see the other two before you decide?" She bit her bottom lip, then nodded.

When they went back down to the others, Dade lifted his eyebrows to Chris in question. He grinned as he answered. "She discovered the Jacuzzi."

Dade laughed. "That would be like a swimming pool to little Kasey."

Kasey laughed. "That's what I said! Of course, I was dancing in it when Chris got there."

Chris sat in his chair and looked at the others. "She chose the smallest room up there."

She picked up her coffee she sipped it before commenting. "I don't need all that space in those other rooms." She looked over at Leena. "The air knife would fit in one."

Owen laughed.

Chris set down his fork and looked at Owen. "Do I want to know what an air knife is?"

Owen shrugged. "You should go to the factory and take

a tour. I learned a lot. Not just about recycling, but I also learned that these ladies play with really big, really scary, dangerous toys every day." The four women laughed at the expressions on the other men's faces.

"You're not instilling a great sense of security here, Owen," Steven said, looking at the women.

Kasey smiled over at Dade. "Dade, would you be able to give me a hand with your van to move some of my stuff sometime soon?" She sat there biting her bottom lip.

Dade gave her a big grin, then glanced down the table at Chris. "Oh man, you are so sunk if she turns that look on you in the middle of a... discussion."

Chris laughed and looked at Kasey. "I know all about it." He winked at her.

Leena sat up. "We can help if you need it. Except next Sunday, we're going to the airport so Owen can meet my parents" Owen took her hand. "They're going to be stopping over for a day before catching another flight to some cruise to somewhere else." She grinned at Owen, who sat there looking nervous. Squeezing his hand, she laughed. "He's worried they won't like him."

Dade winked at Owen, then glanced at Cora. "Coralee, are you all right?"

Cora looked at him for a moment. "I don't know. I've had this feeling off and on all day, and it's stronger now."

The room was suddenly silent. Chris sat forward.

Dade was beside her in an instant. "Can you tell what?"

She sat back and closed her eyes, her hand reaching for the pendant Kasey had given her. She held it in her hand tightly. "I'm not sure."

Owen got up and stood behind her and put his hands on her shoulders.

Everyone just sat there watching and waiting.

Cora opened her eyes. "Chris, call Patrick, and tell him to go to the hospital. It has something to do with Rhonda, but I can't tell what."

Chris was out of the chair heading to the phone. "Keep

trying, Cora." He looked at Kasey. "You join with her and focus. See if you can draw it to her."

Dade stood and walked Cora into the larger sitting room and then sat her down on the floor.

Chris dialed after pausing to recall the number.

Owen followed close behind and kneeled behind Cora, placing his hands on her shoulders.

Kasey took her place beside Cora and placed a hand on her knee.

Rachel sat down on the other side of her.

Leena sat down in front of the three and placed a hand on Rachel and Kasey. Glancing at them, she nodded, and they began the chant they had used weeks before. "Earth and air, set our sight free. Fire and moon, let us see." As they said it the third time, the women physically relaxed into a focused state.

Dade and Steven stood by them, watching all of them carefully.

Chris held his hand over the mouthpiece of the phone. He looked to Dade, who moved towards the women.

Kneeling down, Dade spoke softly. "Coralee, talk to us."

Cora moved her head down towards the floor and opened her eyes. "It's very malicious. I can't see where it's coming from. I can sense them thinking of Rhonda, how she wasn't supposed to live." She took a shuddering breath and continued to focus on the floor.

Chris, still holding the phone, walked over behind Dade and quietly told him that Patrick was at the hospital.

Dade nodded and spoke again in the same gentling tone. "Patrick is at the hospital with Rhonda now. She's fine. She still has guards."

Cora's head flew up, and she looked at him. "Tell him to move her now! Tell him he has to get her out of there! He's angry no one will tell him what's happening with her. He's angry she survived when she had to die to cleanse the sins, so angry..." She cried out and grabbed her head.

Owen's head jerked up, and he wrapped his arms tightly

around her.

"So much pain, make it stop." Cora leaned back against Owen and dropped her head to the side, breathing deeply.

Chris had stood holding the phone out towards Cora. He put it back to his ear. "Did you get all that?" He nodded. "As soon as we do, we'll call. You stay right there beside Rhonda." He pushed a button on the phone and tossed it onto the couch, then knelt beside a shaking Kasey.

Steven was already helping Rachel to the couch. He glanced at Chris. "How did you know together they could do that?"

Dade was setting Cora on the other end of the couch. He then looked up, waiting for Chris to give him his answer.

Chris carried Kasey over and set her in one of the big chairs. He helped Owen to his feet before he reached for Leena. He waited until they were all on the furniture comfortably. He shrugged. "I didn't for sure. It was just a hunch." He reached down and lifted Kasey's chin and smiled at her as he spoke. "This one is a powerful little witch, and I have a feeling she could do just about anything if she wants to." He stood up and grinned. "Put the four energies together, and look out." He motioned to Dade. "Go put the kettle on. I have some herbs in my temple room that should help everyone rejuvenate a bit."

Sitting sipping her tea, Kasey smiled over at Chris. "Temple room?"

He pushed away from the wall and grinned at her. "Yes, temple room. Which you're free to use, as long as you stay out of a few things in it."

She raised her eyebrows. "Oh, sounds intriguing."

Chris grinned again. "Perhaps I'll just remove some items. It might be safer to my home and health that way."

"Afraid I'll blow up the lab? I've only ever done that once, you know."

He squatted down in front of her giving her a puzzled look. "Done what, exactly?"

Kasey shrugged. "I was kind of experimenting, and I set the floor on fire and... well, the oils were there, and things just...happened." She bit her lip and remembered how awful it had smelled.

Chris rubbed the bridge of his nose. "Might double my insurance too while I'm at it." He rubbed his jaw slowly. "We'll work on a quick counter spell lesson sometime soon, before I let you lose in there."

Cora set her cup down. "Has Patrick called at all?"

Chris shook his head. "He wanted you to have a bit of a rest before we try to sort out what you saw and felt, then give him a call and let him know." He looked at Steven. "What are the chances of them being able to move her?"

Steven sat up from where he'd been resting against Rachel's leg. "That's a tough call. She needs round-the-clock supervision and care, catheters, medication. As far as I know, she's still on some pretty serious meds too. I don't know. Unless there's somewhere fully equipped and a really big secret, it's pretty risky to take the chance."

Chris paced to the other side of the room and stuck his hands in his pockets. Kasey sent a gentle brush against the back of his neck, and he looked back at her. She smiled at him sweetly. He grinned back before looking at the others in the room. "There is a place we've used for serious witnesses. Let me make a few calls while you try to figure out what Cora felt." He brushed a hand over Kasey's head in a gentle caress as he walked past her to the phone again.

Cora sat up and took a breath. "The pain at the end, I think it was his pain, a migraine kind of pain but very sudden."

Rachel looked at Steven. "Could that be what you were talking about with tumors and delusions?"

Steven nodded. "Definitely sounds like it. Many psychological diseases have very real physical symptoms." He looked at Cora for a moment. "He was really angry when this pain hit suddenly?"

Cora thought her with her lips pressed tightly together for a moment. "Yes, like that. He was fine, wait, he was angry because no one would tell him how she was doing. I think he's been trying to find out." She looked at Dade. "They have to move her. Has anyone been calling asking about her, asking Justin or Gwen about her?"

Kasey got up. "I'll go get Chris."

She headed down the hall listening to see if she could hear him and not have to go peeking into rooms. She followed his voice into the room that was obviously his library and stood inside the doorway waiting for him to notice her there. She may be moving into the house, but it was still his home, and she didn't want to intrude.

Chris continued talking and was leaning against his desk with his back to her. She sent a gentle brush to the back of his neck, and he turned, smiling at her. She glanced around to see every wall lined with books. A lot of books, she thought. His desk was huge and covered in folders and more books. *Bit of a workaholic*, she mused.

Hanging up the phone, Chris walked around the desk and motioned around the room. "All those are a necessary part of my profession." Stopping in front of her, he grasped her waist and pulled her slowly to him. "Did the tea help?"

She nodded. "Yes. Cora's thought of something, and we need you to call Patrick and run it by him."

He studied her. "In one minute." He lowered his mouth slowly to hers and then kissed her tenderly, lingering for a few heartbeats before he straightened up. "That's better." Tucking her under his arm, he turned them to go back out to the others.

Everyone sat in silence as he spoke to Patrick. Patrick, having heard what Cora said, had come to the same conclusion as they had. "Let us know." Chris hung up and sat down looking around at everyone. "Justin has had a lot of calls with people inquiring after seeing the ambulance. So that's not much help there. The hospital has had someone call a few times. They never ask about her by name, so they have never given out any information regarding her." He glanced at his watch. "I won't know about the other arrangements for moving her for a few hours. It being a Sunday, people had to be tracked down. But if I can get her there, she'll still need medical professionals, so Patrick is working on that from the hospital." He kept his head down and didn't look at Kasey as he added the last part. "I've offered financial compensation for any trained medical personnel willing to stay with her around the clock. But it's up to her doctors to set the ball rolling."

Leena smiled at him. "That's a wonderful thing to do, Chris."

Cora stood up and walked over and kissed him. "A nice thing you're doing." Rachel did the same.

Kasey got up and went and climbed right in his lap with everyone there and hugged him. "I keep telling you that you're the sweetest man."

Chris rested his hand on her leg and hugged her with his other arm. "If that gets out at work, I'll be ruined." He chuckled as he looked around. "So, do we wait, or do you want to know when I do?" He was in no hurry for Kasey to move, so he continued to hold her with her head resting against his shoulder.

Cora was digging in her purse. "If someone will run to the store and pick up a few things, I'll make us something to eat. I'm starving after using all that energy up." She pulled out a notepad and started writing.

Rachel stood up. "The Doc and I will go get it." She stuck her tongue out at Dade. "That leaves you here to help clean up the mess in the dining room for a change."

Steven stepped in front of her and grabbed her chin lightly. "Stick that tongue out again." Her eyes widened at him as she did it. "Well, well, well. Hmm." Steven turned and walked towards the door. "I'll be in the car."

Rachel watched him walk out. "What was that?"

Dade looked at her. "Stick out your tongue." She did.

"Oh, right." He walked towards the dining room grinning. "I'll start in here."

Kasey started giggling. And Cora just laughed when she looked at Leena, who was also smirking.

Chris looked at Owen, who shrugged. He looked down at Kasey. "Someone like to fill us in?"

Cora looked over at the giggling Kasey in his arms. "Steven and Dade just discovered Rachel has her tongue pierced."

Rachel shrugged. "I went with Kasey a few years back when she had her belly done." She grinned. "Hurt like hell, but I've never had a man complain about it, so it was well worth the pain." She winked at Kasey, who blushed.

Chris covered his eyes while he laughed. "Poor Doc." He looked at the dining room. "And I think you shocked Dade, which is hard to do, actually." He looked at Cora and Leena. "You ladies have any piercings you want to share?"

Owen looked over at him and shook his head. "None on Leena that I've found, and I'm pretty sure I've checked everywhere." He earned a smack.

Cora grinned. "I'll never tell."

Dade, who had just walked back in, groaned and walked right back out. Everyone burst out laughing.

Several hours later, Chris stood in his temple room putting several items in a locked cupboard. He didn't tell her, yet, that he hadn't always been on the white side of magic, and he certainly didn't want her to find out accidentally on her own.

It was nice having her here all day, even if it had been to wait on news. Rhonda was being moved to a very secure location. Unfortunately, that meant they may not be able to see her. The hospital offered pay to the three-person staff that would be caring for her, but he'd make sure they got some kind of bonus despite it. Sighing, he glanced around one last time. Everything was away, safely out of Kasey's reach, for now.

Walking over he stopped and picked up the fairy figurine. He studied it. It was said you couldn't catch a fairy and keep it. If you did, it lost its magic. Setting it back down, he hoped that wasn't the case with his little Kasey. Once she was here, he would move mountains to keep her.

Opening his eyes, he looked around slowly. The pain was gone.
He had failed, so he'd been punished with more pain.
He needed to find her.
He needed to finish it.
If he didn't, he'd have to take more next time to make up for it.
He had to cleanse them.
Lying down, he closed his eyes.
He could rest a little longer

◈ **Chapter 14** ◈

Chris pulled into his driveway and smiled when he saw the beat-up little Jimmy truck. *Just what I need after these long last few days*, he thought, *my Kasey*. He didn't like admitting, even to himself, how much he missed her when a few days went by without seeing or talking to her. He grabbed his briefcase and jacket as he glanced briefly at the doors all open on her car. *Probably brought her whole house in one trip*. He grinned as he got out of the car.

He was reaching for the doorknob when she opened it and flew right into him. Dropping his briefcase and jacket quickly, he caught her to him before they both fell off the steps, and grinned down at her.

"Whoa! Sorry!" She grinned up at him, "Didn't see you."

He chuckled. "It's very hard to see anything when you're traveling faster than the speed of light, Kase."

She ran her hands down his arms for a moment. "Didn't hurt you, did I?"

He shook his head.

She glanced down and saw his jacket on the steps. "Oh!" She went under his arm and picked it up quickly. "I hope I didn't get it dirty." She was holding it up and turning it to check.

He had to shake his head to clear the image of her wearing nothing but his large suit jacket. An image like that wouldn't help him keep his hands to himself. "The move has begun?"

Kasey looked up and grinned. "Yes. I packed stuff on Sunday night and all last night. The scary closet holds more than I'd even thought." She pursed her lips and thought for a moment. "I dunno if I'm going to be able to fit it all in the room I picked."

Chris took her elbow and guided her back into the house. "You can use more space than just one room if you need to." He set his briefcase beside the door and closed it. "Or you could just take one of the larger rooms if you want."

She bit her bottom lip. "You wouldn't mind?"

He studied her silently. "No. Other than my bedroom and my library, do whatever you like in the rest of the house. Maybe you can help it to feel more like a home instead of a museum."

Her eyes widened. "Really? You wouldn't mind if I set some of my stuff here and there?" She motioned to the foyer they were standing in. "'Cuz honestly, Chris, this area is about as welcoming as a funeral home."

He laughed and wondered if he'd grow to regret saying that at some point.

Pulling her slowly by the waist towards him, he smiled down at her. He reached to caress her cheek softly before lowering his mouth to hers. When her arms wound around his neck and pulled him down closer, he reached around behind her and straightened, picking her up to his height.

With his lips searching over hers, she angled her head and parted them for him. His tongue met hers, and he felt warmth rush through his entire body. "Mmm. Much better," he whispered against her mouth, still holding her off the floor against him. "A perfect way to end a long, long day."

Kasey grinned against his mouth before kissing him again quickly. "I'll just finish bringing my stuff in while you go relax." She looked down at the floor her feet weren't touching. "But you kind of need to put me down before I can do that."

Chris looked at her for a moment, then shook his head. "No, I don't think so." He swung her up into both arms and carried her into the living room. Sitting down in one of the large chairs, he grinned at her. "First I get to sit here and hold you for a few minutes, because if I set you down, you'll start running again, and I just get tired watching you." She giggled but sat in his lap. "When do you think you'll be all moved in? Because I have to confess, walking in the door, well, trying to walk in my door, and having someone here is a feeling I really enjoyed."

"Well... Dade mentioned being able to get a trailer from work." She chewed on her bottom lip. "I was thinking maybe if the others help we could do it on Friday night."

He looked at her huge green eyes looking back at him, and her lip she'd bit gently with her teeth, and his heart melted. He grinned at her as he leaned down and he licked her bottom lip. "I'm sure we could manage that." She would be here every day after Friday.

She bounced in his lap slightly and smiled.

"Yay!" She kissed him quickly and hopped up and started for the door again. Skidding to a stop she turned around and ran back and kissed him again. "That's for getting Rhonda moved safely, I know it wouldn't have happened without you." She turned again and flew to the door.

He sat there looking at the door. How slow and quiet had his life been before she'd come into it? And how, he thought with a long sigh, was he going to slow her down long enough to catch her? What was he going to do once he did finally catch her? Oh, he had ideas about that. Grinning, he pulled himself up out of the chair and rolled up his cuffs as he went towards the door before she could fly through it again.

Kasey ran past Dade with a box in her hands as he walked back from the van. He stepped aside and watched her put the box in the van and then put her hands on her hips and look at it for a moment. Before he'd taken a step, she walked, no, jogged, past him with a grin.

Chris walked out the door with chairs in his hands and stepped quickly out of her way. Shaking his head, he walked by Dade and put the chairs beside the trailer.

Dade strolled over and leaned against the trailer. "She must be able to get up to full speed in your house."

Chris laughed. "You have no idea. I'm thinking of putting bells on her so I have time to get out of the way."

Dade laughed and glanced towards the door waiting for her to come out again. "Does she move that fast in all things?" He watched Chris's eyes move over his face for a minute, and then he sighed.

"That I don't know."

Dade's eyebrows shot up in surprise.

Chris sighed again. "It's complicated and not something I wish to explore just yet." He glanced towards the door as she came flying through it. "I'm just having a hell of a time trying to catch her at this point."

Dade laughed.

Kasey set down the box, then turned to look at them. She grinned and jumped up to hug Chris. "I'm so happy!" He lifted her into his arms and started walking towards the house.

Steven and Owen went by them carrying a dresser. Steven winked at her. "How come he gets to carry the good stuff and we get the furniture?"

She giggled. "Well, if he hurts his back carrying that stuff, who is going to carry me?"

Dade lifted his eyebrows at her. "I'll carry you, honey." Chris grinned and dumped a squealing Kasey into his arms before he walked back into the house.

Midnight came and went before they were finally finished. Kasey was sprawled out on the carpet in his, no, their, living room. She turned her head to look around at everyone else for a moment. "It would have been much faster and easier if we'd let Leena carry things on air."

Owen groaned and leaned against Leena beside him. "And you didn't mention this earlier?"

Kasey giggled. "Well, physical work is good for you."

Owen smiled. "So is sex, but now I'm too tired after the physical work part."

Leena smacked him.

Rachel lifted her head from Steven's lap and looked at Chris. "Any word on if we can go see Rhonda on Sunday?"

Chris shook his head. "Patrick wants us to wait a week. Then it's going to be a complicated affair of taking different cars and different routes. I had a hard enough time talking him into it at all." He looked down at Cora sprawled out beside Kasey. "He also wants to know if you so much as get a twinge that's not right."

Cora smiled. "I'm having twinges now that aren't normal. Couldn't you have had an elevator put in this place, Chris? My legs are very unhappy."

Kasey giggled. "I've decided when I find a place to move to we're opening the window and throwing it all out on the lawn."

Dade moaned. "I hope you live here forever then."

Chris's heart jerked when she had mentioned leaving. He sat there looking down at the woman on his floor. *Yes, Kassandra, live with me forever, he thought.* "There are two large beds upstairs if anyone is too tired to go home."

"No stairs," Cora whined.

Steven lifted his head off the back of the couch and looked at him. "I am staying right here until morning, I think."

Owen opened his eyes. "We could try a healing circle." He met Dade's huge grin.

Chris shook his head at the two of them. "That is for emotional healing and mental relaxation, not physical exhaustion."

Owen dropped his head back. "You are just no fun at

all."

There were a few quiet snickers.

Cora got to her hands and knees. "Dade, take me home."

Dade stood up. "Be happy to."

"My home, before you go to your home." She laughed at his expression as he pulled her to stand. "Poor man." Patting his cheek, she bent down and scooped up her purse. "Are we doing brunch this week if we can't go see Rhonda then?"

Several nods.

She looked at Kasey. "Shall we have it at your place this week?"

Kasey nodded, then grinned. "Oh! This is my place. Yes, let's do that." She sat up quickly and moved towards Dade.

He held out his hand to ward her off. "Stay!" Then he looked at Chris. "You better start taking some large vitamins, old man, and soon if you want to keep up."

Chris threw his head back and laughed, but in his mind, he was agreeing with him completely.

Kasey pouted. "You guys are not funny." She smirked. "But I understand if you *old* people are all wore out."

Chris's mouth dropped open, and Dade snorted as he quickly headed for the door.

"Better clear out before the battle, people," he shouted on his way out

Chris turned to her after everyone had gone. "Old people?" He leaned back against the door and crossed his arms in front of his chest, trying to look offended.

Kasey bit her bottom lip and turned innocent eyes up to look at him. "I didn't mean it." Her voice was soft and quiet.

He dropped his head down then. When he looked up at her, he was grinning.

"Oh! You!" she gasped.

He tried to reach out for her and hit a wall that wasn't visible. "Kasey, don't start that again." He flicked a hand and stepped through where it had been.

Kasey was backing up across the floor grinning at him. A brush of air pushed against him. He smiled and pushed it away. "Come here, little one. Don't make this old person chase you."

She shook her head and took off down the hallway. She had no idea what was in this direction other than his office, but she ran anyway. When she went to go through the office door, it shut a few inches from her face. She spun around and leaned back against it to see Chris stalking towards her quietly.

"Gotcha." he whispered.

She held her hands up in surrender. "I give. I was just playing."

Chris stepped up and took her hands in his and placed them against the door, trapping her there. "I'm more than happy to play any game you'd like, sweetheart." He looked down at her for a moment. She was panting from running, and her eyes were wide with excitement. "I guess I won this round," he whispered with his mouth almost touching hers.

She nodded silently, not taking her eyes from his. They had gone darker.

"Does the winner get a prize?" he asked, his voice low and soft. She nodded and squeezed his hands that held her arms away from her body against the door.

He searched her eyes, waiting to see if she understood the position she was in. Her lips parted, and her breathing was already shallow. She knew the game, and as far as he could see, she wanted it almost as much as him. He brushed his lips over hers, lingering for a moment, giving her time to stop him. Her lips parted under his and invited him inside. He almost trembled. Taking her mouth with a force that left him burning, he plunged his tongue inside and pressed her back against the door. Her hands clasped his tightly where he held them. Lifting his head, he slowly moved his mouth to her neck wanting to taste all over.

She moaned quietly and leaned into his body. He could

feel the heat of her skin through his clothes. She wiggled her hands again, but he didn't release them.

Chris needed to touch her with more than his lips. Kissing her mouth again in a slower, more sensuous movement, he slid her hands above her head and grasped both her wrists in his one large hand so he could use his other hand to reach around her and pull her tight against where he needed to feel her touching. She gasped when he lifted his head, and he looked down into her glazed eyes. They searched his with an innocence he'd almost forgotten about. He opened his hand and let her wrists go but continued to lean on the door holding her tight against him. "We need to stop."

Kasey looked up at him. Her breathing was as unsteady as his own. She dropped her hand down to rest against his chest "I don't want to, completely."

Chris nuzzled his face into her neck. "I don't want to either, sweet Kassandra, but until you can say that without the 'completely' part, we're going to."

She ran her hands up into his hair and held him tightly. "You make me feel so good, Chris."

He lifted her a few inches and pulled her tight into his hard groin. "It's quite mutual."

She moaned. "I want to be with you so much, Chris, so why does it scare me at the same time?"

Chris took a few breaths before trying to speak. Hearing her say she wanted him did nothing to change his reasoning for letting her go. "I'm trying not to scare you, Kasey. I just came close to doing exactly that."

She put her mouth against his to silence him. "That didn't scare me. I've wanted you to kiss me like that since we were at the cabin."

He groaned against the top of her head. "Don't mention that, not if you want me to let you go. I've done nothing but remember the taste of you, the feel of you against me, your hands on me..." He kissed her frantically, showing her how he remembered. Her mouth moved against his in the same fevered heat.

Growling quietly, he lifted his head. "Either I let you go or I carry you upstairs. Tell me what to do because your eyes are telling me one thing, but your body is saying not to stop." He kissed her with trembling gentleness. "Which one, Kasey?" He almost held his breath waiting for her to answer him. It felt like an hour before she spoke softly.

"I'm going to go take a bath and go to bed, I think."

He closed his eyes above her head and nodded.

"Don't be mad at me please."

He looked down at her and ran a shaking hand gently over her cheek. "I'm not." He kissed her lightly on the lips. "Get some rest, sweetheart. I'm going to get some work done."

She nodded. "I'll see you in the morning."

He smiled and released her.

Chris watched her leave and then opened the door and went into his library. He sat down and picked up a folder. Looking down at it, he tossed it back on the desk. She hadn't even been here a day and he'd almost attacked her. How was he going to do this every day? He leaned back in his chair and let out a long, slow breath. If he used anything other than normal means to persuade her, he might as well open the door and tell her to get out. He cursed and closed his eyes. If she didn't hurry up and catch up with him, want him the way he wanted her, he was going to go insane.

He got up and paced to look out the window. How long would it take her in the bath? There was no way he could go up the stairs and think of her behind the door lying naked in the tub. Groaning, he shook his head to clear that image.

Even while he was still trying to forget it, he found himself heading for the stairs. He'd lock himself in his own room if he had to. He reached his room and went in quickly. The bathroom door was still closed. He stripped off his shirt and tried to ease some of the tension from his body.

He sat down and wished for a drink. Why hadn't he

thought of that while he was still downstairs? *Idiot.* Sighing, he opened the door and had taken one step when he saw Kasey walking away from him in, well, he wasn't quite sure what you'd call it. She wore a white piece of fluff as a top, and a short piece of fluff that barely covered that cute little ass.

Kasey reached her room and turned her head as she opened her door. "Oh, I didn't see you." She smiled sweetly at him.

Chris stood there looking at her bare shoulders where the thin straps rested, and then he moved his eyes down to her skin where the fairy hung, calling to him. Her legs were completely bare. "That's...fine. I was enjoying just...watching." Talk, he told himself.

Kasey looked down at herself. "I guess I should have taken a robe to the tub with me." She bit her bottom lip.

"No. That's fine." He watched her fingers fidget with the fairy. When she started to walk back towards him, his mind screamed at him to tell her to go to bed, but he just stood there looking at her.

"You're teasing me," she whispered when she stopped in front of him.

"What?" *He was teasing her?*

"You. Standing there without your shirt, looking very touchable." She reached up and ran her hand lightly over his chest.

His breath caught in his chest at the feel of her warm hand against his skin. "That makes us even then." He reached out and touched the fairy at her waist. "You know what seeing this does to me." He could barely focus to speak.

Her hand continued to move slowly over his chest. "It wasn't a very restful bath, Chris." She looked up at him with heavy eyes. "I'm beginning to regret being a virgin at my age."

"Don't."

"I don't like constantly feeling like this, when we stop."

He smirked. "No one really does, Kase."

She looked at his chest where her hand rested and then

looked up at him and blushed again. "I just wish, I don't know how to say this." She moved slowly and wrapped her arms around him, resting her cheek against his bare chest.

He knew he shouldn't touch her, but he did, regardless. He stood there and held her.

"I've missed not being able to sleep with you. I enjoyed those few times at gathering falling asleep with your arms around me, Chris."

Chris tightened his arms around her. "I enjoyed it too. But there were six other people outside the door. And here, now, I don't trust myself." He moved back and lifted her chin. "Do you understand?"

She just continued to look up at him with those innocent eyes.

"Kassandra..."

She stretched up and kissed him softly. "I just have dreams since we found Rhonda and..." She looked ashamed.

"Sweetheart, why didn't you tell me?" He hugged her. "I'm just a few doors away now. If they get bad, come wake me."

Kasey nodded, looking relieved. "Thank you." She kissed him softly again, and then walked down the hall to her room.

He watched her every move and sighed when the door closed. Sighing again, he gave up the thought of a drink and went in to try to get some sleep.

Had he slept yet? He opened his eyes and glanced around. He was in his room. Why was he awake? He heard birds, it was morning, or close to it.

When an arm brushed against him, he almost jolted from the bed. Kasey? Why was Kasey beside him? He dropped his head back on the pillow.

When and why exactly was she sleeping in his bed snuggling into him? He lifted his head and looked down at her hair on the blood-red pillowcase. Her skin looked white and delicate next to it. She sighed and moved closer to him, curling into his chest, her small hand resting against his bare waist. He clenched his teeth against the rush in his blood. This was not good.

Moving his hand down, he realized she'd climbed in wearing that white fluff, and he was very much naked. Letting out a slow breath, he rested his hand behind his head and lowered his head back onto the pillow.

He couldn't touch her. Standing fully dressed was hard enough to control. Lying here naked with her nearly naked body against him was a temptation even he couldn't resist. And he wanted to resist, didn't he? Yes. But why was that again?

He decided to just lie there and try to go back to sleep when he heard a sigh beside him again. He looked over to find sleepy eyes looking back at him.

"Bad dream, didn't want to wake you."

He ran his hand down over her hair.

"Do you want me to leave?" Her voice was so sexy when it was sleep-filled.

Oh, there was a question… "No." His voice wasn't very steady. "But if you stay Kasey, I'm not going to be able to not touch you."

She moved so her whole body was against his bare side. "I want you to touch me more, Chris."

He turned, not giving her time to rethink that, and pulled her against him. He ran his hand down the back of her bare thigh, and he pulled her leg to rest over his. Running it back up the soft skin, he ran it under the bottom of the material covering her.

He began kissing her slowly. She moved with his hands and kissed him back in the same slow, relaxed way he was.

Kissing her bare shoulders, he lingered before moving slowly back to her neck. He stroked lightly against the wet flesh from behind her. She sighed against his throat and moved her lips gently against him.

Kasey moved her hand down over his ribs, then back around to stroke over his back. Her touch was hesitant for a moment before she ran her hand down over his butt. He pushed against her gently as she touched him. She had to feel how hard he was through the thin material covering her.

"Show me more, Chris," she gasped into his mouth.

He lifted up on his elbow and brushed his mouth over her shoulder and across her throat. His arm was shaking, but he was determined to go slowly and give her time to adjust to his every movement. Pushing the fabric of her top away with his cheek, he ran his lips over her ribs and up to the underside of one breast. When he ran his tongue gently under it, she gasped and arched towards him.

With soft, teasing strokes, he moved his tongue up to her nipple and licked it gently a few times. She shuddered against him. He moved his hand between her legs, and he rubbed gently over her wetness while pulling her tightly into the throbbing length of him. She groaned and pulled his hair to bring his mouth back to her breast. Sucking gently on one nipple, he felt her rock into him.

He lifted his head and looked down at her as he continued to stroke her. Her mouth was open as she gasped softly between biting her bottom lip. Her eyes were closed, and her head moved restlessly to each stroke against her.

He lowered his mouth beside her ear. "You're so sweet. I won't rush you." He licked around her ear. "Let me show you more, Kassandra." He moved his mouth over her throat. "If you don't want me inside you, let me show you another way." He rested his face against her chest trying to clamp down on his desire. "Don't ask me to stop."

Kasey pulled his head up to hers and kissed him with desperate need. "More." She groaned as his fingers stroked again. "So hot..." Her head rocked back again.

Lifting his head, he gently pushed her onto her back and continued to move his hand along her bare thigh. He shifted down in the bed, moving the sheet aside so he could see her as he ran his tongue along her waist. His arms were shaking with a desire so strong he didn't know how to stop it. He'd waited so long for her.

He moved his tongue around the fairy several times and

felt her rise off the bed to meet his mouth. Leaning down, he ran his tongue over the inside of her thigh and watched her gasp and reach for him. "Let me," he whispered against her hot skin. "Let me taste you, sweet Kasey." Her hand dropped to his shoulder and squeezed.

Moving down, he gently opened her legs and pushed aside the material covering her. When his tongue brushed over the swollen, wet flesh, her hips rose up, and she groaned against the back of her hand.

Using his hand, he held her waist down on the bed and flicked his tongue against her again. She panted. The taste of her was driving him mad with need. He pushed his tongue inside her and grasped her hips to keep her from jolting away from him. Taking his time, he tasted and teased with his tongue until her head was thrashing back and forth on the pillow.

His own hips were thrusting as he fought to keep his word. He couldn't remember wanting a woman as much as he did right now.

With his teeth, he gently nipped her clit, and she cried out, reaching for him. He licked it again before he plunged his tongue inside her hard before moving to and then suck once more. When she cried out loudly, he almost came with her.

Slowing his movement, he lapped and savored her taste and continued to rock her with the aftershocks. He kissed his way back up to her stomach and rested his face against her.

He was sweating from the restraint he'd displayed and shaking so hard he couldn't speak. She moved her hands down to run over his shoulders and face, pulling at them gently to bring him back up to her. He kissed his way up trying to stop from wanting to be rough with her, and right now, he just wanted. He was consumed with need for her.

When he was back up beside her, she rolled and began kissing his neck, moving slowly over his chest. She pushed him gently onto his back and ran her tongue over his chest.

She wasn't entirely sure what to do that he'd like, so she set out to find a way to make him feel as good as he'd made her.

When she lightly bit one of his nipples, he groaned and grabbed her head. "Kasey," he gasped, "don't stop."

Kasey felt his muscles bunch under her hands as she moved them over his stomach. Following them with her tongue, she paused at the top of his thighs. "I don't know how to do this, Chris." He didn't speak, just dropped his hands back on the bed and clenched the sheet in his fists.

He was breathing so fast. She began to marvel at what she could do to him. Moving to kneel between his legs, she ran her hands up his thighs slowly. He moaned, his hips lifting. She slowly wrapped her hand around him. He was so hard she could feel him pulsing.

Leaning down, hesitantly she ran her tongue over the tip of the head, and his hips jerked. He growled and gripped the sheets, pulling at them. She had as much effect on him as he did her. Feeling more encouraged, she watched him as she leaned down and ran her tongue along his length.

"Kasey," he hissed out, gasping to catch his breath.

She smiled to herself and lowered her mouth to him again. She squeezed him tightly in her small hand as her lips nipped along the length of him. With each movement of her tongue against him, his hips would jerk.

She blew gently on the head, and his arms jerked, pulling the sheet free from the bed. She licked her lips before she closed her mouth over him, and he groaned so loudly she thought she'd hurt him, but his hips moved again to pushing deeper into her mouth. Sliding her mouth up and down him, she felt his muscles in his thighs convulse.

He groaned and reached for her head. "I'm going..."

He was trying to pull her mouth off him, so she clamped down hard with her lips and sucked as he'd done. He bucked and tensed, and she felt him come in her mouth with such a force she almost stopped.

He was still pulsing in her mouth when she began to whirl her tongue around the tip. He hissed out a breath and grabbed her hair. "Fuck," he said breathlessly.

She pulled her mouth off him slowly and she licked her lips before hesitantly looking down at him. "Did I do that right?

Chris looked at her, and his heart pounded louder. She was the most beautiful sight he'd ever seen. "You should give fucking lessons, sweetheart." She grinned and climbed on top of him cuddling against him.

He closed his arms around her and glanced at the clock. It was barely dawn. He pulled the blanket up and kissed her gently. "I need a nap. You've just wore out this old man." She grinned and cuddled against him.

He sighed. "I'm going to die if we ever actually make love, Kase."

She closed her eyes and fell asleep in his arms.

✺ Chapter 15 ✺

Somehow, Sunday morning had arrived, and it was time for brunch. Chris hadn't had more than a few moments with Kasey since he had awakened with her in his arms a day earlier. He'd been busy most of the day before, working. When he'd finally wandered from the library, Kasey had been absorbed in rewrites the publisher was requesting.

He lost count of how many times he'd wakened during the night, hoping she'd be there beside him again. He glanced at his watch. Was it too late to call everyone and tell them he wasn't doing brunch?

He had just reached the bottom of the stairs when Kasey came flying out of the kitchen at top speed.

"Hi," she said on her way by him. He had just decided to follow her and see what she was doing when she came flying back in. She pulled his head down for a too-quick kiss and before he could touch her was gone again into the direction of the kitchen.

Maybe, he thought, if he just stood here, he could catch her on the next trip. The doorbell rang, and she was out of the kitchen, flying to open it. She barely stopped to say hello and was off again.

Dade wandered in and stood beside Chris. "Safe path

here?"

"Mmm hmm," was his only reply.

Kasey came flying back in and came to a stop in front of them. "Hi."

It amazed Chris she wasn't even out of breath. He grinned. "Do I want to know what you're doing?"

She chewed her bottom lip, then shrugged. "I was moving the table and stuff, but I had to keep checking the biscuits I'm making."

Dade stood there looking between the two of them.

Chris held up a hand. "Moving what around?"

"The table, now there's better light from the windows where it's sitting." She chewed her lip. "You said to fix stuff."

He pulled her under his shoulder. "I didn't mean…"

"The biscuits!" She ran to the kitchen

Dade grinned. "So how goes life?"

Chris continued to look at the kitchen while he answered. "Mind-boggling and more than a little frustrating."

Dade laughed and headed into the dining room.

Giving up for the moment, Chris turned and followed him.

Kasey talked to Owen throughout most of the brunch, asking questions and talking about scenes, dialogue, and ideas.

Dade sat and watched Chris. It didn't matter who spoke to him, his eyes would move over Kasey every few minutes, which more than confirmed that his friend was completely, hopelessly lost in the little witch. From the looks of it, he had no idea how to handle the situation.

"Chris?"

Chris blankly turned to look at Leena.

She smiled.

"Sorry was lost in thought for a moment."

"Have you heard from Patrick since Friday?" she asked quietly.

He nodded. "This morning, actually. Rhonda is able to

speak a little bit now. Other than what she showed Cora, she couldn't tell him anymore." He looked down at Kasey. She grinned, and he smiled back. "Ah, she is looking forward to us sneaking there to see her next week, though."

"Oh." Leena looked at her watch. "Speaking of sneaking, Owen and I have to get going. My folks will be landing in another hour. We're visiting with them for the afternoon and having dinner with them."

Owen sighed and stood up.

Dade grinned at him. "Be brave, bro."

Owen smiled. "Was fine until she told me both her parents have gifts of sorts. A normal father I can deal with, but one that could set me on fire, I'm not quite sure how to handle." Leena pulled his hand and smiled at everyone.

After they left, Kasey grabbed her cup and moved down to sit where Leena had been sitting next to Chris. She grinned at him as she sat back. He knew he was grinning back at her like a fool, but he didn't care. He reached over and held her hand on the table. Rubbing his thumb back and forth over her in a gentle caress, he felt better with the slight contact.

"Do you think we should try and take another look?" Cora asked.

Chris's head turned slowly from Kasey to Cora. "Sorry...a look?"

Steven put his hand over his mouth and laughed quietly.

Dade was rubbing his jaw trying not to smile.

Cora glared at them, then turned back to Chris. "See if we can try another vision to find out what the killer is planning."

"Oh." Chris smirked at his own empty head and then shook his head to clear it. "We could, but I don't think that's wise without Owen here."

Kasey squeezed his fingers. "We could do it the way I did before." Chris looked at her and let his expression answer her. "Or not." She blushed and bit her bottom lip.

Dade was barely able to contain his laughter. "I dunno,

Kase. Chris is having a hard enough time focusing on a conversation right now. Might be little risky to ask him to focus on a spell."

Steven threw his head back and laughed so hard he had to hold his sides. An unseen hand tipped his chair back gently until he was on his back still laughing.

Dade turned to Chris, who shook his head and looked at Kasey. She had that look. Dade threw his hands up. "Okay, okay I'm sorry, we're sorry." Steven lay on the floor trying to catch his breath. "O'Reily, we're, ah, upsetting mighty Kasey. Knock it off."

Kasey turned to glare at him until his eyes widened, and then she burst out laughing. Dade slapped a hand on his chest. "Don't do that." He sat back and huffed out a breath.

Even Rachel, who had been unusually quiet through all of this, laughed. Steven picked himself and his chair up and looked at her. "You okay, Rach?"

She shrugged. "I'm so tired."

Cora grinned at her. "Another long night?"

All three men swung their heads to look at her.

Steven frowned. "I thought we agreed a long time ago none of you women would go wandering around without someone watching out for you."

Rachel glared at him. "Watching out for us?" She picked up her cup, only to realize it was empty, then set it back down. "For your information, I was with one of the foster children from the community program. He's not well, so I sit with him on bad nights so the people looking after him can get some rest."

She stood up and walked towards the kitchen. "I'm going to make more coffee." Kasey and Cora looked at each other and quickly got up to follow her out.

Steven held up his hands when both men turned to look at him. "Don't say it. I will apologize as soon as she's not standing beside that little scary one that you're making puppy eyes at constantly now." He lifted his brows at Chris.

Chris rubbed his hand through his hair. "It's that obvious, huh?"

Dade nodded. "Thought it would get better when you finally got some time with her, but it's way worse."

"Let's go sit outside. I need air," Chris mumbled as he got up.

The men sat on the deck silently for a few minutes. Chris ran his hand through his hair again, then leaned down with his elbows on his knees. "I'm losing my mind."

Dade smirked. "Losing or lost?"

Chris shook his head. "I have no idea." He looked up at him. "She's so fuckin' amazing, the way she is, not that I can hold her still long enough to tell her that." He pursed his lips for a moment. "One minute she's all quiet and shy. The next she's like a fucking lightning bolt slamming through me."

He sat back. "I woke up with her in my bed Saturday morning. She's been having nightmares. She's all soft and sexy cuddled up to me, and then I didn't even get to see her again until this morning." He held his hands over his eyes trying to center his thoughts.

"You really need to talk to her, man, before you lose it completely," Dade mumbled softly.

Chris nodded. "She's right in front of me now, and it gets worse with each day."

"What's worse?" Kasey asked, stepping out carrying a tray of coffee cups.

Chris dropped his hands and looked at Dade.

Steven shrugged. "Trying to figure out where to look for the killer."

She set the tray down and looked down at Chris. "You look so stressed." She climbed onto his lap and kissed him softly. "I'll have to work on something for you." With Dade and Steven distracted by Cora and Rachel coming out, he leaned down and whispered quietly against her ear, "You could work on climbing back into my bed soon."

Kasey blushed and looked up, smiling shyly. "Maybe." He hugged her to him, then reached for one of the cups.

Steven stood up and gripped Rachel's chin lightly. "Sorry. I just worry about all of you with this maniac running around."

Rachel looked at him. "You can make up for it by using those trained hands to massage some of these knots out of my shoulders."

He kissed her cheek and motioned for her to sit down.

Cora sighed. "I think with Owen missing, Rachel's exhaustion, and," she looked at Chris for a moment, "and whatever is wrong with Chris, we should definitely postpone any circles or spells for a few days."

Chris chuckled. "I'll try to get my head together soon. We can try Wednesday if everyone's up to it."

"At my place." Steven said loudly.

Everyone turned and looked at him with surprised expressions. He grinned. "Kasey's stone more than worked. I actually cleaned my place from corner to corner."

"Okay, Wednesday at Steven's," Cora said softly. "I'll let Leena know."

After everyone had gone, Chris sat in his library looking out the window. Letting out a breath, he got up and went to find Kasey. It was time to tell her a few things. How he was going to, he didn't know.

He paused in the kitchen door and wasn't even surprised to see her standing on the counter putting dishes away. Not wanting to startle her, he used her little trick and sent air brushing up the back of her neck.

She turned her head. "Hi. I think we need a stool."

"Or you could just leave them. I would have put them away." He reached up and placed his hands on her waist and lowered her to the floor.

"You make me feel light as a feather the way you pick me up all the time."

"Sweetheart, you are light as a feather." He kissed her gently. "I thought I'd show you the temple room."

"Oh!" Kasey grinned. "It's been very hard not to peek."

He grinned. "I'm sure it has." He tucked her under his arm and walked down the hall. When he opened the door, she walked in.

Her expression was similar, he thought, to a kid in a candy store.

"Wow." She turned around looking at the shelves.

It was dark, like his bedroom, but in a wonderful magical way, he thought. The shelves were higher than she'd ever be able to reach. Lining the top ones were the volumes of books. There was a tall cabinet with herbs and oils in.

She grinned and touched the little fairy, then wolf, grinning at him over her shoulder. He had almost any stone she could ever have a need for, as well as any magical tool you'd ever want.

Standing back with her hands on her hips, she puffed out her cheeks and looked down at the pentacle on the floor. "Well, you're quite the witch, aren't you, Christopher?" She grinned at him and then walked over to a locked cupboard. "Is this where you hid what you don't want me near?"

He was still leaning against the door and nodded. "Some magic is better left alone," he said quietly.

She walked over and ran her fingers down the spines on a few journals. "And you'd know from experience?" She turned to look at him while he answered.

"Yes."

"So by locking it up, are you saving me from finding out the hard way, or from finding out you did?"

Chris studied her for a moment before he stepped into the room. "Perhaps both." He stopped in front of her and put his hands back in his pockets. "I've told you I was a bad boy, and at one point was a very bad witch."

He walked over and picked up a journal off the shelf. "I began experimenting, in many areas." He set it back on the shelf and waved a hand towards the books. "I've read them all...tried it all."

Kasey watched him for a few moments. "And now?" She put her hands behind her.

"Now?" His voice was quiet.

"What kind of witch are you now, Chris?"

He walked around the room for a moment, pausing to touch something here and there. "An experienced one."

"Do you still do darker things?"

"No."

She searched his face for several moments in silence. "Why did you stop? Most wouldn't have."

Chris walked over until he was right in front of her and looked down at her. "I stopped the day I met you." Her eyes widened. "You walked in for that Wiccan ceremony with Rachel, smiled shyly when she introduced you to Steven and me, and I've never done anything dark since that moment. It took me a long time to not feel unclean when I was near you."

She reached up and touched his cheek. "You are such a sweet man."

He grabbed her wrist firmly, but gentle enough he wouldn't hurt her. "No, I'm not." His voice was low. "If I told you some of the things I've done, you would walk out that door and never come back."

Kasey lowered her hand with his hand still holding her wrist. "Then why are you telling me?" Her voice was barely over a whisper.

He searched her eyes again. "Because I'm in love with you, have loved you for all the years I've known you." She looked at him with those huge, innocent eyes. "I've grown to need your smile, your touch, your laugh."

Chris reached to touch her cheek with a shaking hand. "I need you to keep me right, Kassandra, to show me the right in everything." She hadn't moved. "Everything you do is pure, when you're mad, when you're happy, when you're sad. Your very presence changed me the moment I saw you." He smiled down at her, then dropped his hand. "And now I've frightened you half to death." He released her wrist and stepped back a few feet.

She looked at him for a few more seconds. "No. You

haven't frightened me. Astonished me, maybe, but I've always known there was a dark side to you, Chris." She smiled weakly and spread her arms out. "Look at me. No one gets any cleaner than this, Chris. You even described me as pure. I'm definitely virginal, but why do you think I was drawn to you?"

He searched her face.

"I was drawn to you because of that dark side, Chris. I need that balance too." She paced around the room. "I'm a little overwhelmed right now. To find out you've been in love with me for about six years and never told me." She looked over at him.

"I couldn't."

"Why?"

He looked down at the floor for a moment then back at her. "I had a lot to change and correct before I could." He closed his eyes for a moment. "If I had tried earlier, I would have used what I can do to get you and to keep you." He stuffed his hands back into his pockets to stop from going to her and touching her. "I still have to fight it continuously."

"Even now?"

He nodded.

Walking over, she touched one of the journals. "Is it recorded in these?" She looked back at him. "I'm assuming you'd record everything?"

He nodded. "I did." He walked over to the locked cupboard. He touched the lock for a moment until it opened. He pulled the latch on the door and opened it and then pulled out a thick book. "It's in here." He turned to see her looking into the cupboard.

"Why do you keep all of that?"

He looked down at the oil vials and various tools. "A reminder."

"If this," Kasey motioned between the two of them, "is going to stand a chance, I won't put up with secrets." She held out her hand for the book. He looked down at the book for a moment, then handed it to her silently.

"With your permission?" she said quietly, looking at him.

He inclined his head to give it.

Kasey walked over to the cushions in the corner and sat down.

Chris leaned back against the open cupboard and watched her silently flipping through the pages. He now, after all these years, understood what someone on trial went through while waiting for the verdict.

He saw her hand falter a few times, and she'd flip back a page, possibly wondering if she'd read it correctly.

She looked up at him with an expression he couldn't read. "This is written by your hand?" She glanced at his hands for a moment then back to his face.

He nodded and put his hands in his pockets to hide them.

She looked at him a moment longer and then put her head back down and read further.

Chris didn't move. He stood there, waiting until she'd looked at every page in that journal. He had no idea how much time passed, but it was a thick journal, so it was long enough. But he stood waiting while she read every detail of the spells he had done that no one had any business doing. She read how he could really use his voice and his eyes to get what, or whom, he'd wanted. Everything he'd done when he'd been filled with selfishness and thought of no one else but what he wanted. She'd read how he had used skills he'd developed to watch others and so much more he was now ashamed of. She read it all. When she closed the book, he almost dropped to his knees to beg her forgiveness.

Kasey sat there holding the book. Her heart was pounding. She studied Chris. This man in front of her who had shown her more patience than she'd ever thought possible. She studied the man who had always been able to make her feel good, a man whose hands were so gentle with her. He'd always made her laugh.

This man in front of her had done those things she'd just

read. She knew about dark magic, read some, but never in her mind could she have thought some of those things were possible. She looked at his face. His jaw was clenched, but he didn't speak, didn't move. He just stood there waiting for her to pass judgment on him. She stood slowly with the book in her shaking hands and walked over to him.

He straightened up, his eyes not leaving hers.

She spoke in a whisper. "You will dispose of everything in that cupboard properly. Then lock this book in there to stay. I never want to see it again." She started to turn and then stopped. "If you ever use any of those things I just read about against me or on me, or anyone, ever again, Christopher Larkin, you will be a very sorry man."

He just stood there holding the book, looking at her.

"Do you understand?"

"Yes."

As she was turning to leave the room, he dropped down on his knees and lowered his head

It was dark now, and he didn't care to turn on a light. Chris sat on the couch in his library. He hadn't gone up to talk to her. He didn't know what to say. How could he explain when there was no explanation?

He picked up his drink to discover it was empty again. Setting the glass down, he sighed. It wasn't really helping anyway. He put his head back and closed his eyes.

When he opened his eyes again, Kasey stood in the doorway looking at him. She was wearing only a large T-shirt. Her face was streaked with tears he had put there. Without a word, she walked over to him and climbed onto the couch and curled up in his lap. She placed her arms around his neck and rested her face against his chest.

With unsteady hands, he wrapped his arms around her and held her. He didn't think she'd come to him ever again. Leaning back, he stretched out and pulled her with him to lie down. There were no more tears, there were no words, and they just silently held each other.

When she drifted off to sleep, he got up carefully and took her up to her bed. She sighed when he kissed her. Standing back, he looked down at her for a moment, then turned and went to his own room.

ℰ Chapter 16 ℰ

Chris couldn't remember hurrying home after work before, but he did this day. Kasey had been gone to work the next morning by the time he got up. Pulling into the driveway, he saw her Jimmy parked there. Well, at least she hadn't moved out while he was at work.

The hope he had left when he found a note on the table beside the door. *Gone shopping. Girls' night out. We're all together, so relax. K'*

Relax? He hadn't relaxed since she'd read that journal last night.

He grabbed a beer from the fridge and he went towards his library. Hopefully he could get some work done and make up for not being able to focus on anything at the office all day.

"What are you going to do?" Rachel asked while taking one of Kasey's fries.

"I don't know." Kasey pushed the rest of the fries towards Rachel. "You should have seen him last night. He expected me to throw the book at him, call him names, and leave." She sipped the pop. "I thought of it a few times while reading, to be honest."

"It was that bad?" Cora asked quietly.

Kasey turned to Cora. "Yes, it was horrible, genius, but still horrible. I couldn't believe the man I know, that we know, did all that."

Leena shoved her plate away. "And he told you that you were the reason he stopped?"

Rachel sighed. "Why can't I find a man to say things like that to me?"

"Well you're certainly trying enough. Maybe someday you'll find one." Cora snorted.

Rachel stuck her tongue out. "Thanks, that helps."

Leena reached and took Kasey's hand. "Have you and Chris... slept together, Kase?"

Kasey blushed. "Sort of."

Rachel leaned forward until she was a few inches from her face. "Sweetie, you either did or didn't. 'Sort of' doesn't work in this case."

Kasey twisted the napkin in her hands. "Well, he knows I haven't ever, and he's been pretty patient. We do other things. Then he holds me and lets me sleep with him."

Rachel fanned her face. "Does he have a brother? Kasey, adult males don't wait."

Leena smirked. "Not if they're with you."

"Hey, is this pick-on-Rachel night? 'Cuz if I'd gotten the memo, I would have made other plans."

Kasey leaned her head on Rachel's shoulder. "You're so lucky, Rach. Being my age and still a virgin is really beginning to suck."

Rachel leaned her head on top of Kasey's. "Not from where I'm sitting. The man is taking his time with you. He's been so completely honest with you. He's completely friggin' reformed for you." She looked at the other two women. "How does that suck?"

Cora busied herself by taking a drink, and Leena smirked. "It doesn't, to be honest."

Kasey sighed. "I wish I could just climb into his bed and stop being so scared of everything."

Cora lifted her eyebrows at her, and Leena smiled.

Rachel leaned over again. "So, why don't you?"

"Oh, I couldn't." Kasey blushed.

"But didn't you already once?" Cora asked quietly.

Kasey shrugged. "Yeah, but it was from having a nightmare."

"So, do it again, and put yourself and him out of your misery." Rachel reached for Cora's fries while winking at a blushing Kasey.

"Well... I could... but I don't know what to do, really. Well, I do, but not really."

Leena chuckled. "I'm pretty sure Chris does, and will help in that department."

Kasey put her hands on her hot cheeks and let out a slow breath. "I can do this," she said more for herself than the others. She looked at them. "What do I wear?"

Rachel shrugged, "A paper sack, ripped t-shirt, he won't care!"

Cora pushed Rachel over out of the way. "Oh, I have just the thing. I bought it only to get it home and find out I was too tall to wear it. We'll swing by and get it before I take you home."

Kasey just nodded and took deep breaths.

"Subject change!" Rachel threw in. "Tomorrow night at Doc's, are we going to do things the same way as last time?"

Cora smirked. "Yes, except Kasey and Chris aren't allowed to be next to each other."

Leena nodded. "And Owen can't be beside me. I swear that man is in heat or something the last few days. He's finished another book, and I'm exhausted!"

Rachel scowled at her. "I don't need to hear you're getting *that* lucky." She turned to Kasey. "And now Kasey is too. I ask you, when is it my turn?"

Chris heard her come in and tried not to run out to see her. Failing, he thought, as he found himself walking out anyways. He found her shoes and purse by the door. There were a few bags sitting at the bottom of the stairs, but no Kasey.

Walking slowly up the stairs, he found her walking out of the bathroom. She jumped when she looked up and saw him standing there.

She looked past him, and then at him briefly. "Hi. I was going to have a swim. Unless you want the tub, then I can wait."

Chris put his hands in his pockets, trying not to touch her. She stood looking at his chest and not his face. "No, go ahead." He waited to see if she'd look at him. "How was shopping?"

She shrugged and turned towards her room. "Fine. Found lots of interesting stuff." She gave him a quick smile over her shoulder. "I forgot something to put on after my bath." Then she quickly walked to her room.

He watched her walk away from him, again. She couldn't even look him in the face. Hadn't he thought this would happen? What possessed him to tell her? He took a shaky breath. Because it was better to lose her now than to lose her later? But was it?

He turned around and walked into his room and closed the door quietly. He went over stretched out on his bed and held his arms across his face. What will he do without her?

He didn't know how long he stayed that way. He heard a quiet tap on his door and turned to look and see Kasey standing in the doorway. He swallowed. She stood there with the light from the hallway shining behind her. She was wearing some sort of black teddy. The front was low cut with no material over her stomach, just two thin pieces running down her sides to a small ruffle of black lace.

He bolted upright but couldn't move as she moved slowly towards him. Was this some dream? He had to be sleeping. This was not the same Kasey who had practically run from the sight of him in the hallway.

"Chris?"

He swallowed. "Yes?" She stood at the edge of the bed now as he looked over every inch of her. His heart was beating in his throat, and he couldn't think of how to speak.

Kasey put one knee up on the bed and leaned down closer to him. "Love me," she whispered in a shaky voice.

His quickly looked at her face. She moved closer to him. Reaching out slowly, for fear she wouldn't really be there, he held his breath until he touched her cheek softly with the tips of his fingers. Leaning closer, he searched her eyes for the fear he'd seen the night before. There was none.

He placed his hand behind her neck and gently pulled her closer while he feathered kisses across her cheek. "Yes." She came up on the bed on her knees. He reached to place his other hand on her cheek as he feathered light kisses over her lips next. She was shaking, or maybe that was him. He wasn't sure. He kissed her lingeringly for a few moments.

Pulling her into him, he leaned back so she lay across him. He was nervous and couldn't believe he still knew that feeling. Caressing a hand down her back, he held her gently against him. He shifted more onto his side.

He touched her neck with his lips and trailed teasing kisses at the delicate, delicious hollow. She held on to his head, holding it tightly to her.

Gripping her hips, he rolled so she was on her back. His face was buried in the warm valley between her breasts. He inhaled her scent, and his blood heated. He lifted his head and kissed her again, plunging his tongue into her mouth and exploring all of it.

He kissed her with a feeling of desperation. He'd thought he'd lost her. She kissed him back with the same heated desire, and he thought his heart was going to burst.

He moved his mouth down her throat and then lifted his head and looked down at the black lace covering her. He had been so shocked when he'd seen her dressed like this he hadn't even noticed the fairy framed by the material against her skin. Leaning down over it, he rested his head against her warm skin as he swirled his tongue around the fairy before kissing just underneath it. She hissed out a breath. He teased her with his tongue just above the lace before skimming his mouth over her bare hips.

When he cupped one knee gently and bent her leg to run his mouth along the inside of her thigh, she moaned and relaxed her leg for him.

He breathed against the wet material between her legs, and she moaned again. Running his tongue along the outside of the lace, he moved over to her other thigh and kissed it softly. When he licked slowly along her other hip, she groaned and the sound vibrated through him.

"Chris..."

He kissed along her ribs and licked just under the material beneath her breast. She hissed and ran her fingers into his hair. Licking a hard nipple through the fabric, he felt her arch against his mouth.

With her other hand, she reached and released the clasp holding the top in place and pushed it down so his mouth was against her bare breast.

Holding his head, she arched her back until her breast was against his open mouth. He cupped it in his hand and sucked the nipple gently. She panted and squirmed against him.

Pushing up on her elbow, she buried her face in his hair and wrapped one leg around him. With impatient hands, she tugged at his shirt impatiently. He lifted up so she could unbutton it with shaking hands. Then he shrugged out of it. Her mouth ran over his throat and across his shoulder. She bit him gently, and he threw his head back and moaned. Pushing him back, she fumbled and undid his pants while trying to push them off his body.

He rolled and got rid of them before moving back to lean over her. She was so lovely, her lips swollen from his kisses, her neck red from his mouth, the black lace was resting around her waist.

Kasey looked up at him and then pulled his head so she could kiss him. Her mouth was hot against his. He began to push the lace down over her hips while he kissed her back with the same urgency. As the material moved down her thighs, he waited for her to hesitate but she just lifted her hips so he could pull the material off.

Sliding his hand back up her leg slowly, he ran it inside her thighs to feel she was wet with wanting him. Stroking over her softly, he heard her groan deep in her throat, and she dropped her head back. He pushed a finger inside her and almost cried out with his own pleasure to feel how hot she was.

Devouring her breasts, he quickly brought her to a shattering climax, needing her ready for him, not wanting to wait anymore. She vibrated against him and then pulled him back up to her. He fumbled to reach the night stand and get a condom while she kissed his throat, it wasn't helping his coordination. Getting one he put it on with shaking hands as she pulled him closer and opened her legs to let him move between them.

When he felt their bare skin touch against him, his whole body tensed, and he had to fight not to plunge into her. Slowly he pushed against her, allowing her time to adjust to the feeling. She gasped and pushed her hips towards him. He gripped her leg to stop her from moving. He didn't want to hurt her.

He moved his mouth to her throat, he sucked it gently while he pushed farther inside her. She was so tight. He didn't know how much longer he could wait. Sensitive muscles pulsed around him, and he panted, trying to go slowly. Her breath was coming in short gasps when she suddenly gripped his hips and thrust up onto him. He almost exploded from the feeling of being all the way inside her.

Kissing her roughly, he tried to stay still, for a moment. She opened her legs wider and wrapped them over his hips, pulling him into her. Unable to stop, he began moving quickly into her. He didn't want to hurt her, but he couldn't stop the hard thrusts of his hips. He'd waited too long.

She began to whimper against his neck. Her fingers dug

into his back as she met his thrusts, causing him to reach that unstoppable point. She began to make squeaking noises into his ear, and he couldn't hold back any longer.

As her muscles clenched tight in orgasm around him, he came with such force his whole body shook. She went lax in his arms, breathing as hard as he was.

"Wow," she gasped against him.

He pulled her so they could lie on their sides, but didn't want to pull out of her. "Mmm" was the only reply he was capable of making.

He kissed her eyelids softly, and then her cheeks, before kissing her lips. When he looked into her eyes, he saw the smile before he looked at her mouth. Turning his head, he saw silver sparkles dusting their way down towards their heads. He smiled. "I'll have to try for fireworks next time."

Kasey smiled. "Sparkles were all I could manage right now." She snuggled against his chest.

He rolled onto his back, still trying to catch his breath as he turned and kissed her gently. "Old man needs a nap again."

She smiled and cuddled against him and closed her eyes. "Me too."

Chris woke to an empty bed. Did she run as soon as her eyes opened? Glancing at the clock, he saw he still had an hour before he had to leave for work. Groaning, he got up and went to take a shower.

He was leaning against the wall, letting the water wake him up, when two arms came around him from behind.

"I went to put the coffee on and came back to find you missing."

Turning in her arms, he smiled down at her. "I woke up to an empty bed." He kissed her tenderly. "Are you very sore this morning? I wasn't very gentle last night."

"A little, in a good way. And you were gentle enough when needed." She kissed his chest and ran her hands down his flat stomach. "So, how does this work in the shower?"

Her hands ran down his thighs and back up over his hips.

He kissed her while picking her up. Her legs immediately wrapped around his waist. "I'll show you."

He sat looking at his knife.
Why couldn't he find her to finish what he'd failed to do right?
He needed to free her before moving on to the next.
He dropped his head into his hands and rocked.
The pain had been so bad since he failed.
No one would tell where she was.
Didn't they know she needed him?
She had come to him to save her from the sins she'd committed.
The pain was back.
He had to find her.

৵৶ Chapter 17 ৵৶

"Kasey, we're going to be late," Chris called from the bottom of the stairs and then turned to see her jogging from the temple room.

She stopped in front of him. "I borrowed some oils of yours. Is that okay?" She chewed her bottom lip.

"Anything you need." He grinned down at her. "Are you taking your giant dish?"

"Oh! I almost forgot it." She went running towards the dining room.

"It's in there now?" He didn't get an answer until she came back out with it.

She nodded as she struggled with the large piece of copper. "It looked great in that empty corner."

He took it from her and followed her to the door. "Everyone's going to be waiting." He admired the way her jeans hugged her hips and bottom as she opened the door for him. Amazing was all he could think.

Kasey jogged down the steps and went and opened the car door for him. "I still can't believe we're doing this at the Doc's."

Chris put the dish inside and then closed the door and turned, pulling her against him. "He has an empty carpeted basement. It will be perfect." He grinned at her. "But first I need something." He kissed her, hard and breathless. Lifting his head, he grinned again. "Much better."

She smiled up at him. "We need to do a lot more of that when we get home."

He watched her get in the car. "Anything you need."

"Oh, this is perfect!" Kasey squealed and ran to the other end of the large room. Stopping and spinning around before she ran back towards the others. "I need my bag." They all watched her fly back up the stairs.

Chris turned to Leena and grinned. "Does she run this line at work single-handed?"

Leena laughed. "Pretty much, her team just stays out of her way and tries to pitch in from time to time."

Dade laughed and smirked at Chris. "How the hell do you keep up with her?"

Chris lifted his eyebrows at him. "Like this." He stood to the side at the bottom of the stairs as she came through the door at the top. She ran down the stairs digging in the bag with her head down. When she was two steps from the bottom, he reached out and pulled her against him by her waist. She shrieked and grabbed around his neck, laughing.

She kissed him and then smiled at him. "Hi." He set her back on the floor slowly. "Thought those were planned for when we get home."

"Then too."

Steven cleared his throat. "Focus!"

Rachel laughed. "Yeah, you two are not allowed to be beside each other this time."

Kasey blushed and walked quickly over to the edge of the copper dish. "Does everyone remember what to do?"

Owen nodded. "We're doing it exactly the same as before?"

Kasey was reading a folded piece of paper. She shrugged. "Pretty much the same. I'm going to be doing something slightly different than last time. Hopefully it will show us more. But all of you do the same thing." She looked over at Chris quickly, then away. "And let's be sure not to touch each other this time."

Cora, who had been sitting quietly with her head down, looked over. "Are you using the same stones? They worked so well last time."

Nodding, Kasey stood up rubbing oils into her palms. "Uh-huh, I recharged them."

Chris watched her carefully for a moment. *What was she doing? Why was she so nervous?* He walked over with the intention of massaging some of the tension from her shoulders.

She jumped away from him and then smiled. "No touching. I need to focus this time, Chris."

Everyone stopped in their preparations to turn and look at him.

Chris held up his palms and went to stand by the dish and wait. "Okay." *What oils did she have?* The scents were familiar, but he couldn't quite place them. It was a mix, but of what? He smirked. She was probably trying to increase her vision strength. He had to shake his head to not laugh out loud and distract everyone. If she gained any more strength in her magical abilities, he was going to be in serious trouble.

Kasey sat a few feet from the dish with her head down, breathing deeply. The salt was down, candles burning.

Leena moved quietly, lighting the incense.

Owen came over with the smudge. Kasey shook her head, refusing. "I've taken care of that another way." She moved to kneel by the dish. "Owen, I'd like you on my right and Cora on my left.

Chris jerked his head up and looked at her, searching her face. With her eyes closed, he couldn't see her thoughts. Inhaling, he took in the scent of the oils again. A sweet smell, it was so familiar, but what was it?

The water was dark and glossy.

Everyone was in place and began to chant quietly with a smooth rhythm, increasing in volume each time.

Kasey opened her eyes and looked into the dish. *Let me see something to focus on.* She needed something personal, something direct.

A calendar floated to the top of the dish. This was no surprise to see the Lammas date was circled.

The hand wearing the ring was holding something in it. Breathing deeply, she focused on the hand, trying to bring it closer to the surface.

A pill bottle...it was a pill bottle! His thumb covered the name of the medication. Leaning forward, she focused on the image. "Take me there." Humming under her breath, slowly trying to focus more, and reach further inside the vision. *Let me see the name. Who was the prescription for?*

The hand set the bottle down. *No, pick it up!* She began whispering the chant she'd memorized under her breath, and then added, "Take me there. Let them see..."

Pick up the bottle. She pushed the thought towards the image of the hand that now rested on top of a Bible.

Pick it up! Look at the bottle! Show me the name! The hand moved off the Bible. Kasey felt the sweat run down into her eyes. "Show me!" she hissed. The hand stopped in front of the bottle it clenched, then opened a few times. "Show me!" she whispered. *There! Lawrence C. Pr.*

The hand dropped and picked up the knife beside the Bible, gripping it so tight the knuckles were white.

Chris looked up at her suddenly. He knew the incantation she was mumbling. He closed his eyes and tried to remember.

Bayberry mixed with astral oil? Chris jerked his head towards Kasey just as she collapsed onto the floor.

"No!" He slapped a hand into the water, splashing it everywhere, and went quickly to her. "Kasey!" He ran his hands down her arms gently. "Kasey, let go! Come back!"

Steven dropped to his knees and checked her pulse. He looked up to Chris. "What has she done?"

Chris's hands were shaking. Looking over at the bag she'd pulled from her purse, he reached over and grabbed it. Quickly dumping the contents onto the floor, he pushed the oil bottles to see the names on the labels. "No, Kasey, why did you try this alone?" he whispered. Careful not to jar her, he pulled her into his arms and held her gently to him.

He knelt there stroking her face softly. "Come back, sweetheart. Let it go, and come back." Tears ran down his face as he looked up at the others.

Leena dropped down beside him and ran a hand across Kasey's sweaty brow. "Chris, think! What do we need? You know. How do we bring her back?"

He tried to focus on her face through blurred eyes.

Cora crawled over to her and placed her hands on Kasey's arm. She gasped and pulled them away. "Chris, where is she?"

The tears rolled down his face. He looked down at her pale face. She looked only to be sleeping. "In between," he whispered.

Rachel was shaking as she put a hand on his face to make him look at her. "What do we need, Chris? Tell us what to do. Help us bring her back."

He looked around at the fear in everyone's expression and closed his eyes for a few moments. "We need… ahh!" he spat in frustration. "Uh... vervain, plant or oil will work, and dittany." He looked at Leena. "Tell me you have your case of herbs with you?"

Leena nodded, looking to Owen. "It's in the back of the Jeep."

Owen nodded and ran up the stairs just ahead of her.

Chris let out an unsteady breath trying to stay calm. "I haven't done this in years."

Rachel moved closer. "Chris, you are the only one that knows about this. What else do we need?"

He reached for the paper Kasey had been reading and opened it with one hand. Holding her against his chest, he read what she'd written. "Kasey, why did you try this alone? I would have come with you, to watch over you," he whispered again. Turning, he looked at Rachel. "We'll need four white candles and four blue ones."

She looked up at Steven.

Steven nodded. "I've got those. I'll show you where." He knelt and checked Kasey's pulse again, nodding to Chris, and then got up and went with Rachel.

Dade knelt in front of Chris. Looking down at Kasey, he whispered, "I have the ability to see spirits, as you know. I'll see her coming back until she reaches a certain line."

Chris looked up from the soft skin he'd been caressing. "Can you guide her back?"

Dade shook his head. "No, it's too risky. I might not get just her." He looked over at Cora and then back to Chris. "I can call those that have crossed over but not one that has a living body."

Chris nodded. "Watching for her will be enough."

Dade nodded. "I'll go get my rattle from the van."

Cora touched Chris's arm briefly. "What else can we do?"

Chris glanced around. "Move the smudge closer." His hand was shaking as he ran it though his hair. "We'll need black salt. Can you see if anyone has any?"

He wished for the supplies in his temple room. "I'll need a moment."

They both nodded. Taking Cora's hand, Dade walked to the stairs.

With the candles lit and herbs in place, Chris finally looked up at the others. "I'll need you to circle the two of us with the salt. Do not cross it, regardless of what you see."

He took a deep breath. "Circle around us, and clasp hands. I don't want you to see us. I want you to focus on seeing her return to her body."

Steven knelt in front of him. "Wouldn't it be better if she were in the circle alone? We'll need you outside with us."

Chris shook his head. "I am not letting her go." His tone

was a clear warning.

Steven nodded and held out his hand for the salt.

"Wait!" Rachel rushed forward and knelt in front of Kasey. She lowered her face to Kasey's and kissed her cheek. "Come back to us, Kase." Looking up, she touched Chris's cheek. "Bring her back." She stood up slowly and moved back, taking her place in the circle. Steven made the thin line with the salt around Chris holding Kasey's lax little body in his arms.

Chris kissed her lips lightly and then lifted his head and closed his eyes. He began the incantation under his breath until he felt the flow of it move through him. He looked down at her fragile body as he continued it in his head.

Come back to me, he willed her.

The others stood looking down at them in the center of their outstretched arms. The candles flickered shadows over Kasey. Sweat rolled down the back of Chris's neck, and his arms were shaking trying to hold his focus.

Dade shook the rattle softly and stared into the air above them and waited, hoping. A light glimmered and then faded. Without moving his eyes away, he whispered in a low voice. "She's trying to return."

Chris closed his eyes and concentrated harder, murmuring the chant inside his head *faster, clearer!* If he had been speaking it out loud, he would have been screaming it loud enough to shake the walls. The body in his arms jerked a few times

"She's almost there," he heard Dade say softly.

Kasey began to vibrate in his arms, and then he heard a breath escape her small mouth. He continued the chant until he felt resistance in the body he held in his arms. Opening his eyes, he lowered his head and looked down into the most beautiful green eyes he'd ever seen.

Kasey blinked and then tried to lift her heavy head. "Did it work? Did I do it?" she whispered with a voice that cracked.

Chris lowered his head to rest on hers. "I am so very

angry with you right now," he barely had a voice as emotions choked him. He kissed her hair.

She lifted an unsteady hand to hold his head against hers. "I knew, *knew*, you'd be able to bring me back. I knew you would."

"Remove the circle!" Dade paced around it.

Lifting his head, Chris held his hand over the line of salt. With a flick of his fingers, the salt flew out and away from them.

Rachel and Cora dropped to their knees and looked at Kasey's still trembling body.

Rachel leaned over her. "You are in big trouble! You scared the hell out of me!"

Dade glanced over Chris's shoulder and grinned down at her. "You're one scary green-eyed witch, Kase, but never do that again!"

Steven was checking her pulse and her eyes as he spoke. "As soon as my own blood pressure returns to normal, I'm going to lock up all of your toys, young lady."

Owen nodded to that. "You promised to break me in gently, I am not happy."

Kasey just rested her head against Chris's shoulder. "I get it, guys. Bad little witch. But what you're not saying is whether it worked or not."

Cora stroked her hand down the back of Kasey's damp hair. "We have part of a name, Kasey. Lawrence C., and the last name began with Pr."

Kasey opened her eyes. "We can check the lists? See if that's on it?"

Chris shook his head. "The only thing you're going to be doing is drinking the tea Leena's going to pour into you, with a funnel if she has to." He stood up with weak knees and began walking towards the stairs. "Then you're going to stay in bed for at least the next twenty-four hours. No work! No, and I mean *no* magic! Nothing but rest!" He stomped up the stairs.

Kasey slowly lifted her arm up to rest her hand on his

cheek. "Oh, Chris, I love you," she whispered

Chris stopped in the middle of the stairs, causing everyone else following to stop in line behind him. Looking down at her with a tear rolling down his cheek, he smiled. "Your timing in finally telling me really sucks, Kassandra." She smiled faintly as his trembling lips brushed against hers. "You really scared me, sweetheart. I didn't know what to do."

Kasey brushed her fingers over his lips. "I knew you would, Chris." She sighed. "Now you had better move before they start pushing us up the stairs."

He turned his head to look, having forgotten the others were behind him. Everyone stood there smiling at him, not one in a hurry for him to move at all

◈ Chapter 18 ◈

The phone beside her rang again. "Hello."

"Hi, sweetheart, how are you doing?"

This was the fourth time Chris had called today. "Fine. I've been telling everyone that. Everyone has called me all day. Cora's called twice, Rachel once, Leena once. Dade sends me text messages, in case I'm resting, so the phone doesn't ring and disturb me. Owen offered to come over and sit with me." She laughed. "Doc called to see if I'm drinking enough and of course to see if I'm going to the bathroom often enough. I'm ready to scream, Chris!"

"I know. I would have stayed home if I could have. I couldn't postpone this court date without notice. Have you been resting, though?"

Kasey sighed. "I passed out in the car last night and don't remember anything until you kissed me good-bye this morning. I've rested enough."

"Where are you?"

She looked around guiltily. "Downstairs in the living room."

He cleared his throat. "I thought we agreed you would stay in bed all day?"

Kasey laughed. "No, you decided I would. I didn't agree

to that... request. I was going stir-crazy there in your dark lair, Chris. So, I grabbed my laptop, and I'm slumming in the living room now."

He let out a loud breath. "Just don't rush it, Kasey. You were gone far too long last night."

"I'm okay, Chris. I've done rejuvenating baths, and drank all the tea Leena gave me,"

"Have you eaten? I should have thought to have something delivered."

"I'm fine. Just finish what you have to do and come home." She lowered her voice. "I'm bored and lonely."

"I'll be there in about an hour. Try to have a nap. Everyone is going to be coming over after dinner tonight to see you."

"Oh. Okay, I'll behave and rest."

"Good. Kasey?"

"Yeah?"

"I love you."

She smiled into the phone. "That's just what I needed to hear. I love you too, Chris, now get back to work."

"I will. See you later."

"Bye." She set the phone down and turned to scowl back at the lists on her laptop. With over forty pages, it had taken her almost two hours, between phone calls of concern, to highlight all the names with Lawrence or a first name with the initial *L* in them, all the names with *C*, and any last names with the first two letters being *Pr*.

She pouted. *I had to lose it before I got the last name, didn't I?* Now what was she supposed to do with the twenty-eight highlighted names? Chris would know.

Chris came through the door dropping his jacket and briefcase on the floor much like Kasey did every time she entered the house. He walked quickly to the living room to see her. She wasn't there. Maybe she was lying down upstairs again. He turned around and headed back towards the stairs.

"I'm in the kitchen," she called out to him.

He turned around again. "How are you resting if you're…" He stopped and stood in the door. Kasey sat perched on the counter with her legs crossed. Wearing only the anklet and little fairy he'd given her.

"I thought about making dinner, and then realized I wasn't hungry for food."

His eyes drifted over her slowly. He should be angry she wasn't resting, but his heart began beating very loudly in his chest, distracting him. "No?" Walking towards her, he grinned. "Other appetites?" She nodded and reached to circle her arms around his neck. "What are you hungry for?" he asked against her neck.

"You."

He kissed her shoulder gently. "Feeling better then?"

"Mmm." Her lips brushed over his throat as she pulled his tie off. "Uncomfortably so." Uncrossing her legs, she pulled his hand from her hip and placed it between her legs. "See?"

He'd never gotten so hard this quickly in his life. Just feeling the heat between her legs had him hissing out a breath. "I could hurt you this way."

She pushed his shirt down his arms, cuff links hitting the floor as it went over his hands. She ran her hands down his chest roughly, stopping when she reached for his belt. "Let's try and see." She licked one of his nipples. "I missed you today."

Chris waited for her to push his pants over his hips, then gripped her hips tightly. Lowering his head until he reached her breast, he bit it gently. "I thought I'd lost you…" He moved his lips over and sucked the other nipple greedily. "I need you so fuckin' much, Kassandra. Don't ever do that to me again." His voice was low.

Kasey pulled his mouth up to hers as her small hand closed around him. "Show me." She bit his bottom lip. "Now."

He was vibrating with needing her as she stroked the hard length of him. Briefly he thought of how he'd almost lost her as he pulled her hips to the edge of the counter he held her there as he reached down and aligned their bodies. Grasping her under the knees, he thrust into her without warning. He shuddered from how wet she was. As she threw her head back and moaned, he lost all reasoning he was struggling to hang on to.

"Yes," she growled.

He thrust into her harder, groaning as her muscles clenched around him. Thrusting faster, he lowered his mouth to pull her nipple with his teeth. She cried out and grasped his head. He pulled her harder to meet each thrust. She groaned and bit into his arm as she came violently.

Panting to breathe, he kept thrusting into her, holding her still, until he shuddered and hissed as he came so hard it almost hurt.

Pulling her damp body tight against him, he took a deep breath and waited until he could speak again. "Did I hurt you?" He panted against her neck.

She licked his shoulder. "In a very delicious way," she gasped.

He pulled back to look at her heavy green eyes. "I think I've created a very wanton little witch."

She smiled and ran her tongue over his lips. "Is that bad?"

Chris pulled her from the counter, still inside her, and carried her on shaky legs towards the stairs. "Oh no, that's very good." He kissed her roughly. "I have six years of fantasies to act out."

Kasey chuckled against his shoulder. "Do any of them involve my mouth? Because I'd really like to try that again." He groaned and started walking up the stairs faster.

After everyone arrived and she had assured each one she was completely fine, she settled in Chris's lap. "So, I had lots of time today to..." She looked around the living room before remembering she'd taken her laptop upstairs. She jumped up from Chris's lap so fast she teetered for a second before she literally ran out of the room. "Be right back," she called over her shoulder.

Dade laughed and looked at Chris. "Well she didn't stay down long."

Chris grinned. "No." He looked around. "We have about a minute before she flies back in. Would anyone like a beer or wine?"

"I'll help," Dade said, getting up.

Steven grabbed Chris's arm on the way by and looked at the marks on his bicep. "You should put something on this, you can die from human bites."

Chris grinned. "But what a great way to go."

Dade grabbed the beer while Chris poured the wine. Chris stood for a moment looking at the counter.

"Larkin? You okay?"

Chris turned. "What? Oh, fine, just got lost for a minute there." He patted the countertop. "I love this counter." He grinned at Dade.

Dade looked at him curiously, and then at the counter, and sighed. "Please. Teeth marks, counter obsessions, I can't bear to know."

Chris laughed and walked out carrying the tray of glasses. Grabbing the beer, Dade followed him. Just before he reached the living room, he stopped and held out a glass. Dade stopped abruptly behind him.

Kasey flew around the corner with a handful of papers. "Oh!" She stopped and took the glass from him, then reached up and kissed him. "Thanks." She smiled and walked in to join the others.

Dade chuckled, following behind.

"Okay." Setting the wineglass down before she spilled it, Kasey sat on the floor. "I was bored silly this afternoon, so I went over those lists again."

She hopped back up to her feet. "I highlighted all the names with Lawrence or *L* and with *C* as an initial, same for the last names beginning with *Pr.*" She paced, flipping through the pages. "That gives us twenty-eight possibilities instead of six miles of names."

Chris reached out and pulled her, with the pages, onto his lap. "This is great." He looked through a few pages. "I can see if we can dig up anything on these." He grinned at her. "And we'll send them to Patrick." Passing them to Owen, he looked around the room. "Have we reached any decisions about Lammas?"

Cora looked around at the men. "What do you mean?"

Steven lowered the beer from his mouth. "He means are we going? Do we really want to place any of the four of you women in danger again?"

Leena looked at Owen for a moment. "Couldn't we have been involved in this discussion also?"

Steven opened his mouth, then closed it and looked at Dade.

Dade shrugged and was about to speak when he turned and Cora glared at him. "I just spoke to Gwen today. We are going to Lammas, and that sick man will not hurt another woman!"

Dade closed his mouth.

Kasey squirmed off of Chris's lap and picked up her wine to sip. "I agree." She looked at Chris with that look that dared him to defy her decision.

He glanced at the four women. Sighing, he rubbed the bridge of his nose. "Justin said there's a cottage on the site large enough for the eight of us."

Steven ran his hand over his face and looked over at Rachel. "Who is going to make the shopping list?"

Cora smiled sweetly at Dade. "Have any of you made a *decision* on how and when we're getting to the location Rhonda is at this weekend?"

Dade lifted a hand toward Chris.

Chris shook his head. "We'll be going in four different cars, all taking different routes. Patrick is going to call me with the rest of the details Friday night."

Kasey rested against his legs. "Has he said how she's

doing?"

Chris smirked. "Yes. He said she was easier to watch over when she was unconscious."

All the men laughed into their drinks, earning several scowls.

$\mathcal{S}$ **Chapter 19** $\mathcal{S}$

"Where are we supposed to meet him?" Kasey squirmed in her seat again. "I can't wait to speak to her."

Chris reached over and picked up her hand. He gave it a gentle squeeze before bringing it to his mouth to suck gently on a finger. She stopped and sat still, looking at him. He smiled. At least he'd found the secret to getting her to sit still. "We're about ten minutes away. Relax."

She smiled and let out a huffed breath. "Is everyone else going to be there by then?"

Chris nodded and checked his rearview mirror again to make sure no one was following them. "Yes, we'll pull the cars into a little barn and leave in the van with Patrick."

She leaned back. "I hope everyone else is okay."

"I'm sure they are."

The eight sat silently in the windowless van as Patrick drove them to the house, only Chris knew the location of. Kasey was so nervous, she clung to Chris's hand.

When they walked into the little house, they saw a dark-haired nurse sitting at the table reading a book. "Back so soon, Mr. Blaine?" She smiled at everyone. "Rhonda is in the sitting room in the La-Z-Boy."

Patrick raised his eyebrows. The woman shrugged. "She refused to see anyone lying flat on her back."

She turned and studied them. "It's good to see her looking forward to something. It's been very frustrating for her with all the therapy. Of course, she still can't bend a great deal. The wounds on her back are still too tender." She sighed and sat back down. "I keep telling her it's going to take hard work. But she acts like she'll magically heal overnight." Tsking to herself, she picked up the book. "Call if you need me."

Steven nodded. "Of course." He turned his back to her and wiggled his eyebrows at everyone else. "Let's go see if we can boost her spirits."

The woman half reclined in the puffy chair did not look like the scared woman in the hospital room a few weeks earlier. Her strawberry blonde hair was neatly combed down and spread out to her shoulders. The scars on her face weren't as angry-looking. Her brown eyes weren't as wide and frightened. Kasey looked around at everyone else for a moment and then looked back at Rhonda.

Rhonda smiled a tiny smile. "Hi. I'm so glad you came." Her voice was soft and raspy.

Patrick frowned at her. "Why aren't you in bed?"

She turned annoyed eyes towards him. "You go lie in bed, Patrick."

Everyone turned to Patrick.

He shrugged. "She's been going a bit stir-crazy. It makes her a little snappy now and then." He went over and sat near the window.

Rhonda smiled. "Sit, everyone. I'd sit up a bit, but it's still a little difficult."

Cora smiled. "Just seeing you almost upright and breathing is enough for us. How are you feeling otherwise?"

Kasey nodded to no one in particular as she sat down.

Rhonda smiled briefly. "Pissed off mostly, as you well know, Coralee."

Everyone turned to look at Cora.

Cora laughed. "Rhonda is able to send me thoughts or images from time to time, after us being so closely connected." Then she grinned at Rhonda. "Yes, I got those messages loud and clear."

Rhonda nodded slowly. "Good. And you're all right with that?"

Cora nodded but didn't say anything.

Kasey looked all around the room, and Rachel began picking invisible lint off her skirt. Leena just smiled and leaned into Owen.

Kasey nervously watched Patrick glance at each woman, and then he glared at Rhonda.

She ignored him. "Owen, I was wondering if you would hold my hands again. My back I can be patient with, but not being able to pick up anything is getting a little frustrating."

Owen smiled and stood up. "Be happy to."

"Whoa." Rhonda smiled, "You really are as big as I thought I'd remembered."

Owen knelt beside her. "But gentle as a lamb. Isn't that right, baby?" He winked at Leena.

"If you say so," Leena said with a smirk as she watched him hold Rhonda's hand for a moment. "Oh, I've brought more tea for you. Have they been helping?"

Rhonda nodded. "They're wonderful. Of course, Mr. Blaine wants me to only drink the ones that put me to sleep." She threw him a cold look.

Patrick turned and looked out the window again.

Steven stood up. "I'm sorry, but the doctor in me has to look." He waited for Owen to move around to the other hand, then picked up the one Owen had just released. He turned it over and checked both sides and flexed her fingers. "They've done a great job here."

Rhonda nodded. "Yes. I'll just go Goth and wear some sexy gloves when I go out."

Everyone laughed.

Kasey sat to the edge of the chair. "Have Leena design you some outfits. She has a knack for flaunting the good and hiding the bad."

Chris snorted. "Sweetheart, there isn't a bad anything on you."

Kasey blushed and turned back to Rhonda. "Have the stones been helping? I brought a few new ones so you could switch them from time to time."

Rhonda reached with the hand as Owen released it and pulled the chain out of her shirt. She stopped. "Oh!" Turning her teary eyes to Owen, she whispered, "I can pick up the chain now. Thank you!"

Owen looked bashful as he went and sat back down. "I'll have a go with your back before we leave if you like."

Rhonda nodded. "We'll see how I feel. I go from awake to drained very quickly." Trying to adjust her position, she hissed out a breath. "To be truthful, my back is really starting to ache being in this position."

Dade stood up. "We can help you go stretch out."

Rhonda smiled. "Please." Chris was on her other side before Dade could nod. Slowly they helped her get to her feet. She grinned. "Don't let me fall on my face, but let me walk on my own, please." Each placed a gentle hand on her arm.

Rhonda winked at Cora as she moved slowly towards the door. "I think you girls are the luckiest I've ever known. To have all these..." she looked at Chris and then Dade up and down slowly. "...big, sexy men looking after you all the time."

Cora held the door and laughed. "Oh, they have their moments."

Dade whispered close to Rhonda's ear. "So do they. It's all fair in the end."

"I think it's amazing the way she is now compared to a few weeks ago," Kasey said, barely able to contain her excitement as they stood in the small barn.

Patrick leaned back against Dade's van and smiled at Cora. "You lovelies wouldn't be planning something, would you now?

Cora smiled sweetly at him. "A woman must have some secrets, Detective Blaine, or fantasies."

Patrick almost blushed at her tone. "Let me know when all of you are back safely." Then he got into the van.

Dade nodded and gave Coralee a curious look. She smiled sweetly and got into the van. He glanced over at the other men. Each one clearly caught that, just as they had back at the house. They now had five sexy witches in their lives who were definitely up to something.

The women were out of the vehicles and into Leena's house before they had them in park. Chris got out and leaned against the car waiting for the others to come over. "Is it just me, or is there something going on we haven't been apprised of?"

Steven nodded. "I have never heard Rachel talk so much, *ever*. I couldn't get a word in edgewise all the way home."

Dade stuck his hands in his pockets. "Coralee had me talk about work and the maintenance I do at the retirement homes. Which is definitely a first."

Owen scowled. "Leena went to sleep, or I think she was."

They turned to Chris. He shrugged. "Kasey was silent and sat still all the way home."

Something was going on.

Dade ran his hand through his long hair. "Do we risk asking?" He smirked. "If we piss them off, well, we saw what Kase can do. The four of them together could be a little more than we can handle. Do we take the chance?"

Chris nodded. "Oh, yes we do. After Kasey's stunt earlier this week, I don't think I'd survive another one."

They walked into the house, and not one of the women was present. "Lee?" Chris stood in the living room.

"We'll be down in a second, just showing them something."

Chris's eyebrows went up as he looked at the other men.

"They know," Cora whispered.

Rachel bit her lip. "How?"

Kasey shrugged, even though she wasn't feeling very calm about it. "I'm not about to say something. I'll get locked up until after Lammas." Then she looked at them. "I still can't believe what we're planning. The guys are not going to be happy at all."

Cora licked lips. "I don't think we really have a choice, do we? I can't go through what I did at Solstice. If Rhonda hadn't been able to project to me... we may not have found her until it was too late."

Rachel lowered her head. "It's sad she didn't even get to go to her friend's funeral."

Kasey frowned. "We can take her to the grave as soon as she's well enough."

Cora sat on the edge of the sewing table. "If we don't go through with our plans for Lammas, Rhonda is never going to be able to go out again. Not with the killer being so mad that she lived."

Rachel sighed. "So, back to the men, how do we prevent them from asking too many questions? If they even suspect, we'll all be in serious trouble."

Leena grabbed some material. "I'll try to distract them from it, I hope."

They walked in to find the men were sprawled in the living room. "What were you showing them, baby?" Owen asked her quietly.

Leena smiled and walked over to Chris. "Designs for new outfits, for Lammas."

Owen grinned.

Leena stopped in front of Chris and held up a sheer dark green material. "Chris, maybe you can help. I can't decide whether to dress Kasey in this." She held up a bright pink see-through lace. "Or this."

Chris looked over at Kasey and then back to the materials. "Either one instills many pleasing thoughts in my mind." He smirked. "I'll leave it up to you. Anything you've ever made is...perfect for her."

Kasey came over and sat on his lap. "You're so sweet." She snuggled into his arms. He kissed the top of her head while looking over at Dade.

"Coralee, Rhonda hasn't been sending you any more images that would help, has she?" Dade watched her carefully.

Cora shook her head and looked down at her hands for a moment before answering him. "No. I can't explain all of it, a woman's confidences and everything, but most are just from frustration. She and Patrick are rubbing each other the wrong way."

"Last question." Steven looked over at Rachel, who was playing with her lip, causing her tongue ring to pop in and out of her mouth. "Are you ladies planning some secret spells or such for Lammas?"

Leena sat down beside Owen. "Of course not. What we're planning, I'm sure you gentlemen will enjoy very, very much."

Owen pulled her against him. "Yeah, baby?"

"Of course," she whispered against his mouth.

Dade cleared his throat. "Well, that's what I need, more fantasies. Thanks, ladies." He stood up and looked at Cora. "Do you want a ride home?" Dade stood without moving as she got up and started to walk by him, then stopped and kissed him on the mouth.

"Let me know if you need fuel for those fantasies, Dade Jones."

Watching her walk to the door, he grinned. "Honey, just watching you fuels more than you'll ever know."

Steven watched the two walk out and turned to Rachel with a grin. "I need refueling too." She turned and looked at him, then walked over and picked up his hand. His eyes watched her as she licked his palm slowly. "That should help." She winked at him, then walked to the door.

Steven silently sat there until she had left. "Yep, that'll do it." He sighed. "I'll see everyone Wednesday." Getting up slowly, he glanced at Chris. "You'll have the results of the lists?"

Chris nodded without looking away from Kasey. "Yes. Although none of them match either Beltane or Solstice's attendance, but we still might get lucky."

Kasey pouted. "Does everyone use their real names at gatherings, though?"

Steven paused near the door. "They do, Kase, for emergency purposes. You can't phone someone and say your daughter Moonbeam Fluffy Bunny has fallen drunk in the river and hurt herself when their daughter's name is actually Tiffany."

Kasey sighed. "Well, there has to be something on them that will match an address, or something."

Steven shrugged at her and walked out the front door.

Chris ran a soothing hand down her arm. "We're still checking, sweetheart." He didn't want the risk she'd put herself in to be for nothing either. Kasey smiled at him. "Let's go home." Biting her bottom lip, she grinned at him again and leaned closer to him. "Take me to your lair, Christopher."

Chris grinned as he stood with her still in his arms. "We'll see you Wednesday at Cora's."

Owen sat for a silent moment. "What are you four up to?" He stroked a hand down Leena's long hair. "I don't have to read minds to know there's something going on."

She leaned into him and nuzzled against his neck. "We were discussing the possibilities for a handfast date."

His eyebrows went up. "I told you, you decide, and I'll be there." He rubbed his jaw. "And also letting me know how this happens might be good too."

She smiled. "I was thinking New Year's Day, pagan New Year's, that is. November first." She kissed him. "A new year, a new life together..."

Owen pulled her into his lap. "If that's what you want,

baby, then November first it is."

She hugged his wandering lips to her. "Would be nice if Kasey and Chris decided to get married too, then it could be a double. Wouldn't that be nice?"

He didn't reply, couldn't for a moment, and then he grinned at her with his boyish smile. "Let's go to bed."

She smiled. "I'll be there in two minutes." She had to send a message to the girls and tell them she was getting married on New Year's Day.

ಌಲ **Chapter 20** ಲಌ

Chris tried again to catch up to Kasey. Since Leena sent the message that the handfast date had been decided on, she was beyond calming. "Sweetheart, come here." He pointed to the spot right in front of him.

She turned and came back down the hall. "I just want to go look some things up. I'll need to start working on a gift for them." She stopped a few feet from him and smiled. "It's so wonderful! Leena has been so happy with Owen, and she deserves it. Now she's going to be his wife!" She turned again.

He laughed. "You have three months to figure out a gift. I'll buy ten of everything if that's what you want."

"It's not the same," she called out going into the temple room.

Frustrated, he walked slowly towards the door she'd gone through. By the time he got there, she was leaning over his worktable flipping through one of his crystal books. The energies of sheer happiness and excitement came off her in waves. She was barely able to stand still as she read, that perfect bottom under her short skirt teasing him with each movement.

She mumbled the odd thing as she went through the

pages.

He went up behind her and bent over her, pulling her tight against him. "I thought you wanted to go to my lair?" he whispered against the back of her neck.

Kasey paused. "I do. I'm just so excited I can't stop."

He ran his hand down over her stomach to rest between her legs and pulled her gently back against him. "I'll help you settle down, Kassandra."

Her arm reached up and circled his neck, pulling him against her. "We could make use of all those nice cushions over there."

Chris bit the back of her neck as he ran his hands up to cup her breasts through the little top she wore. "We'll get there eventually." She pushed back into him, rubbing against him. He ran his hand down over her bare thigh and back up, pulling the skirt up out of his way.

Her skin was so soft he moaned against the side of her neck. "I want you here, now, like this," he growled.

She trembled at his touch. Smiling, he loved that he was able to make her wet just with a few words. Reaching, she pulled her top over her head and then dropped it on the table in front of her. He immediately ran his hands over her breasts and began kneading them gently.

"Show me," she whispered hoarsely, turning her head so she could bite gently against his neck.

"I often sat in here thinking about you, until I shook with wanting you, Kasey." He moved his hand to stroke between her legs. "Every time I'd look at this perfect, sexy body of yours, I'd get so hard it took my breath away." She gasped as he continued to rub. He leaned down so his mouth could devour her throat. He undid his jeans with a quick hand and pushed them to the floor.

Pushing his hard length between her legs from behind, he rocked gently, rubbing against the damp material covering her.

She pushed back against him, leaning farther over the table.

"Chris, you make me want you so much, with only a few words." Her breathing was already fast. "Show me." She moaned as he squeezed one nipple through the lace covering her. She reached down between her legs and ran her fingers over him. He gasped when she touched him.

He slid his hand down her back and reached under her skirt to grasp the thin material. Leaning away, he pulled the material with one jerk from her flesh and heard her whimper and drop her head. Stroking her, he pushed two fingers inside her and almost lost control when he felt how wet she was.

He leaned over forward and bit into her neck. "What do you want, sweet Kassandra?" She pushed back against him and moved her head to give him access.

"You." She panted against his arm resting under her on the table. "Now."

He rubbed himself back and forth over the wetness and pushed the head of his erection against her. She pushed back against him, whimpering. He continued to tease her, and himself, several more times, until she was pushing back against him, trying to push him inside her.

"Now?" he whispered against her ear.

"Yes." She panted. "I want you inside me, Chris." She pushed back into him. "I need you inside me."

Hearing her words, he slowly pushed into her, wanting to feel as he pushed through her soft folds. She was even tighter in this position, and he groaned when he was all the way inside her. She pushed back against him, squirming, trying to get him to move.

"Slow, I want to take you slow." He pulled back out slowly and had to grip her hip with one hand to stop her from moving quickly.

Kasey was gasping against his arm resting under her and biting into it with each slow movement he made. When her small hand touched between their legs, he moaned. She was never shy and always wanted to feel.

As he stroked in again slowly, her hand bushed against him and cupped him when their bodies fit tightly. She kneaded gently with her hand.

He growled. "Witch, I can't go slow if you do that." She squeezed again as he pushed into her. Pulling himself more upright, he gripped her hips and looked down at their connecting bodies. His heart pounded faster. The sight of him taking her would not be something he'd ever tire of. Hissing out a breath, he pushed into her harder. She squeaked against the table. The noises she made broke his control every time.

Placing a gentle hand on the small of her back, he held her in place as his other hand grasped her hip, and he pulled against her quickly. She was panting and moaning as each thrust got harder. When her muscles contracted against him so tightly, his legs tensed, and he heard himself cry out with her.

Caressing her back, he took a few breaths. "Fuck, Kasey! I'm going to have to tie you down if I'm ever going to make love to you slowly."

Kasey sighed. "I don't think I'd live through slowly."

Pulling away from her, he turned her in his arms and held her against him. "You deserve slow and long... but then you touch me, and I'm lost." Her hands were pushing his shirt up over his head.

Realizing he was still half dressed, he threw the shirt to the table and stepped clear of his jeans. He scooped her up against his chest and carried her over and settled them on the cushions.

She sighed against him. "Well that table certainly proved useful, huh?"

He kissed her mouth lingeringly. "Yes, and as soon as I've caught my breath, we're going to see if these cushions are useful."

She grinned and pushed him back, straddling his larger body. Running her hands down over his chest slowly, she licked her lips. "Well, you just lie there and rest then. I'll find something to do until you're ready." She balanced herself on his chest and rocked her hips slowly over him. "Oh. Hmm. I think I need to try it this way, Chris."

Chris watched her bite her lower lip and felt himself stirring back to life under her. "My own sexy, wanton witch." He grinned. "Take off that bra, and let me watch, sweetheart." Her hands shed the bra and sent it flying behind them.

Watching her rock over him with her eyes closed and wearing only the short shirt, he groaned. "You're so fucking beautiful, Kassandra. I can't breathe when I look at you." She smiled down at him with heavy eyes, and he growled when her hands ran slowly down over her body. "Fuck," he whispered, pulling her mouth down to his.

"I love you," she whispered against his lips.

He kissed her hungrily. "Show me."

Chris didn't know how long he'd been lying awake beside her. She was curled into his body and sleeping, with good reason. By the time he'd carried her up to bed, she'd done a very thorough job of tiring them both out.

She looked so innocent in sleep. *His.* The word kept coming back in his mind. She was finally his, and each time he looked at her, he couldn't believe it. How he had managed it, he still wasn't sure. He did know he'd spend the rest of his life making sure she was happy. He wanted to hold her like this every day, every night, every morning.

He let out a slow breath and kissed her softly. Would he ever not feel like if he turned his head she'd disappear? He didn't think so.

Grinning to himself, he finally pulled her tightly against him and rested his head above hers. He had some plans to put into motion tomorrow, which would involve many favors on a Sunday.

Kasey woke alone. Rolling over, she looked at his pillow to see a note. He couldn't be working on a Sunday, could he? She focused, trying to read the note.

Had some things to take care of. Rest so I can tire you out again when I get home. Love, Chris.

She smiled thinking of the night before.

Stretching, she climbed out of the big bed. She could get those rewrites finished this morning while waiting for him to return.

She had just settled down on the floor with her laptop in the living room, with a hot coffee in her hand, when the doorbell rang. Sighing, she jumped up. When she opened the door with a smile, there was no one there.

Stepping out, she looked around. Were there kids in this neighborhood? Hmm.

Glancing down, she spotted an envelope. She picked it up and kicked the door closed. Slowly she turned the envelope over looking for a name. It wasn't addressed to anyone. Shrugging, she opened it. Chris couldn't blame her if she opened a blank envelope.

Her breath caught in her chest as she read the words.

You should have let her die for her sins.

Dropping the note, she ran to the door and locked it.

Flying through the house, she locked all the rest of the doors and then ran upstairs to her room and closed the door. She took a few breaths and grabbed her bag, digging in it for her cell phone. She opened it quickly and dialed Chris's cell number.

"Good morning, beautiful,"

"He was here!"

"What? Who?" The radio in the background disappeared. "Who was there?"

"There was a note on the front steps." She heard his car accelerate.

"Where are you?"

"I'm in my room. I locked all the doors. Chris, come home."

"I'm on my way. Stay there. Don't open the door to anyone. I'll be there in fifteen minutes." She heard him turn quickly around a corner. "It's going to be all right, sweetheart. I'll be there shortly.

She slid into the corner and sat there. "Okay, hurry!" She hung up the phone.

Chris didn't remember ever driving so fast in his life. He pulled in and jumped out just as Dade pulled up. Not bothering to close the car door, he ran across the lawn.

Dade caught up. "Don't touch the doorbell. Kasey told me he rang the doorbell."

Chris nodded and stuck his key in the lock. He wasn't all the way through the door when he started yelling. "Kasey!" He heard a door slam and her running. He met her halfway up the stairs and caught her in his arms.

"I was so scared," she whispered into his chest.

"I'm here now." He turned, carrying her down with her legs wrapped tightly around his waist. Dade stood looking at the note on the floor where it had fallen. "Don't touch it."

Dade looked up and nodded. "Get me a piece of paper and tape. I want to cover the doorbell until Patrick gets here. He was already headed this way when I called him."

Chris walked towards the living room still holding Kasey. "Paper's in the library." He sat on the couch kissing her face gently. "It's okay, sweetheart. I'm here now."

"How did he find us, Chris?" She was shaking.

"Well, it's easier to find us then for us to find him. We weren't exactly hiding." He scowled. *But would they have to hide now?*

Rachel flew into the living room with Cora right behind her. "Is she okay?" She dropped down beside him.

"Just scared. He rang the bell and left the note."

Cora covered her mouth. "He knows where we are?"

Chris nodded. "Apparently."

Cora jumped when Dade came into the room. He walked over and hugged her against him. "What are we going to do, Dade?"

Dade stroked his hand down her back, holding her against him. "Let's wait until Patrick and the others get here, honey, and we'll figure it out."

A teary-eyed Leena walked in with Owen's arm holding her close. "Kasey," she whispered.

Kasey turned and looked at Leena. She climbed out of Chris's arms slowly and then stepped quickly into Leena's. "He knows us," she said as the other two women hugged them.

Steven came running in, still wearing his hospital scrubs. "Patrick was pulling in right behind me." Rachel went to him and hugged him tightly against her. He wrapped his arm around her and pushed her head gently against his shoulder.

A tired-looking Patrick walked in. "Leaving the door wide open may not be advisable at this point." He looked around the room. "Did anyone other than Kasey touch the note and envelope?" Everyone shook their head. "I've got some guys on the way over to check for prints. We'll need those from each of you if you haven't already."

Kasey turned and looked at him. "How are we supposed to live when he knows where we are?"

Patrick sat down while making notes. "We don't know if he knows where all of you are." He motioned towards Chris. "If he was present during the commotion that morning at Solstice, he'd know Chris found Rhonda, and Chris isn't exactly hard to locate. The note could have just been for him."

Everyone turned to look at Chris.

Chris shrugged. "I'd be more than happy to discuss this with him face-to-face."

Kasey shrieked and climbed back into his lap. "You will not do any such thing!" She hugged his neck.

Leena set her purse down. "I'm going to make coffee. We left so fast I wasn't even sure if I had all my clothes on properly until we were halfway here."

Patrick waited until the other detectives left before herding all eight witches into the living room again. "So, you need to make a few temporary living arrangements." He motioned to Cora and Rachel. "You two are the only two women living alone."

Owen hugged Leena against him. "They can stay at my house. I'm at Leena's most of the time, and Dade lives about four minutes away."

Dade nodded. "I've got no problems with that."

Cora sat there for a few moments and looked around. "I don't like having to change my entire life because of some maniac."

Rachel nodded but didn't speak.

Kasey bit her lip. "I would feel better knowing you two weren't alone."

Cora smiled at her. "Well, Owen does have a really nice kitchen at his townhouse."

Rachel leaned back against Steven's legs. "And it is closer to the community center." She looked over at Patrick. "But what do we do with our present homes? How long are we expected to rearrange our lives for this sicko?"

Patrick closed the notebook and put it in his pocket before speaking. "I can't really answer that. I wish I could tell you we're closer to catching him, but we're not. Even with the information you keep giving me, I'm running into dead ends." He looked down at his hands. "Those names we ran didn't turn up anything we can use. Several people have either passed away or don't even live in this country." He sighed. "Two of them seemed to have vanished without a trace, no records of any kind." He shrugged. "People change their names every day. Without doing it on paper, there's no way to find them."

Chris ran a hand down over his face. "Any addresses match any of them you have?"

Patrick shook his head.

"Can you get into tax records? They have to file taxes, don't they?"

Patrick nodded. "They do, but that doesn't mean they are." He grinned. "People aren't as honest as you lot."

Dade laughed. "Well that's the first time I've be accused of that."

Cora threw at pillow at him. "You couldn't tell a lie if you needed to, Mr. Dade Jones. You just flirt your way out of trouble."

Chris sighed and pinched the bridge of his nose. "This is not the day I had planned." Standing, he put his hands in his pockets. "I'll do some more digging." He grinned at Patrick. "I have some contacts that honest police don't use."

Patrick raised his hands. "I don't want to know, but if it will help me nail this bastard, then by all means pass along anything you find, Larkin." He got up and looked around. "I have to get back. Rhonda felt so good after you left yesterday we almost had to chain her to the bed to make her stay put." He ran a hand along the back of his neck. "I don't know what I'm going to do to keep her safe once she's at full strength again."

Chris studied the man for a moment. "Oh, I'm sure it will come to you."

Patrick winked at him. "It will at that." He headed to the door. "All doors stay locked at all times. No wandering around alone, you know the drill. I'll be in touch." There was silence as they watched him close the door.

Everyone jumped when they heard a crash.

Dade was the first one to reach the sitting room again.

A picture, which had been on the wall, now lay face down on the floor. Kasey stood looking at it with her hands on her hips. "I'm so mad! This psycho is out there running around able to do whatever the hell he wants, and we have to stay locked up like we've done something wrong!" She flung her hands out away from her body, and all of the pillows flew off the couches into the air before hitting the walls.

Dade looked from her to Chris, who was standing there with a stupid grin on his face. Personally, he was debating on taking cover, and the besotted idiot was standing there grinning.

"Kassandra. Calm down. You're scaring Dade," Chris said quietly with a smile on his face.

Kasey turned and looked at Dade and then to Chris. He was smiling! "Oh, you can smile. You're big enough to just squash anyone that presents a problem. I'm not so lucky."

Chris put his hands back in his pockets and leaned against the doorframe. "Sweetheart, if this maniac had any idea what you were capable of, he'd run to the nearest cop and confess everything."

He pulled his one hand out of his pocket and looked down at it. "This was not the day I had planned or the way I intended to do this, but I think now is a good time." He opened his hand, and a shimmering silver orb floated above his palm.

It moved slowly by everyone, towards the vibrating woman at the other end of the room.

Kasey watched the orb with suspicious eyes until it hovered right in front of her face. She couldn't see what was inside the small sphere. She looked over at Chris.

Chris placed his hand over his heart and smiled at her. "I don't have the right words as Owen does, or Dade's smooth style. I can't charm you as the Doc could, Kassandra. I just know I've loved you since the first moment you smiled at me, and for more than six years now, I've waited to show you." Her huge eyes glanced at the orb and then back at him. "Hold out your left hand, Kasey."

Kasey held an unsteady hand in front of the orb. The shimmering light ran up over her fingers.

Chris was having problems focusing on the orb and watching her sweet face at the same time. "You've only to say you will be my wife, little green-eyed witch, and let me have a lifetime to make you happy."

Kasey turned happy eyes towards him and whispered, "Yes."

The shimmering stopped, and left in its place was a gold ring with tiny diamonds shaped like a fairy. She looked at it and then smiled and ran towards him.

Chris caught her without a stumble and kissed her with

every ounce of love he felt for her at that moment.

"Talk about being outdone," Owen mumbled from beside them.

Chris hugged her and glanced at the happy faces. "It was either that or let her blow up half the house until she was calmed down."

Bright fireworks flew over their heads before floating slowly down until they shimmered and then turned to dust.

Dade patted him on the back. "I still say you'd better start taking vitamins, old man. She'll have you wore out in a month."

Chris grinned. "I hope so."

He couldn't blame the lawyer.

He didn't know the woman had sinned.

In any other instance, saving a woman was the right thing to do.

Now he would know why she was to have died and wouldn't stand in the way of punishing a woman's sins.

Now he would know

✺ **Chapter 21** ✺

Kasey kissed Chris and climbed out of the car. She was just going to the entrance when she spotted Owen's Jeep pull up, followed by Steven's car.

Once the four women were inside the building, they stopped and looked at each other.

Leena looked at Rachel and Cora for a moment. "Did anyone know about this escorting-us-to-work plan?" They shook their heads.

"He was outside my building when I came out this morning," Cora griped.

Rachel quirked an eyebrow. "I'm all for suggestions on how to correct this situation. Am I supposed to take one of them with me if I'm on a date?" She jammed her hands into her back pockets. "I thought if we agreed to stay at Owen's for a few weeks they'd settle down."

Kasey sighed and wanted to kick something. "There was no chance of me getting out of the house alone this morning. I even tried sex."

Cora smirked. "Well, that's the first I've heard that from your mouth."

Kasey blushed. "I'm sure I could shock you quite easily now."

Rachel put a hand on Kasey's shoulder. "No distracting me with talk of sex, sweetie." She looked at Leena. "What are we going to do?"

Leena was silent for a moment, then looked at Kasey. "Chris's little temple room well stocked?" Kasey nodded. "Good. Whichever male shows up to take us home tonight is taking us to Chris and Kasey's. We have work to do."

Cora rubbed her hand over her forehead in frustration. "It better be good. Lammas is a week away, and I don't think I can deal with one of them following me around for longer than that." She looked down at her feet. "And what we have planned for Lammas had better work, or I will have a nervous breakdown."

Chris came out of his library to see the three men sitting in his living room. He paused and looked around. "Did I forget about a meeting?" *Where were the women?* "Where is everyone else?"

Dade leaned forward and rested his elbows on his knees. "We were instructed they were coming here after work, and they have been locked in your little magic broom closet for the last hour."

Chris raised his eyebrows. "Doing?"

Owen lifted his hands. "Won't say."

Steven slumped down on the couch. "They're not too pleased being driven to and from work."

"I see." Chris turned and started down the hall. "Let's see what they're up to."

The men got up and followed him.

He tried the doorknob to find it locked. "Kase, unlock the door."

"Soon," she called to him through the door.

He stood there glaring at the door. They'd locked him out of his own room in his own home. *We'll see about this.* He stepped back and slapped an invisible command at the door.

Sparks flew off it, and the door remained closed. "What the..."

Dade grinned. "Quite the little witch you have there, Larkin."

Steven whistled out a breath. "Just how much trouble can they get into with all your stuff in there?"

Chris still scowled at the door while he answered. "A lot." He tapped the door with his hand. "Kassandra, unlock the door."

A gentle breeze blew over all four of them.

"That would be a polite no," Dade said quietly.

"Like hell I'll be locked out of my own temple room," Chris hissed. Stepping back, he stared at the door. The handle shook. When he thought it was going to open, it started to pour rain on the four of them. He waved a hand to stop it and looked at the men beside him. Dade's long hair was soaked, and the expression on his face was similar to how he was feeling about the whole thing.

"And that would be a mind your own damn business," Owen said, sticking his hands in his pockets.

Chris looked at Steven. "You have any ideas?"

Steven shook his head trying to get the water to stop dripping in his face, then took a step away from the door. "Oh no. I'm plenty happy enough to wait until it opens on its own. You might like lightning striking you, but I'm not too open to trying that."

Chris shook his head. "Are you all afraid of them?"

Dade nodded. "I've seen what each one can do alone, especially your little innocent there, my friend. The four of them together scare the hell out of me."

Chris sighed and looked back at the door. "Kasey?"

"Yes, Christopher?" Her voice came through the door again.

"You're making me angry, and I don't want to do something I've promised you I wouldn't."

A gentle breeze ruffled his hair. "I know you won't, Chris. Now go away. I'm trying to concentrate here."

His jaw dropped. Sighing, he looked at the others. "Beer?" They nodded and followed him down the hallway.

"Seems you're a bit afraid of their wrath too, counselor," Dade mumbled behind him.

"Shut up," Chris growled and walked into the kitchen.

When the women walked into the living room, they were met with four glares.

"Oh!" Kasey jumped and pulled the gris-gris bag from under her shirt. She looked at the women. "Wow, do they ever work." The other three nodded. Turning her head, she looked at Chris. "You need to calm down."

"Do I?" he said softly.

She frowned at his expression, then put her hands on her hips. "Yes, you do." A chair came across the room and nudged the back of her knees.

"Have a seat and explain to me why I was locked out of my own temple room." He hadn't moved a muscle.

Sparks flew towards him.

He glared at her and the sparks vanished with a simple wave of his hand.

Kasey watched the other women sit quietly, obviously not wanting furniture to come at them.

Cora held up a hand and stared at the men. "Did you really think we were going to just sit by and let the four of you tell us where we could and couldn't go, and be escorted quietly?"

Dade leaned forward. "Yes. We are not targets of some maniac out there."

She turned cold eyes towards him.

"Would you rather we don't say a thing and wait until it's too late, Coralee?" he asked her.

Cora sighed. "No. But you have to let us breathe." She looked at the other women for a moment. "We're not used to having to answer to anyone. You have to give us some room to breathe, Dade. Rachel and I have agreed to move into Owen's and not be alone at night until this is settled. The occasional ride to and from somewhere is also welcome. But are you going to sit at the mall and watch us shop, then usher us home, too, every time?"

Dade crossed his arms over his chest and sat back. "If I have to."

Kasey watched Rachel turn and glare at Steven. "How do you plan on babysitting us with your schedule?"

Steven shrugged. "I can switch things around if you need to be somewhere." He leaned towards her. "Although dating might get tricky." He grabbed at his mouth as if something were covering it.

Rachel grinned at Kasey. "Oh, that's awesome. Thanks for the lesson."

Kasey smirked and then looked over at Steven.

Rachel turned back to him. "If I require someone to go with me on a date, and I do plan on having a life still, I will double with Cora if need be."

Dade snorted.

Steven looked at Chris with angry eyes, still trying to brush the unseen hand from his mouth.

"Enough!" Chris waved a hand so Steven could speak, and looked around at the four women. Kasey sat there in the chair he'd shoved at her with her arms crossed looking every inch the witch. "Slapping magic at each other isn't going to solve anything. Now explain what you were doing and what you said when you came out. What have you done?" He watched and waited.

Kasey sighed and got up to pace. "It took quite a while to get it, and it required all four of our skills to do it. We've charmed the gris-gris bags to be warning systems. They'll warn us if there are any angry or evil intentions towards us. They should work at a fair distance too." She grinned at Chris. "As soon as we were finished and placed them on, we could feel your emotions before we opened the door. The closer we got to you, the stronger it became."

Chris sat back and looked at her, his anger fading quickly. Of course, it annoyed him when it was replaced with pride, because he really wanted to be mad at her right now.

"Fine. We'll give you a bit of space, but if any one of you feels even the slightest twinge of anything, I want you to get someplace secure and get a hold of any one of us." He looked around at the other men, who obviously weren't happy either. "Deal?"

Kasey shrieked and landed in his lap. Grabbing his face, she kissed him hard. "Deal," she whispered against his mouth.

"Can we take this opportunity to get the list and any plans for Lammas organized?" Steven grumbled. "I have to start pulling favors and shifts to cover for me so I can go away for a few days again. Half of me is happy to get four days instead of three. The other part of me isn't really comfortable with vacationing alongside a killer."

Rachel smiled at him. "I'll keep ya safe, Doc."

He rolled his eyes at her.

"So, who is doing the shopping? And I think it would be more cost efficient if we didn't send Owen this time." Leena laughed, looking at him as she said it.

Kasey wiggled out of Chris's lap and slipped onto the floor. Holding her hand up, Kasey grinned when a pad and pen came around the corner into her hand. "I've really been practicing," she said to Dade, who groaned. "Okay, so who needs what? Chris and I'll do the shopping this time around."

"Are we following the same vehicle arrangements as well?" Owen inquired, looking around to see shrugs and nods. "Alrighty, then." He glanced at Chris. "It would make me feel much better if you were to tell me you've made some sort of connection or have some kind of lead with that list of names."

Chris ran his hand down the back of Kasey's hair. "I wish I could. All we can hope is he makes a mistake this time and we get to him before anyone is hurt."

Cora leaned forward and said in a tone that had everyone holding their breath, "He won't harm another woman again."

The three women looked over at her and met her determined look with an understanding of things to come.

This Lammas gathering would be one to remember always.

KEEP READING FOR AN EXCERPT FROM
THE NEXT BOOK IN THE MAGIC SEASONS
ROMANCE

Book 3

By Jacqueline Paige

ꙮ Chapter 1 ꙮ

Rachel sat there in silence, her mind filled with too many thoughts. They had to be bordering on insane, all eight of them to go to a third gathering—knowing the killer was going to be there again. Although unlike the Beltane murders, one had survived the attempt at Solstice. She felt sick to her stomach when she thought of Rhonda barely surviving the attack. Would she be able to go through something like that, and still carry on after? She didn't know. How Rhonda was managing to not lose her mind since having to hide, she'd never understand. The scars she'd been left with…and knowing your friend died and you survived… Rachel didn't know if she could ever be as strong as Rhonda.

Cora nudged Rachel's arm and showed her a text message.

Keep in touch. Would be there to help if I could. Blow their minds. Rhonda

Rachel snorted. "Easy for her to say she won't be there." Remembering the men in the front seat, she grimaced at Cora. "I think it's so wonderful, a double hand fasting at New Years. I'm so jealous." She pouted. "I hope they start making babies soon so I can be Aunt Rach and spoil them rotten."

Dade glanced at her in the mirror. "Most people like to wait until after they're actually wed before they make those babies, Aunt Rach."

Steven turned around and leered at her. "I have no problems with children before marriage. Just let me know if you want one of your own, sexy witch. I'll be happy to help in any way I can."

Dade snorted. "It amazes me you aren't black and blue from using those lines, Doc."

Rachel leaned forward. "I actually could use your help, Steven." She said it seriously.

Steven's eyebrows shot up. Both men looked at each other and then he turned back toward her. She kept her voice quiet. "My little foster guy isn't doing all that well, would you be willing to do a consult when we get back?"

Steven tapped the side of his head and grinned. "You had me dreaming for a second, angel," he smirked. "I'd be happy to."

Rachel smiled. "Wonderful. It's just so sad. To be six and not have the energy to run breaks my heart. The clinic has done a few tests, but nothing shows up. He just keeps getting thinner and weaker. I don't think they're really looking." She rubbed her hands together and studied them for a moment, before looking back up at him. "He had a really bad case of the flu last fall and he's never really been the same since. You know how crowded the ward homes are... His caregivers have been trying *everything*." She glanced to see a sympathetic look on Cora's face. "I almost didn't come this weekend, but Ricky told me to go and celebrate for him." She sniffed and reached into her purse.

Dade gave her a wide-eyed look in the mirror before he glared over at Doc.

Steven turned sideways in the seat to face her. *Does she know how much he wanted to hold her?* "Do you know anything about his medical or family history?"

Rachel nodded as she played with the edge of her skirt. "His mother was a drug addict, she didn't want him."

Steven sighed and unbuckled his seat belt. He knew what the child of a Drug addict usually meant. Improper eating, no prenatal care and the list of illnesses the children suffered from were longer than he wanted to admit. He pushed between the two front seats and half kneeled, half squatted in front of her. He'd worry about being stuck later. "You get him in to see me. Don't worry about an appointment, just show up whenever it's good for you." He caressed her cheek softly. "You know I'll do anything humanly or otherwise possible for him, don't you?" *For you* he added inside his head.

Rachel gave him a shaky smile. "Thank you. I just worry."

He leaned up and kissed her softly on the lips. "That's a good trait in a mother, angel, foster or otherwise." He kissed her again and turned before he pushed his luck too far.

Dade looked at him solemly. He glanced in the mirror at the women again.

Cora looked over at Rachel, who had turned to look out the window, then peered into the back of the van. "Dade, did you bring your base djembi along?"

Dade's eyes met hers in the mirror. "That and a couple others, honey. Why do you ask?"

Coralee gave him a sweet smile. The kind of smile he usually had to work really hard to get. "I think I'll want to hear that one at the Saturday night revel fire."

He grinned then winked at her. "I would love to play it for you, it makes my mouth water when you dance." She smiled again but didn't reply. *What are they up to?*

Rachel sat turned towards the window. Steven had given her some hope, at least. Between worrying about Ricky and quivering nerves over the plan she and the other women concocted, this was going to be one very long weekend. She watched the fields go by, the crops of corn and beans were deep green and ripening each day. Lammas, the celebration of the first harvest.

Smiling, she looked up at the trees scattered along the road here and there. They were full and green, and looked so alive. The last thought sobered her. Glancing at Steven she smiled, if anyone could help Ricky it would be him. *Does he know how much his always being there when I need it means to me? Probably not.* Steven had been her shoulder to cry on since she was a silly teen, and she hoped she would always have him.

Steven turned to look at Rachel again. The short skirt rode up with her legs crossed, he'd almost dropped a kiss on the witch tattooed on her thigh. He turned back, couldn't even look at her now without thinking of her witch. Or worse, every time she licked her lips all he pictured was that tongue ring and what she could do with that. Where were all the fairy godmothers when you needed one? He had only one wish, and she was in the back seat.

He rubbed his hand over his brow. Would she hold it against him if her little buddy were as ill as he worried? Warning bells had gone off as soon as she'd told him that he'd never bounced back from the flu.

Catching Dade glancing at him, he sighed. Hopefully it was something simple, a nutritional deficiency, not uncommon for children of addicts, their bodies had complications like that all the time. Shaking himself out of doctor mode, he grinned back at the women.

"So, are we going to need bibs to sop up the drool seeing you all in Leena's latest outfits?"

Cora grinned at him. "I think that's the only reason you come along with us, Steven. To see what Leena's created."

He bobbed his head in agreement. "That and I love looking around the fire and noticing every male there watching the four of you walk away with *us*. Does wonders for a man ego."

Dade was chuckling quietly. "Wouldn't do much if they knew the truth."

"Yeah well, that's privileged information," Steven mumbled.

Rachel smiled, "It's a half-truth now if it makes you feel better. Owen and Chris get to be with some of us."

Steven playfully patted his heart and grinned at her. "You are a nasty witch, angel. Stomping on a man's dreams like that." Hearing her laugh made his burden lighter.

Dade leaned forward. "Somewhere on this road between fields, there is a lane we need to be turning down. Call out if you spot anything that looks like that."

Climbing out of the van Rachel stretched up then bent down to touch her toes. Long nights of sitting in chairs watching Ricky had her stiff and sore. Riding in the not so comfortable van didn't help. She bolted back up at the whistle behind her.

"You make me glad I'm a man, Rach."

She turned to grin at Steven and let her eyes slowly appraise his stocky build from head to toe, "You most certainly are a man, Dr. O'Reily." She stepped over and ran her hand over his large bicep. "How does a Doctor have time to make a body like this?"

He looked down at her hand briefly before looking back at her. She watched his eyes follow her tongue, running across her lower lip. "I work out whenever I'm not working. Let me know if you need to see more, I'd be happy to show you, angel."

Dade walked up. "Quit before you make her mad."

Rachel ran her hand down his arm again before stepping away. "Oh, Dade, I don't know, I might have to take him up on that offer someday." She flicked her tongue making her piercing stick out before grinning and walking to join the others.

"I want to fall to my knees and beg every time I see that damn stud in her tongue," Steven whispered when she was far enough away.

Dade nodded. "They do it on purpose to drive men crazy."

Chris stopped and watched Kasey as she went over to the women. "Do what to drive men crazy?" He asked quietly.

"Get things pierced," Steven muttered.

Chris grinned. "Works fine too. I can't think every time Kase has hers showing."

Dade grunted. "Well, at least you get to *appreciate* it closely. The rest of us just stand back and dream."

Chris put an arm around each man's shoulder as they turned towards everyone. "When it comes to Kasey's piercing, that's all you'd better ever think about doing."

Kasey turned and sent him a look. "Christopher, play nice."

"Always, sweetheart." Chris winked at Steven as he hugged her from behind, his hand possessively resting over the little fairy in her belly button.

Rachel looked from Chris to Steven. "Did I miss something? Chris is all puffed out and you two look like you left your favorite toys at home."

Steven winked and put an arm around Rachel, slowly pulling her up against him. "I'd smile again if you'd help me forget my lost toy." He leaned down and nuzzled his face against her neck. She smelled so good.

Rachel laughed and hugged him. "I'll give it some thought." She leaned back and looked up at him. "What is up with you today? Normally you sleep the whole time in the car, unless you're driving, and that's questionable sometimes, and you're being a bigger hound dog than usual."

He ran his hands up and down her sides gently. "I can't help it. You look so good today, angel."

Owen cleared his throat. "Would you please hurry up and strike out so we can register and go find the cottage."

Everyone laughed and patted Steven on the back walking past him towards the small building. Stretching up against him Rachel ran her tongue up his neck and then smiled and followed the others.

"Nasty witch," he whispered as she walked away.

Justin and Gwen stopped what they were doing as they came through the door. Gwen went around the table to hug everyone. "I'm so happy to see you all!"

Despite her words, the stress of the last few months showed on their faces. How Gwen projected her usual happy energy, Chris had no idea.

He lifted Kasey's hand and held it out towards Gwen. "Look what I caught." Kasey leaned back against him.

"Oh! Isn't that wonderful!" She walked over to them. Hugging Kasey she smiled. "I expect you're able to keep him in line, dear."

Kasey blushed. "I have a hard time keeping him in line from time to time, but it's nothing I can't handle." Chris pulled her back against him and kissed the top of her head, grinning down at Gwen.

Gwen turned and gave everyone an inquiring look. "Any other engagements?"

A shocked expression crossed Cora's face. "Is it contagious?"

Gwen smiled and hugged her. "I spoke with Rhonda this morning, she sends her best." Her look sobered for a moment.

Cora nodded. "Thank you." She glanced at Rachel and Kasey briefly.

Leena stepped away from Owen. "Is Patrick going to be here this weekend?"

Justin nodded. "He'll be here in a few hours. He had to wait for someone to replace him at the safe house."

Chris studied the women and hadn't missed the looks that passed between them. "Will we be able to see the attendance list later tonight?" Chris asked quietly.

Justin nodded. "I'll bring it down to the cabin before the opening circle." He smiled over at his wife. "Gwen has the cabin all ready for you. I'll take you over to see it when you're finished here." Justin kissed Gwen on the cheek and went out the door.

"Sweetheart, could you sign us in? I need a word with Justin before he gets too busy," Chris asked Kasey.

She nodded. "Sure."

Chris walked outside and stood beside Justin. "Your lovely wife has been acting funny too, Justin?"

The older man nodded. "Yes sir. They're up to something and I've tried everything I know to find out."

Chris put his hands in his pockets. "Well, if you catch wind of anything, please pass it on, we'll do the same." He glanced at the door and then back. "They're taking bigger chances and try as we might, we never can seem to stop them."

Justin slapped him lightly on the shoulder. "Wished I had some couple wisdom for you, but I'm still working it out myself." He shrugged, "it's only been forty years, I'm still hoping."

Chris laughed. "That's not comforting." He paused. "We almost lost Kase a few weeks back, she tried to do an astral search and connect to him, I don't know what they're planning, but I'm pretty sure we're not going to like it."

Justin just nodded as Kasey came out.

"We're ready for you to lead the way Justin."

Steven stood back shaking his head.

"It's so cute." Kasey giggled.

"It's *pink*." Dade stated loudly.

"I think it was probably at one time more of a red tint." Chris smiled at Dade. "Going to offend your manly nature to stay in a pink cottage?"

KEEP READING FOR AN EXCERPT OF

SALVATION

By Jacqueline Paige

Chapter One

He watched the child in silence, not that he could be heard even if he wanted. If his math was correct, she was three years old now. Stepping into the room and away from the window, he watched her small body shake as she pressed an ear against the door. He couldn't see her face with the fall of wavy black hair covering it. But he knew the face under her messed hair was round and angelic.

From the other side of the door she was carefully leaning against, he could hear the yelling...again. Her parents spent most of their time screaming at each other and breaking things. He'd sat with the child many times in the last year while the adults in her world showed her all the wrong ways to live.

It worried him that she no longer cried; no longer curled her tiny body into the corner and tried to make herself invisible. At least the quarrelling adults had never brought it to her; he didn't know if he could stand to see her hurt in any way. He closed his eyes and cursed himself; what could he even do to help if they did?

A loud crash brought him back to the moment; he opened his eyes to see the girl remove her ear from the door. Her face was visible now and it pulled at his heart to see tears rolling down her round cheeks. It made her dark brown eyes seem blurry and vague. She hugged her tiny arms around her middle, trying to comfort herself. A small part of him wanted to take her in his arms and shelter her from the sadness, not that he knew how to hold a child.

She took two steps back from the door but still watching, as if she was afraid it was going to fly open. She sniffled once and raised her face, then looked right at him. Did she actually see him? He was tempted to look behind to see if there was something there that would catch her attention, but he was afraid to look away and go back to being invisible to all.

She blinked and cleared the tears from her eyes yet continued to look right at him. With her chin up she used her sleeve to wipe across her face, then raised her chin with a determination he knew all too well. Her eyes appeared as if they were looking right into his, causing his heart, if he truly still had one, to jolt inside of his body.

Finally, she turned from him, went to the little table in the corner, and sat on the small chair. She opened a book, took colored sticks from a messy carton, and scribbled in angry motions over the outline of the picture in front of her.

Sighing, he closed his eyes. She would be fine. He really did need to stop coming here.

He had tried to stay away, as he knew he should, and had been able to watch from a distance. But the child lay on the bed with her face hidden, shaking and distraught. He didn't know what he could do, but he liked to believe his presence would be sensed and she would somehow be comforted.

Glancing away from her, he noticed papers crumpled up on the floor. He couldn't pick them up to look at them, but he could read part of one. "*Happy 7th birthday.*" She was seven already? Had not only a few months passed since she was that tiny cherub-faced child? He frowned. How had he lost track of four entire years? What did he have to keep track of except time? All he *had* was time, endless expanses of time.

Shaking his head, he stepped closer to the bed. If only he could offer a calming touch to let her know she wasn't alone. But in truth, she was; he could hear the screaming outside of the walls of her room, and knew that she was very much alone in this world.

She rolled onto her back, clutching something to her chest. With an angry swipe she wiped across her face and took a long shaky breath. He leaned down to see her better and was surprised to see how she had grown since he last let himself get this close. Gone was the childish softness. In its place, the beginning of a more mature form was now visible. He sighed and stepped back; this small one was going to be a world of trouble for some man in the years to come.

Looking back he found her eyes looking right at him, as only she had ever done. He stepped back in shock. He told himself she was just staring into space and it happened to be in his direction, but her eyes moved over his body in a slow, measured way. If he spoke would she hear him? He clenched his jaw; hadn't he spent years trying to be heard by others? He wouldn't waste one more ounce of energy on that ever again.

When she stood up, he almost stepped back again, afraid she'd go right through him and make him feel undetectable. Instead, she stopped in front of him to look up at his face. Inside his head he smiled at her, but the movement did not show on his face. She couldn't really see him; he must be creating this from years of desire. She turned and walked to a shelf in the corner. He hesitantly took a few steps to follow her.

He was astounded when she turned and motioned to a ship sitting on the top shelf. He looked at her for a moment and then moved his eyes to the ship. He smiled; it was a small model of a galleon. While it looked quite like a real one, very majestic and formed well enough, he frowned. Why would she want him to see that? Why would a young girl of seven even want a scale model ship? He looked back to see she had calmed and wasn't the distressed child she'd been just moments ago. He noticed the tilt of her chin and recognized that determined glint in her eyes. He smiled at her and hoped by some fanciful miracle that maybe he was partially responsible for this.

So he was a completely spineless man, he thought as he entered her room yet again. He had not lost track of time and knew she was twelve years older now. He had only allowed himself to come this close while she slept over the last few years though, for he was uncertain of what her ability to see him actually meant. She stormed past him, opened her door, and screamed obscenities that he'd only ever heard from older, weathered males. She shocked him, made him wonder whether he should really be here. The door slammed, and he turned to see her take a leap and flounce onto the bed.

She had definitely lost that helpless, angelic look. Her dark eyes turned to him and he had no choice but to stand there and watch her look at him. She bounced off the bed, straight up as if she were pulled by a rope, and walked past him to the shelves along the wall.

He turned slowly. Gone were the childish toys and trinkets. There were no more coloring sticks in this one's life. His eyes moved over the top of the shelf. She had, over the last several years, added to her galleon, and it now held a detailed frigate and shebec model. If he were the size of a mouse, he could have lived on them, they were that detailed. She had associated him with the ships, and he supposed she was observant to have done so.

With a hesitant movement he raised his eyes away from the ships he'd last seen in their real and true form to look back at her. She smiled at him, or possibly it was a snarl; it wasn't easy to distinguish, but the point was she could really, truly see him and he was once more left to wonder what it meant. He heard a door slam downstairs and watched her turn quickly to the window.

Stepping closer so he could see, her mother was leaving, and with her was a man. Even though he had never seen this man before, he knew it was the sort of man any woman was better not getting close to.

Hearing her heavy sigh he turned. She had walked back over to the bed and was putting tiny drops with wires attached to them in her ears. He'd noticed most children of her age walked around with wires coming from their ears. Somehow he doubted it was to lessen the sound of cannon fire. He watched her for a moment longer, decided she was well enough for now, and left without further hesitation.

The sound of sob haunted him once again, without intending it, he found himself inside her room. In the last four years he'd managed to stay away, but in an odd moment of weakness, had spent a few brief moments here, just to assure himself she was well enough. The room had undergone enormous change; it now assaulted his senses to be in it. It was a mix of bright and dark, contrasting with each other in ways that it made him dizzy. Gone were the pretty pinks of childhood; in their place was black with blood-red splatters.

He stopped beside the shelf and wanted for one moment to touch the ships. Two more spectacular replicas displayed on the top shelf. A caravel, which, he thought with a smirk, looked as pieced-together in this size as he had always thought they were in the real versions. The man-o-war filled him with longing, just as the real thing had once done. There wasn't anything that could compete with the force of it, the sheer threat its appearance on the horizon had wrought. Bringing himself from memories of a past long gone, he turned to find her sprawled half on, half off the bed. She was talking low into a phone; yes, he knew what a phone was—now.

"I hope he falls and breaks both of his legs and has to spend the rest of the year hobbling around on crutches! He's such a loser; I don't know why I even bothered." She sniffled.

Pausing, he raised his eyebrows and tried to understand what she talking about. A male was no doubt involved; he was not so long gone that he didn't recognize the tone that every female adopted when a male had done wrong. What he didn't understand was the word *loser;* had there been a race? He shook his head and decided he needed to observe more television in his wanderings. It had been his only way to discover a world outside of his confinement. The only link that let him feel as if he were still part of the human race, not a lonely drifter who felt no peace. Of course, the first time he saw the wondrous thing they called a television, he was intrigued by such a puzzling contraption.

"Yeah, okay, later!"

Turning, he watched her hang up the phone and hop off the bed. He knew his eyes bulged when she stood up and walked over to close the door. He felt like he'd just been broadsided! What was she wearing? He seriously doubted she should even leave the building. Her shoulders were bare, as was her midriff, and his throat practically seized shut when he realized she was no longer a child in any sort of way. She had breasts! When had she gotten those? His eyes traveled down to see bare womanly legs beneath a short skirt. If he actually had such a thing as saliva left in his body, it would have dried right up inside his mouth.

She walked over and touched the man-o-war ship with a feminine hand, and he suddenly felt like an extremely old man. Turning with her hand still on the ship, she looked directly at him, and he froze, not knowing how to react. She was past sixteen years now and more than womanly, but he felt saddened to realize that she had never been allowed much of a childhood.

His eyes traveled the length of her again, noting that she was just a little more than a hand's span shorter than his own height, but it was her eyes that swallowed him. Her dark hair hung to her shoulders, untamed waves of thick silk. Her deep brown eyes had been highlighted with coloured powders, and the result completely robbed him of air, or would have if he still breathed. A child of this age should not know how to look at a man the way she was looking at him.

He watched without movement as her hand ran over a sketch of a face propped behind the ships, he would swear it was a likeness of his own face—himself in a looking glass, the way he remembered looking. He moved a hand to touch the scar that ran from his temple to cross his cheekbone. The sketch was of him, including the scar. He glanced back at her and had so many questions, but none he would ever ask. She could see him, but how? And why?

Inclining his head to her, he turned to leave before he could change his mind, making a silent vow he would not return again.

❧

Miranda got out of her faded, rust-covered car and slammed the door. "Great!" She looked down the dirt road only to kick the tire as she walked to open the hood. "You couldn't die where there are actual people or traffic, could you? It had to be in this scenic, stupid, middle-of-absolute-nothing spot!" She propped the hood open and leaned on the front of the car, looking in. "Nothing's smoking, sizzling, or hissing...which means I am so screwed! I can't even fiddle with anything to make you start again, you stupid piece of—" She took a deep breath and tried to calm down. With a sigh she turned around, feeling defeated. "Okay, Randy, you just need a little reflection time here to come up with a new game plan." She walked across the shallow ditch, and headed toward a large tree. "No need to stand in the sun and bake your brain while you do."

Dropping to the ground, she sat with her back against the tree. "This has not been one of my better days." An orange butterfly fluttered down to sit on the top of some weeds a few feet from the tree. She watched it for a moment. "It started out bad enough. Can you believe he dumped me? I mean, seriously, he was hardly the catch of a lifetime or anything, but to leave me a message, breaking up with me on the phone? That is so low!"

The butterfly's wings flitted a few times, making her feel as if it were responding to her dilemma. "Apparently, I'm too blunt, and that bothers him." She snorted and shoved her heavy hair back from her face. "I just tell it like it is. It's not my fault most people prefer to be lied to." The butterfly moved to another plant a few feet away.

Randy sighed. "I should have taken that as a sign and just stayed home, called in and played dead, or something... Going in to work in the mood I was in was such a huge mistake." She beamed at the frantic fluttering from the creature. "But you won't tell anyone I screwed myself right out of a job, right?" She shrugged. "The job sucked anyway. I should have left there a long time ago. I mean, really, I was hired to work in the art department...which for some silly reason I thought might have something to do with art...but, nooo, was I wrong or what? I spent all my time being the flunky and running this here and that there... I don't think I was even allowed to contribute to more than a handful of projects the whole time I was there"—she huffed out a breath—"and the boss...what a chauvinistic asshole!"

The butterfly seemed to pause in its movement, and Randy nodded. "Yeah, you're right. Telling the boss man that I was not his personal gopher was probably not the best way to go about it." She pulled her knees up and rested her chin on them. "I'm single and unemployed all in one day. Oh, and let's not forget that stupid piece of crap sitting over there." She looked at her car on the road. Looking back, she watched the insect flutter up and hover for a moment at her eye level before it flew off in the direction of the car. "Yeah, I better see if it will start...not that I have anywhere to be, but I'd rather sulk at home than in the middle nowhere." She got up and brushed off her pants.

She tried looking under the hood again. "Maybe you just needed a break, huh?" she said to the car. "I'm going to try to start you now, and if you can just be nice and get me home, I promise I'll call someone to fix you up." She patted the car gently before climbing in behind the steering wheel. "Impress me," she whispered as she turned the key.

Three times she tried and although it made noise like it wanted to start, it didn't quite seem to have the energy to complete the task. "Well, at least you're not completely dead. I'll just give you a few more minutes to get it together." She got back out of the car and leaned against the side, peering down at the motor. "I should have taken shop in school instead of art," she mumbled to herself.

Sighing, she closed the hood with a loud bang. She glanced up at the sky to see dark clouds rolling in fast on the breeze, covering the sun. "Oh, that's just what I need to complete my—" The rain began so quickly she had to close her mouth to stop from swallowing it. It pelted her, soaking her before she could get to the door of her car.

Hopping in quickly, she slammed the door shut and brushed wet hair out of her face. "Perfect!" It was hitting the windshield so hard she couldn't even see the road. She wiped her wet hands down her drenched pants a few times before she realized it was useless; they weren't going to dry. "I have seriously pissed off the world today, haven't I?"

Waving her hands around she tried to dry them before she dug into her purse for her phone. She held it in her hand and squeezed her eyes shut as she opened it. Opening them slowly she almost laughed. No signal. "I'm shocked," she mumbled without emotion as she tossed the phone over her shoulder into the backseat. The rain ended as fast as it had begun.

Grasping the steering wheel, she slowly lowered her forehead to rest on it. A strange, yet familiar feeling prickled across the back of her neck. She didn't raise her head, just smiled into the steering wheel. "You could do something to help."

She lifted her head slowly, afraid to move too fast, and turned to look beside her. She watched the image of the man she'd been seeing for years become clearer. If she focused hard enough, he almost appeared to be real. Many times over the years she thought she was seeing things, possibly ghosts, but it was only ever him.

He gaped at her, his shock more than obvious. "How...you can see me? Truly?"

Randy sat there wanting to reach out and hug him. Hallucinations didn't talk—did they? His voice was rough and deep, and she'd never been happier to hear someone speak. "I more or less sense you most of the time, but if I focus hard enough I can see you." She looked at the scar across his left cheek. "You're very clear today."

He frowned. "And you can hear me?"

Randy tried not to grin. "I'm answering you, aren't I?"

"That's impossible..."

"And yet, here we are talking and being all visible-like." She looked at him, from his long ebony hair down to his black worn boots. "I have a lot of questions, mostly pertaining to whether I'm sane, but right now...I don't suppose you know anything about cars?"

Dark eyebrows shot up, he opened his mouth and then closed it for a moment "I have never actually been inside one until this moment."

"Ah. I figured as much." She reached around and grasped the key. "If this happens to start, I'll be driving like a speed demon to get home ASAP, so will you be able to chill right there and come with me or am I gonna watch you poof away again?" Serious pale blue eyes looked over every inch of her face.

"I don't think I comprehend the meaning of what you just said." He said it softly, still frowning.

Randy laughed. "Sorry. I want you to come to my house with me, is that possible?"

He opened his mouth then closed it for a moment, a serious look in his eyes. "I am not certain I will remain with your car when it's moving, but I will come to your home later on if I cannot."

She bobbed her head a few times, smiling. "Cool." She let out a quick breath. "Cross your fingers."

Frowning again he looked down at his hands. "For what purpose?"

Randy chuckled. "Never mind!" She turned the key, it groaned a few times, a bit faster than before. She tromped on the gas and the car roared to life. Without looking beside her, she threw it into drive and slammed her foot on the gas, trying to get home as fast as she could just in case it died again.

"I believe I will meet with you at your home. I do not like being in this thing while it is moving," he murmured between clenched teeth.

Randy glanced beside her and swore her ghost was slightly green and suffering from motion sickness. "Okay... Hey, what's your name?" She looked back at the road and gunned the gas pedal again.

Closing his eyes briefly, he opened them again quickly and swallowed. "Jareth Blackwood." He inclined his head to her. "Until later."

She glanced over to see him gone already. "Jareth," Randy whispered. Her ghost had a voice and a name; maybe today wasn't such a sucky day after all.

After
the
Silence
Volume 1

BREE

By Jacqueline Paige

Chapter One

I was nineteen when the world went crazy, nothing that was would ever be again.

Remnants of a familiar world remained, but not enough to instill those warm, fuzzy feelings you get when life is comfortable and predictable.

I'm Bree Taylor. This is an account of what I remember, how things happened when life changed forever and I managed to survive. There is so much to tell, a thousand pages wouldn't be enough to explain it all, but someone has to tell it. There needs to be a record so if we, as a planet survive, others will have the history. If we don't, then the next species to invade earth will know what we did wrong.

It is now just a few days after my twenty-second birthday, I'm standing looking out the window and wishing my brother, Shawn, well in the afterlife. A seemingly small laceration on his leg became so much more and took him away from me, leaving me to figure out this world on my own. If I have relatives left living, I wouldn't know. All that I cared for are now ashes spread over the dirt and just memories inside my head.

I am alone.

"Bree?"

I turned towards Darren, one of my adopted brothers, and gave him a look to tell him we were done discussing my decision. He didn't heed the warning.

"Are you sure this is what you want to do?"

His voice was filled with grief and worry. *Was I? Yes, at least eighty percent certain.* "Darren, I can't stay here. Being in the city is dangerous enough as a family, never mind a single girl."

A desperate look appeared in his eyes. He was probably wishing at this point that some of the other brothers were still alive, but only Bobby and Darren were left out of my six older brothers.

"We'll move you closer to us, keep you safe."

We, being his very old mother and wheelchair bound brother. I gave him my most stern look. "I think you have enough to worry about, you don't need me to add to that list."

Darren's eyes strayed to the picture I still held. The one of my family and me before life was forever altered.

"Shawn would have wanted me to. I feel like I'm letting him down."

I offered him a smile that said I had accepted it, even though I really didn't. "Shawn is gone and I have to go and try to find my own place now. You guys did all you could to prepare and teach me to fend for myself, your job is done.'

He stuffed his hands in his pockets and leaned back against the wall. "Where will you go?"

I turned and looked out the window. "I think the mountains."

A sound came from him that told me he thought I was too much of a girl to survive that. "The crazies hide there."

I chuckled and slowly turned back, rolling my eyes at him. "And they don't in the city?" His expression pleaded with me. "Darren, I know you have always been close to my family, you're like family. So I know that Shawn probably told you I changed after the virus." The fear in his eyes confirmed my suspicions. He knew the truth. "I have to find out what I've become, before others do. I need to know if I'm a good thing or a bad thing. And I need space and solitude to discover this."

"Bree, you could never be bad."

My heart warmed from his words. "I hope you're right."

He sighed loudly. "Fine, but you're taking Tremor and Shawn's weapons – otherwise I'm going with you."

I knew he wouldn't, we both knew it, but it was his way of feeling like he had done all he could. "I don't have to take Tremor. I can walk."

He shook his head sending his black hair scattering around his face. "We have LadyBell and her colt; we don't need any more than that. Tremor's fast and loyal and he'll get you through the bad times."

I was hoping the bad times would be few, naive I know, but I could hope. My heart strained as I fought to keep my resolve. He loved his horse and to know he was sending him out there with me meant more than I could express. "Thank you." I wanted to hug him, I really did, who knew when I'd have any friendly human contact again. If I hugged him now I knew I would fall apart, and I needed to keep my head out of the emotional whirl that was already threatening to suck me in. "I should get ready. I want to leave early enough so I can be out of the city before darkness falls."

Darren nodded, even though his entire face told me he didn't agree. "I'll go get Tremor. You get your stuff packed up." He looked at me for a long silent moment before he rushed back out the door.

I stood there looking at the door long after he'd gone. In my head I wasn't at all sure this was a good plan. I was following my heart and it was telling me to get out of town and find out where I was meant to be. Of course my head was saying that was a load of crap, but I was still going to do it. I couldn't explain why I needed to be outside and away from all the buildings and people, it just felt right.

Darren didn't know I was already packed. When I knew Shawn wasn't going to recover I started to gather up what I would need. Before Shawn was too far away from me, we had discussed my plan. He agreed I needed to leave. He had also said he was coming with me as soon as he was on his feet. I think by that point we both knew he would never recover.

I swore to follow the least traveled path. I promised to stay away from crowded places. I vowed to him I would survive and then I tucked the blanket around him and went off to cry by myself until my eyes felt like they were going to split in half.

I'm done with the crying and ready to take on what's left of this planet and the series of trials I know it will throw in my path. Tale of a colony of peaceful people live high in the mountains, it's my plan to find them. I hope the stories of the crazies that live between here and there are just that, a farfetched creation of some idiot's imagination.

Going into my room, I quickly headed to the closet to pull out the packs that had been sitting ready for me. I didn't need a lot. I could live off the land if needed, but one entire bag contained dehydrated food, just to be safe. As I swung the largest pack up onto my shoulder I caught a glimpse of myself in the mirror. Would this be the last time I saw the woman looking back at me? I looked into my now green eyes, a leftover from the virus. I stared until I saw it; determination, hidden just under the surface. Sighing, I ran a hand through my choppy red hair and debated, very briefly, if I should dye it a dull brown and tone it down. I knew that would never happen. I wouldn't trade in my brilliant hair for anything. It was a statement and if I couldn't do anything else I was definitely going to make one.

Closing my eyes, I prayed for my spirit to stay strong. When I opened them I didn't look at the mirror again, just picked up the other two bags and walked out of my home for the very last time

Darren stood outside holding the reins and crooning softly to Tremor. I couldn't see his face, which was a blessing, I didn't have to see his eyes begging me not to go again. The large horse's ears flicked as he listened attentively. No doubt he was receiving instructions to keep me safe and out of harm's way. Darren lifted his face away from the animal and looked over at me. "He's quite happy you're getting him the hell out of this city." A halfhearted grin appeared on his face. With a tilt of his head he motioned to the other side of the porch. "We're going to walk with you until you're outside the city limits."

I turned and looked to see Bobby leaning against the side of the house. I couldn't help but smile when he wiggled his eyebrows at me. Bobby was the clown of the group that grew up together. I often wondered if anyone else ever sensed he was too serious inside and that was why he joked around as much as he did. Bobby was my first crush when I was thirteen. It never went anywhere, for obvious reasons, but I still had a secret place for him in my heart. I was grateful he was coming along; it would prevent Darren from pleading with me to change my mind, again. "Hey, Bobby." He pushed away from the wall and sauntered in his easy way towards me, his long leather jacket making him look like he floated.

"Hey, Brat. You didn't think you were going to sneak off without saying bye did you?"

"Wouldn't dream of it."

He pulled the bag from my shoulder. "Good to know."

Darren came over and took the bags, taking them to secure to Tremor's saddle. "I think you should walk with us for a while and then he won't be too tired to haul ass when you need him to later." He didn't look at me when he spoke.

"She'll be fine, Dare, we taught her." Bobby's tone sounded annoyed.

Silently I hoped he was right.

Stepping in front of me, he looked me over. Without a word he moved and took off the coat that I couldn't ever remember him not having. "You're going to need something to keep you dry and warm." He held the coat out to me.

I opened my mouth to say something, but nothing came out. Pulling my hands out of my pockets I took the jacket and looked up at him. Bobby was a good six inches taller than my five foot five making me wonder if the leather was going to drag on the ground when I put it on. He continued to stand there and say nothing so I put my arms quickly into the sleeves. It hung about three inches off the ground. He gave me a triumphant grin and then moved around behind me, pulling at the material muttering about straps as he did. When he was finished the coat didn't gape away from my body as much as it had.

"There's a nice custom pocket on the inside left." Leaning around me, he flipped the coat open to point to it. "And this…" Bending down to the cuff of his jeans, he pulled up the material to reveal a knife handle sticking out of his boot. "Fits in it perfectly." I knew my eyes were wide as he slipped the knife into the pocket.

He stepped back quickly and jammed his hands into his pockets like he was afraid of grabbing me if he didn't. As he looked down, just before his shaggy blonde hair covered his eyes, I thought I saw a tear running down his cheek. "Find a better place, Bree," he whispered, so softly I almost missed it.

I swallowed the lump that lodged in my throat and nodded. "Thanks."

"Let's go." Darren urged from where he stood. "I want you to have more than enough time to find somewhere to stay when it gets dark.

I wanted to take a huge breath and build the courage to take this final and first step, but I couldn't bring myself to do it in front of them.

"Mom sent a bag of things." Darren patted the small one tied to the back of the saddle. He didn't elaborate what kind of things. Running his hand to the front of it, he flipped open the small pack. "Shawn's hand-gun is in here and there's enough ammo on the other side to last a long time." He looked down at the ground and said nothing further.

I moved around to the front of Tremor and looked up into his big eyes. "We're going to be just fine aren't we?" I ran my hand down the blackness of his coat over his neck and picked up the reins. His ears flicked and he brought his mouth down to nibble at my shoulder. As far as encouraging signs went, that one worked for me.

I couldn't stand the looks Bobby and Darren were giving each other, so without prolonging this any further, I turned and started to lead the way down the street, thankful we weren't far from the nearest border.

I kept Tremor at an easy trot until we were far enough away that I wouldn't be tempted to go back. Stopping, I turned him and looked back to the two men that stood exactly where I'd left them a few minutes earlier. I waved my arm at them, silently thanked them and wished them well. Turning the animal in the opposite direction, I prodded him with my heels to get us out of here. He complied without hesitation and carried us quickly away from the city that was filled with nothing but heartache that I could no longer face.

About Jacqueline

Jacqueline Paige lives in Ontario in a small town that's part of the popular Georgian Triangle area.

She began her writing career in 2006 and since her first published works in 2009 she hasn't stopped. Jacqueline describes her writing as *all things paranormal,* which she has proven is her niche with stories of witches, ghosts, physics and shifters now on the shelves.

When Jacqueline isn't lost in her writing, she spends time with her five children, most of whom are finally able to look after her instead of the other way around. Together they do random road trips, that usually end up with them lost, shopping trips where they push every button in the toy aisle, hiking when there's enough time to escape and bizarre things like creating new daring recipes in the kitchen. She's a grandmother to nine (so far) and looks forward to corrupting many more in the years to come.

Jacqueline also writes under the pseudonym of J. Risk

Jacqueline loves to hear from her readers, you can find her at

http://jacquelinepaige.com

Author note:

Did you enjoy reading one of my books?

If so, PLEASE help spread the word on social media. You can help by sharing on Facebook, tweet about it, post something on Instagram, Pinterest. Posting a review on your favorite book sites go a long way to help authors. With your help in keeping my books "out there", I can continue writing to keep those stories coming.

Writing and promoting can be very time consuming. I love talking to readers, but the hours spent on keeping so many social media outlets current can become overwhelming and time for writing pays the price. If you can take a few minutes to help, that would be awesome. Thank you!